PRAISE FOR THE CLEANSING

"Out of place, stranded, surrounded by secrets — you had me at creepy little town. Even better: the idea of a pulp horror story set in the 1930s era of those wonderfully garish magazines — *Weird Tales*, especially — where it might have appeared with a Hannes Bok cover of cats and witches, snakes, dark woods. *The Cleansing* delivers all this, plus the taboo fascination of reading somebody else's mail. Writers have been telling horror stories through letters ever since Mary Shelley set quill to paper. Robert A. Brown and John Wooley bring back that quaint old object, the typewriter, and find it haunted by history."

— RON WOLFE, AUTHOR OF *HELLRAISER* AND *KNIGHTS OF THE LIVING DEAD*

"...like entering a time machine and reading a great pulp magazine from the 1930's!"

— BRUCE HERSHENSON, MEMORABILIA DEALER AND PUBLISHER

"*The Cleansing* will bear mentioning in the same breath with Lovecraft and Robert Bloch and Robert E. Howard, with as compelling a voice as any such Architects of the Weird."

— MICHAEL H. PRICE, AUTHOR OF THE *FORGOTTEN HORRORS* BOOK SERIES

SINISTER SERPENT

THE CLEANSING: BOOK 3

ROBERT A. BROWN
JOHN WOOLEY

BABYLON BOOKS

First edition by Babylon Books

To the original OAFs — we were all crazy then.

August 10, 1939
late Thursday night

Dear John,

I've been giving a lot of thought to the cats and Ma's circle of friends and what it all might mean for me, and I've come to the inescapable conclusion that I've been put under some sort of protection from her and her old-lady friends. Rennsdale, who travels with me everywhere now, is a big part of it. Hell, for all I know every cat in town may be a part of it.

Do I know how it all works? Hell, no. But I've studied enough magic to know that witches have "familiars," animals that spy for them and do their bidding. I hesitate to call Ma and Mrs. Davis witches, but if what Pat saw is true and they were all huddling over a pentagram, then I don't know what other word would fit.

I've learned not to ask direct questions in this town, even of friends like those two old ladies. As Ma's quick to intimate, there are things about Mackaville that no outsider is supposed to know. So the best thing for me to do is keep my mouth shut and my eyes and ears open, speaking only when I'm spoken to, occasionally asking a right question. Maybe I'll find out enough to get to the bottom of it.

If I live that long.

And even if I don't get to the bottom of it but manage to get out of here intact and breathing, maybe I'll be making my exit from Mackaville sooner than the WPA schedule dictates. I've been knocking out interviews like a wild man, and if I keep it up I'll have the assignment all wrapped up and tied with a shiny bow well before the October 1 deadline.

It's tiring to keep pushing myself like this, but it's good for me, too. When I'm out flying down the roads on the Indian, headed to see some ancient geezer or dame who's happy for the company, I feel like I've left Old Man Black and the Gabbers and the crazy secrets of their town behind. Sure, I feel a little trepidation when I'm done and have to go back home, but I've gotten where a part of me is always listening acutely to what's going on inside me, so I'm instantly alert to the very beginnings of any seventh-sense warning. I've learned to distinguish that sense from just the normal (again, if anything's "normal" in this town) fish-out-of-water apprehension I often get when I return from my travels in the hills. I can't help but think this heightened sensitivity is a very good thing.

The weather was hot as usual yesterday, and the big storm from a few days ago seems to have kept the humidity up, but the roads have dried nicely. I finished about four in the afternoon and headed to Foreman's Drug

Store to cool down with a cherry phosphate and see if there were any new pulps on the rack. His magazine shipments come in on Wednesdays, and in the past few days I've gone through my whole stack as well as Ma's copy of Lost Horizon. Despite the energy I'm expending on these interviews and working with Pete, I'm often having trouble falling asleep, so I've been doing a lot of nocturnal reading. I make a call to Pat – who's still quarantined – every evening after supper, and then I head for the room, with MacWhirtle usually padding along at my heels, and get lost in a pulp for a couple of hours – with my antenna always up, as I said.

I was sitting at the glass-topped counter with my drink and thumbing through the new issue of Adventure when Mr. Foreman eased onto a stool beside me. As usual, he was dressed immaculately. His white suit went with his white moustache and Van Dyke. He and I and the teenaged soda jerker were the only three souls in the place, and in a moment the kid sidled up and asked him, since business was slow, if he could make a call and check on his sick mother. Mr. Foreman nodded his assent.

We both watched the kid go into the phone booth and drop in his nickel. In a moment, he was talking animatedly and then, seeing that we were watching, he pulled the glass door shut.

Mr. Foreman grinned. "I've never seen a

boy quite that excited about talking to his ma, have you?"

I grinned back. "Nossir," I said. I liked Mr. Foreman. Maybe he was another of the few I could trust in this town. He always seemed congenial and ready to visit every time I came to the store, and I couldn't help but remember he was one of the people who'd come out four-square for me after that fight with the Black twins they started in his drug store. (Damn, that seems like a long time ago.) Plus, he seemed to be a kind of intellectual, well-read and articulate.

I don't know if I've told you about this, but in one of those weird coincidences, it turns out he and my dad were in the same division during the Great War. We figured that out a few weeks ago, and ever since, he's been telling me war stories. As part of a machine gun team, he witnessed some grim and gruesome things. The one story of his I'll never forget was about the horses they had with them.

"Men were there because we enlisted or were drafted and we understood, at least a little, what could happen," he told me. "But a horse expects you to take care of him. I can never get the screams of wounded horses out of my nightmares; after all these years, their cries still wake me up at night."

Just typing that gave me the chills all over again.

Yesterday, though, the war wasn't on his

mind. With a friendly smile, he asked, "How's the story-gathering coming along?"

"I'm getting some real pippins," I told him. "Just got back from hearing an interesting yarn about some kind of spooks dropping rocks and stones on the roof of a house."

"That'd be old man Tabor's grandfather's house, wouldn't it?" His lips turned up in another grin.

"Yessir."

"I figured. I've heard that story from him at least a dozen times. Other old-timers have told me the same thing happened to their grandparents and great-grandparents. They've been handed down for so many years that no one knows the truth, really."

I nodded.

"Of course, it's not your job to dig through and get the unvarnished truth. You're just taking them down for posterity. And it's not that I think they're just made up. I suspect they're just distorted. They get shared and passed on and embroidered and while there's truth at the core, here's a lot of other stuff, too. Everybody grabs that truth and stretches it a little, to cover their own ideas about things." He looked around conspiratorially and even though there was no one else in the place besides the preoccupied soda jerker in the closed phone booth, he lowered his voice. "I don't say this to many folks, but I 'spect you might be able to say the same thing about the Bible."

I guess he figured I wasn't a holy roller or Baptist or anything, or maybe that I was more of a freethinker, being a "writer" and all and from outside the town. Plus he'd seen me at the Presbyterian church.

"I wouldn't be a bit surprised," I said.

John, I don't know why I said what I said next. Maybe it was the way he seemed to accept me as his intellectual equal, another inquiring mind, but for some reason it just popped out.

"I wonder, Mr. Foreman. Could you say the same thing about the Cleansing?"

If he was shocked, he didn't show it. "You know about that, eh?" he said, his eyes studying my face.

"I've heard some things. But everybody's awfully mysterious about it."

He nodded. "It's very mysterious. It's mystery — and history." Then his eyes narrowed. "Robert, I know you well enough to know that you're a truth-seeker, just as I am. I will not advise you to stop that activity. What I will advise you to do is watch out for Jack Johnson. I don't want you going phut."

About that time the bell rang on the door, and a middle-aged man in overalls walked in and looked around until he spotted us.

"Mr. Foreman," he said in a kind of whine. "Becky's got th' miseries again."

Mr. Foreman nodded. "See you later, Robert," he said softly. "Remember what I said."

In case you don't recall your old man's slang from the War to End War, Jack Johnson doesn't just refer to that great colored boxer, but also to a huge enemy shell. And "going phut" is going out, buying the farm. Dying.

With that chipper thought, I headed over to Pete's and put in another couple of hours. At the end of the day he slipped me a pair of aces. I made a protest, but he waved it aside.

"Ain't much," he said, "but you've put in more hours these past coupla weeks, and I wanted you to have a little somethin' extra."

Since Patricia is still quarantined with her grandma, the two bucks'll probably go for pulps or a few stag trips to the picture show. Maybe I'll treat Pete and Diffie to another journey to the movie house in Harrison.

Last Pat told me, Dr. Chavez said it was 50-50 for scarlet fever. Mrs. Davis still has a really sore throat and a little bit of a rash, but not a bad enough one, I guess, for the doc to make a sure-fire diagnosis. Also, it's pretty rare for older people to get it, and it can really lay 'em low. I hope Mrs. Davis gets through it okay.

After receiving a lot of garden-variety stories about hardships and hearing a bunch of passed-down platitudes, I've recently run into a couple of pretty interesting tales. There was the one I told Mr. Foreman about, with the spooks dropping rocks on houses, which is apparently ingrained in the folklore around these parts. And then this morning, I ran up about ten miles through the hills north of here and listened to a Mrs. Ligntener tell me about her grandfather and how he used to hang "witch balls" on the east side of his house to keep the ghosts and bad spirits away. She claimed that these little glass balls actually captured the evil that was in the air and pulled all of it into the space within themselves, which is why her grandpa replaced them every so often, carefully burying the old ones in a special area. Her son, who apparently lives with her, was gregarious enough – as these mountain folks can be – but she was a stiff-backed old thing who wouldn't even give me her first name (although it's on the list the WPA sent me). She could tell a story, though. And she herself had a witch ball hanging on her porch, so the tradition continues.

When I finished the interview, it was about one o'clock. Not quite as warm as it's been, and a beautiful day with a bright blue sky. It felt almost autumnal as I rode back toward town, Rennsdale on guard in the sidecar. As much as I was enjoying the ride, I suddenly felt the seventh sense kick in as I negotiated a sharp bend. I was on one of those "improved" roads, which meant it had a thin layer of gravel over asphalt or tar, which makes for a smoother surface and easier ride than I get on the dirt roads. I slowed the bike down, dug under Rennsdale and the tarp with one hand, and pulled my shotgun up within easy reach. I didn't spot anything in the undergrowth to my right, which was sparse enough that I could see a good distance up the hill. On my left, the road, as usual, dropped off at least a hundred feet into the valley below.

The seventh sense still buzzed, but damned if I could see anything unusual. As I took another bend, I noticed there was what looked like a sheen of water on the road ahead, so I cut the engine down even more – then I slammed on the brakes and spun the bike around hard. The back wheel slid a little, but as soon as I had the Indian pointed back uphill I gave it the gas and burned the tires, lurching forward. Then I jammed the brake again and jerked to a stop.

Rennsdale wasn't happy about the wild ride and laid her ears back, staring at me with what looked like disgust as I dismounted and pulled the bike onto its stand.

"Sorry," I whispered to her as I lifted the shotgun from beside her. "Couldn't be helped."

Her expression remained unchanged, and I left her and walked to the section of the road covered by that sheet of liquid. Sure enough, it was just as I'd thought when the rainbow-hued spots had suddenly gleamed up at me, reflected in the sun's light. It wasn't water at all. Someone had dumped gallons of crankcase oil over the road. If I hadn't stopped in time Rennsdale and I would've shot right over the edge.

I stood there looking at it and wondering what to do when I heard a car coming down the road behind me. I turned, ran back, and wheeled the bike around so it blocked the road. A red pick-up jounced to a stop, the same old Chevrolet that had been parked outside Mrs. Ligntener's place. Her son – Richard, I remembered – climbed out and, shielding his eyes from the sun, took a moment to recognize me.

"Hey, gov'ment man," he said. "What the hell's going on?" He sounded unsure of whether he should be angry or not.

"Come over here and take a look at this, Mr. Ligntener. Some fine citizen spilled a bunch of oil all over the road. You or I hit that, we'd do a brodie into the canyon."

He stood there, looking at the glittering, viscous mess, his thumbs hooked in his overall straps. "Shee-it," he said finally. "How in hell did that happen?"

I was pretty sure why it happened. I'd already started mentally cursing myself for not taking an alternate route home, as I'd been doing. But the day was so nice, and I felt good...

"Probably some fool with a barrel of oil in his truck took the curve too tight and spilled it," I said.

He spat in the roadway. "Mebbe so. Shore can't leave it like this, though."

"You got a shovel in your truck?" I was pretty sure he would; it's standard equipment for folks who travel on dirt roads, and his farm was six miles off this "improved" one.

"Shore," he said. "Got two."

"Well, the only thing I see to do is spread enough dirt on it to soak up the oil and make it safe to drive across."

He spat again. "All right," he said, and headed back to his pick-up to get the shovels. For the next couple of hours, we worked together, digging dirt from beside the road and smoothing it onto the oil, after scraping as much liquid as we could off the left-hand side down the mountain. A car and another truck pulled up while we were at it and their drivers spelled us for a while until it was all done. There was a lot of not-so-good-natured conjecture about what "idiot bastard" had left that death trap behind, but among us we made a good job of it, and everybody finally went on his way.

By the time I made it to Ma's it was time for dinner, and Dave and I were the only ones there. I entertained him with some of the stories I'd collected in the past couple of days. He always seems to enjoy the yarns and maybe even envies me a little for getting to do this for a living. Anyway, I told him about the spooks and the rocks and the witch balls, and by the time I got to my adventure on the roadway we were having a big slice of Ma's pecan pie. (Of course, I didn't let on to him that I knew the oil spill was no accident.)

Afterward, I drove over to Pete's and helped him for just about an hour, until he closed up. I told him about the oil trap that I figured had been set for me and, during a momentary lull, wondered out loud which of my two nemeses might've done it.

"I ain't sayin' anybody did it," he told me, as we stood just outside the door of his office, watching the street. "But if somebody did, it'd likely be a Gabber. Sometimes when they want to do somethin', they ain't exactly direct, if you know what I mean."

I'd been thinking along those same lines. Maybe, after I'd given him – or, rather, his effigy – that warning stab, Old Man Black had decided to be a little bit more subtle and he or his sons had laid the trap. But then I figured maybe that was giving them too much brainpower credit. It could just as easily have been the Gabbers, who, if they really wanted me defunct for whatever reason, had never made any threats to my face about it. Quite the opposite. So while I wasn't sure about whom to put my money on, I figured if push came to shove I'd go with the Gabbers.

After he shut off the Skelly sign and his

pump lights, Pete invited me to stick around for a visit. Ever since I showed a preference for Cleo Cola, he's kept a few in the pop box, and he offered me one, took a Coca-Cola himself, and turned on his radio. It's a nice one, wood with a streamlined cabinet, and he's very proud of it, always referring to it by its full name, the "General Electric F-63."

The radio gets real good reception, but the news coming out of it tonight was not so good.

Because he's hooked onto a big antenna on the roof of his building, he can pull in a lot of channels; lately, if conditions are right, he's been able to tune into the short-wave stations. That's what he was trying to do when the sheriff's car pulled up into the bay and honked.

I stiffened, but Pete just laughed.

"Relax," he said. "He's not here because of you. Sometimes he comes in and listens to the war news on the short-wave with me."

The bell on the spring rod above the door jingled, and in waltzed Sheriff Meagan. He nodded to us, fished a Mandalay Punch out of the box, flipped a nickel to Pete, and sat down in the only other chair in the little office.

"What's happened in Poland today?" he asked Pete.

"Don't know yet, Sheriff," Pete responded. "I'm just now trying to bring in a signal."

Sheriff Meagan nodded and reached into the front pocket of his uniform. It looked to me like he was fishing for a cigar, so I slid off Pete's desk and went around to the glass case that held not only candy, but a small assortment of cigarettes and cigars. Pulling out a couple of rum-cured crooks, I went to the cash register, put in a dime, rang up the sale, and presented one of the cigars to the Sheriff.

"Allow me," I said. "I think I owe you one anyway."

The sheriff smiled as he took it. He looked a lot better when he wasn't pissed off. "Thanks," he said. He paused to light it, took a drag, and then held his Ronson out to me so I could fire up my own cigar.

"Run into any more nekkid wild men, Brown?" he asked, exhaling a stream of smoke. I gaped at him until he broke into laughter, slapping his knee.

"No," I managed to say. "No, sir."

I had no idea where he was going to take the conversation, but just then Pete picked up the BBC European Service and we turned our attention to the announcer, who was talking in a deep British accent about the latest developments around Danzig. That was the hot spot, I knew, the place where the fuse was going to be lit for the next war, and the news reader didn't do much to dissuade me from that thought. Hitler and his Heinies had Danzig pretty much surrounded, and it seemed a foregone conclusion they would try to take it away from Poland. But, said the announcer, the Polish Legion was celebrating the 25th anniversary of its entry into the Great War, and the country's top dog – whose name is a jawbreaker I won't try to spell, but you know who I mean – was telling the crowd of "perhaps 100,000" that "violence inflicted by force must be resisted by force."

The sheriff shook his head at that. "Those sons-of-bitches'll be goin' at it before the month's out. Dammit."

There was a little more about it, including crowd noises and cheering, but Pete lost the signal then and clicked the radio off. All of us took the last swigs of our pop and set the empty bottles in the wooden carton.

Outside, a wind had come up, and for a moment it actually felt chilly, especially for August in Arkansas.

Sticking his hands in the pockets of his khaki slacks, Sheriff Meagan said, "You know, men, I was over there in the Army of Occupation. I was just a kid, but I saw enough combat to find out those damned krauts are tough bastards. This is going to be a long-assed tough mother of a war."

Shaking his head, he said good night and got in his car. Pete and I watched him drive off and then each of us wordlessly left for home.

The chill stayed with me, lodged in my

bones, all the way to Ma's. And once I got here, I just couldn't go to sleep; that's why I decided to write you. I guess that's also why this is a lot windier than my usual letter.

I'm going to try again now to get some shut-eye. It's almost two a.m. I wonder what time it is in Danzig?

Your faithful correspondent,
Robert

August 12, 1939
Saturday morning

Dear John,

Yesterday it rained hard all day so I stayed inside and finished up transcribing my interviews – and there were a lot of 'em. Now, the sun is shining, there's no wind, and the air is as thick as Jell-O. I'm sitting at my desk with the window open typing this missive to you, and then Rennsdale and I are going to take it and the big manila envelope full of transcriptions over to Harrison. (I've told you repeatedly, I know, that I don't trust Barney Gibson, the Mackaville postmaster, especially after hearing him talk during that meeting out at the plant. So I save up my reports for a few days, and then motor them and whatever letters I have for you to the p.o. in Harrison, which stays open 'til noon on Saturdays.)

I've had to get used to not being around Pat, although I talk to her every day on the phone, and I'm finding that I miss her a lot. She says she and Mrs. Davis may be quarantined for another couple of weeks or so, that even though Doc Chavez isn't 100 percent sure it's scarlet fever he's not taking any chances. Lately, I've been worried that Patricia might get it, whatever it is, but I try to push thoughts like that out of my mind. I'm kind of heartened, however, by the fact that I'm worrying about somebody besides myself. To me, it means things around here are quiet.

And they were, all day yesterday. Almost. I polished my shoes and leather leggings and read your latest letters again, MacWhirtle curled up on the bed beside me. (Before I forget: Your new story, or novel, sounds great. I know you don't want to say too much about it because you don't want to talk it to death, but I'd love to hear more.) It was great to lie around and be a bum, and I was doing just that until about an hour and a half before supper, when I heard Ma yell for me. When I got downstairs, she was holding the telephone.

"It's the 's,'" she whispered, passing the instrument to me. Mister Clark was sitting on the sofa near us, reading a book and listening to a hill-billy music program on the radio, and I guessed she didn't want to say "sheriff," even in a whisper, in front of him.

Oh, hell, I thought. Now what? "Yes sir," I said into the receiver.

"Robert. This is 'S' Meagan." There wasn't quite a chuckle in his voice, but close enough. "Can you drop by the office for a minute? We'd like to talk to you."

"When?"

"Soon as you can get here."

Well, what could I say? "On my way," I told him and, hanging up, nodded at Ma that it was ok. Mister Clark was looking up at us from his book, and I expect he was going to stick his nose into our business, but I left quickly so he didn't have the chance.

As I headed up the stairs to get my rain coat, I wondered who the "we" was going to be. I also wondered if I was going to get "sugar" Sheriff Meagan or "shit" Sheriff Meagan – I'd sure as hell seen both. I was still wondering when I hurried out into the drizzling rain, pulled the big Indian out of the shed, and took off. Rennsdale, interestingly enough, was nowhere to be seen. I could only figure she drew the line at rainstorms.

It only took a couple of minutes to reach the court house. I hated to leave the bike out in the rain, but I did have my handy all-purpose tarp in the sidecar and threw that over it.

This time, the prune-faced old lady at the desk actually smiled at me. "Go right in," she said. "They're expecting you."

A collective pronoun again. <u>They</u>.

I opened the door to Sheriff Meagan's office and stepped in to face a middle-aged state trooper in jodhpurs and gleaming high-topped riding boots as well as a heavy-set, jowly guy I vaguely recognized. Sheriff Meagan introduced the latter as Chief Lawson, and as he shook my hand I recalled seeing him around town and, I remembered, leaving the sheriff's office the first time I'd been summoned here. Then the sheriff introduced me to the trooper, whose name was Best or Vest or something. I stuck out my hand, and before I could mutter any greeting he said heartily, "I'm happy to shake your hand, young man. You did a damned fine thing yesterday." The way he talked he almost sounded like he was from our part of the country and not the South. Then Sheriff Meagan and the chief started throwing in their two-bits' worth and I was going nuts trying to figure out why I was the hero of the day.

"He's talking about how you blocked that road and took charge of getting it cleaned off and covered with dirt," said the sheriff. "You probably saved some lives, Brown. Good thinkin' on your part."

He had his own hand stuck out, so I shook it, too.

"Sit down. Sit down," said Sheriff Meagan, and I did, while all three of these minions of the law smiled paternally down at me. It felt weird, but it beat the opposite response.

"I was just telling the trooper and Chief Lawson that you've had some pretty rough sledding since you've been in town," Meagan said. I was for sure getting "sugar" sheriff this time. "The state police got the call about your good work on that highway, and the trooper here wanted to personally thank you. I do, too. That area's in my jurisdiction."

His eyes narrowed a little. "There's something else we'd all like to know. We don't think it was any accident with oil barrels or some damn thing like that. We think it was premeditated. You have any thoughts about who could've done it?"

Of *course* I did, John. But even with all the *bonhomie* in the air, I was hesitant to put the finger on anyone. The Gabbers' roots run deep and tight in this town, and I didn't have any proof it was them anyway. Then, Old Man Black – well, unless I presented some pretty unbelievable evidence involving pigs and snakes and a voodoo doll, I really couldn't make much of a case for *him*, either.

So I decided to be honest, within bounds.

"I don't know who did it," I said, "but I think you're right about the premeditation. I think someone laid a trap for me and didn't give a tinker's damn if anyone else got hurt."

"You were right, then, Sheriff," said the trooper. Then, to me, "Robert – you don't mind if I call you Robert?"

"'Course not." It was certainly preferable to most of the names I'd been called the last time I'd been in this office.

He nodded. "Robert, you know when you come into a little isolated town like this there are certain people who can be very hostile to strangers. People can be touchy for all kinds of reasons. They got stills runnin' up in the woods, maybe, or they got something else to hide. Can be just about anything. Could be they just don't like the way someone looks.

"I've heard from several folks that you've had some close calls before this one," said the trooper. Involuntarily, I glanced over at Sheriff Meagan – and damned if he didn't wink at me.

"Just scare tactics, more or less," I returned. That was kind of a lie, but I was caught up in wondering why the hell this bad-assed sheriff had just winked in my direction. It seemed so out of character that it was almost funny.

"Yeah," said Sheriff Meagan, "and as long as it was just that I didn't see no need to interfere."

"But," added Trooper Best (or Vest), "when someone dumps gallons of oil on a steep curve up in the hills, on a state road, that's a different story. Now, think hard. Anyone you figure it might have been?"

I could tell that the grilling might be getting a bit more intense, so I needed to put a halt to it right then. Considering quickly which suspect might go over better with this trio, I said, "Well, Old Man Black's had it in for me ever since I fought his twins outside the drug store." I guess the devil made me say what I said next, but when I suddenly remembered the uniformed figure I'd glimpsed who did nothing to stop that melee, I turned to the chief.

"Seems like I saw one of Mackaville's officers watching while we were having it out," I said. "Wasn't you, was it?"

"Nope," he said. "Heard about it later, though."

"Prob'bly heard he kicked both their sorry asses, too," the sheriff said from behind his desk. He was smiling at me like I was a prizefighter he'd won money on.

"This Black – he the guy you mentioned to me, Trout?" asked the trooper. I didn't know who the hell "Trout" was until Chief Lawson answered.

"Might be our man, Calvin," Lawson said. "I can give you his route number and a map to his place. It's just a few miles from where the oil was spilled, and he's got a truck that maybe could have hauled in that much of the stuff."

The chief opened a notebook and started drawing what I guessed was a map, while the trooper said, "That's fine. I'll take a couple of the boys and we'll pay a visit to Mr. Black. He's prob'bly got shed of the oil barrel by now, but maybe we'll get lucky and find it."

The idea of calling down the law on that old bastard was deeply satisfying, but I felt I'd better give the patrolman a tip-off.

"You'll want to be careful," I said. "There are a lot of rattlesnakes around his place."

He thanked me, everyone exchanged handshakes, and "Trout" Lawson and the trooper left the office. When I started to follow them, I felt Sheriff Meagan's hand on my shoulder, stopping me.

As soon as they left, he shut the door and took his seat again, offering me a rum-cured crook and lighting one up himself. Except for the sizzle of the matches and the sounds of a couple of puffs, it was quiet in there for more than a minute before his poker face split into a wide grin.

"You're good, Brown," he said, exhaling smoke in a tight stream. "You know that? You're damn good. You sounded as innocent as Little Nell. Hell, you almost had me believing you."

I started to open my mouth, but he waved a hand at me.

"You think I don't know about you and Old Man Black? Who the hell you think hauled you to Doc Chavez's back in June, after you'd got shot up there in the hills around Black's place? And I know a few things that's gone on since, too."

I wondered just how much, then, that he knew. Did everybody in this damn town know everything? Were they just playing with me like a cat with a half-dead mouse? Did they all already know what was going to happen to me, whether I was ever going to get out of this God-forsaken burg or not?

He took another puff on his stogie, and I did likewise. I wanted to just let him talk and maybe find out some of what he did know.

He was probably too canny to reveal much, but I didn't have any other plan of action.

"He's a tough, stringy old bastard, but a visit from a couple state troopers ought to shake him up," said the sheriff, flicking ashes into the cut-glass tray on his cluttered desk. "But you know, Brown, this'll call down the lightning. He'll _really_ be on your ass now."

I nodded, wondering if the little doll I'd regained from Ma would be enough to hold him back. "Yeah," I said, "but I actually do think he dumped that oil. Him or his sons, or all three of 'em." In fact, although at first I'd fingered the Gabbers for the deed, the more I thought about it the more I thought the sheer chicken-shittedness of it might point in Black's direction.

"Haven't seen them goofuses around lately." The sheriff blew a smoke ring. "But, yeah, I think Old Man Black's behind it. He's the kind of guy who wouldn't give a shit if he killed other people, just as long as _you_ got the kiss-off." Putting his crook in the ashtray, he pulled open a drawer and pulled out a half-empty pint of Four Roses and a couple of glasses. "I didn't ask, but I figure you're human," he said.

"You didn't need to. I am."

Grinning a bit, he poured each of us about four fingers, a pretty stiff drink for me. Or it _used_ to be. Ever since I got introduced to the 'shine around here, I figure I could drink gasoline and not feel it.

Turns out that's not exactly true. He threw his down in one gulp and I followed, and when he put the bottle and the glasses back in the drawer I figured it was time to say adios. I found myself grinning too widely at the wrinkled old receptionist, and when I opened the door and the drizzle hit me, I realized I had quickly become about half blotto. By the time I got back to the boarding house I felt ok, but Ma, who met me at the kitchen door, turned up her nose and told me I smelled like a distillery.

I blamed it on the sheriff. He'd offered and I couldn't very well refuse, I told her. She said to eat some Sen-Sen before I came to the table so as not to let the other boarders know there was a drunk at the table, and then she turned back to the stove and the pork chops we were having for supper.

A good day.

Your pal and faithful comrade,
Robert

August 13, 1939
Sunday afternoon

Dear John,

As if there hasn't been enough hell breaking loose around me, I got another dose of it today. Normally, I'd just slough it off, but this is Mackaville, and I don't think I need to say any more.

Yesterday, after I'd taken your letter and my reports to the Harrison post office, I drove to Pete's Skelly station and helped him for a few hours. It was getting near closing time when he told me out of the blue that he wanted to go to church this morning and asked if I'd go with him. Seems as though he hadn't been in a while.

Now, I'm not sure what was responsible for this attack of religion, but I couldn't very well say no, so I agreed. He's Baptist, so I had to tell Ma I was going with him instead of with her to the Presbyterian church this time, and while I could tell she wasn't thrilled about my being a "turncoat," she allowed as to how it was a nice thing for me to do.

"But don't you let them Baptists get you in no altar call," she told me. "They're pretty persistent folks, and lotsa people get spooked bad by all that hellfire 'n' brimstone."

Of course, you and I both know something

about the Baptists, but they're a lot more numerous here than they are back in Hallock. When Pete came along in his Hudson and drove us down to the church, I could see that the folks had really turned out. It was that Baptist church just off Main Street that I'd looked at and almost gone into my second day in town but hadn't thought much about since. We had to park a couple of blocks away, and as it was misting a little bit, both his black leather jacket and my dress coat were pretty damp.

The church is a lot bigger than the one the Presbyterians have, and it was packed from front to back. We were sliding into a space in the very back row when a couple of ladies came in and Pete nudged me. Stepping back, we gave them our seats and stood up against the back wall, along with another seven or eight people, all men.

The service started off not too differently from the Presbyterians', with a welcome and a couple of hymns. They had a choir and the congregation had some good loud singers. But there weren't any corporate prayers like I've gotten used to at Ma's church. This preacher was different, too, kind of a jivey guy with slicked-back hair and an expensive-looking suit. He could just as easily have been a salesman.

It didn't take long to see – or hear – that his delivery was going to be miles away from Rev. Venable's, and his sermon was going to be real different, too. He started out talking about how the devil could be anywhere, even right in your own back yard, and he kept raising and lowering his voice, thundering and then quieting.

"You don't want Satan calling on you, you'd better get square with the Lord!" he shouted, and then started talking about Jesus, drawing out that name until it was nearly three syllables long. He went on and on for I'll bet a good 45 minutes, and then the choir started singing "Just As I Am," and he came down on the floor from his pulpit and started in again, talking about being saved and rededicating your life and repeating again his theme about the nearness of Old Nick. People responded, too. I'll bet he got nearly a dozen to walk down the aisle to where he stood and do whatever it was they were supposed to do. A couple of the women were sobbing and sniffling and one wailed a little bit.

I vaguely knew that this was SOP for the Baptists, but there was still something unsettling about it, especially that part about old Satan hovering around the back yards of Mackaville. So I was glad (after about 10 choruses of "Just As I Am," the last two with only the piano playing) when the preacher figured everybody that wanted to go down the aisle had done it and released us. Pete and I were the first two out the door.

"'Bout like I remembered," he told me as we walked away.

"All that stuff about the devil, though," I said. "Is that usual?"

His reply was squelched by the arrival of Diffie, who ran up to us. He was dressed in his Sunday best: a dark suit and bolo tie with a silver clasp.

"You guys hear? What do you think?" He was so jacked up that Pete had to stop, grab him by the shoulders, and steady him.

"Easy," Pete said. "What are you talking about?"

Diffie looked from Pete to me. "You're kiddin'. No, no, you're not. I can tell."

Leaning in, he affected a stage whisper you could hear a block away. "The pigs," he hissed, looking around at the clusters of people passing us by. "There's some kind of monster running around the pig farms. I think that's what the preacher meant; that it's somethin' out of Hell, sent by the devil." He swallowed. "It tore up two of my cousin's big Poland China sows – just left 'em layin' there, dyin'. Killed four or five pigs over at the Raleigh place."

He paused for dramatic effect. "And," he whispered harshly, "it tried to break into Jube Gabber's house – smashed a panel right out of his door. If he hadn't blazed away through the door with his shotgun, it would've gotten in."

By this time, most of the crowd leaving

the church had passed us, and I said, "Just talk normal, Diffie. Nobody else is listenin'."

He nodded. Diffie's not the sharpest blade on the pocket knife, but he's not one to make up stories, either.

"This monster – it got some of Black's pigs, too, and I hear it went after him, tryin' to get in his house. And I'll tell you something else." He looked again from me to Pete, his eyes wide. "I don't think it'll be long at all before it gets to town."

Thus endeth the sermon, with annotations by Diffie. I think I like the Presbyterians better.

Your pal and faithful correspondent,

Robert

August 17, 1939
Thursday evening

Dear John,

Once again, there's a lot to tell you. I may get it all in this one letter; I may not. But I'll do my best.

Monday started out a little rainy, but it cleared before I even got out of town – thank goodness, seeing as how I had to run out south for three interviews. Rennsdale, you remember, doesn't like rain, so when she showed some reluctance to get into the sidecar I took off without her. Funny. I saw movement in my rear-view mirror and when I looked she was running toward me like she'd changed her mind. I almost stopped; I probably should have. But it was raining, and I didn't feel there was any need for her to suffer. I was sure I could do just fine without her, Mrs. Davis's admonitions to the contrary.

Remember my telling you that people around here suddenly seem to want to talk to me when I'm over helping Pete? That's extended to my government work as well. People who were on my "won't talk" list are now willing and even eager to share their stories. Somehow, something has thawed with regard to old Robert. The damned thing is, I may never find out why. These people may have gotten more voluble with me, but they still play it close to the vest.

Anyway, the folks in each house I visited had evidently heard about Diffie's "monster." Of course, they didn't come right out and tell me that. In fact, when I asked, the most I got out of any of 'em was, "Yeah, I heard somethin' 'bout that." But, you know, every house had a shotgun propped up beside its door, and that spoke volumes.

By the time I made my last stop, it was getting pretty late in the afternoon, and the elderly man and woman I interviewed invited me to stay for supper.

I've written you before about how some of the food around here is, well, different, and I always decide whether to accept dinner or supper invitations on a case-by-case basis. This house seemed clean enough, but I was kind of eager to get back home, too, so I politely turned 'em down. But Mrs. Gabber — that's right, they're more Gabbers; he's a third cousin to Jube and Jeb — grabbed my arm and dragged me into the kitchen.

"Just looky there," she said, gesturing to a sideboard that held about twenty cut-up squirrels and a huge bowl of purple hull peas, a small mountain of food with a lard pail behind it. "Pa and I ain't gonna be able to get around that mess of goods by ourselves. You get back out there and hep him with the wood awhile, and then wash up. I'll commence to fryin'."

She clearly wasn't going to take my no for an answer, and truth to tell I like both squirrel and purple hull peas; I don't think we have them in Minnesota, but I've eaten them a couple of times here and compared to them, black-eyed peas taste like cardboard. So I went out back and found Mr. Gabber, who was just getting ready to chop up some stove wood. He seemed to be kind of a frail old man, rheumy eyed, and I thought he might appreciate my doing a little work for my board.

"Tell you what, Mr. Gabber," I said. "How about you let me have that axe, and I'll do some chopping while you tell me about the history of this place."

"You know how to use this here tool?" he asked.

"Yessir. I grew up doing it."

Handing me the axe, he nodded none too confidently. "All right, feller," he said. When I quickly split a neat billet of wood, he sat back in a wooden chair and grinned.

"You'll do," he said, pulling out a corncob pipe. "What all you interested in?"

I picked up another piece of wood, which had already been sawed into a proper length, tapped it with the edge of the axe, and then split it neatly in two.

"Well," I began, "I guess I'd just like to know about things that happened around here when you were younger. Bigger stuff, you know. Whatever stands out to you."

That was all the encouragement he needed. I learned about "barn burners," mean S.O.B.s who'd sneak over and set a man's barn on fire for the slightest offense. I also learned that if they got caught they might well be lynched on the spot. Then there were regular old-time hangings and horse whippings, the last of which had been administered by a woman's father to her cheating husband only about three months ago. I heard about shotgun weddings, too, which are very real in these parts.

Then he dropped the bomb shell.

I was just finishing up the last few chunks of lumber and tossing them in the wood box, a shed with a slant roof next to the back door of his home, when he said, "Then, 'course, there was that riot over in Mackaville."

He could've hit me across the back of the head with one of those pieces of stove wood and gotten the same effect. He was talking about the Cleansing! Had to be.

"That right?" I asked.

"Yeah." He hit his pipe against the arm of his chair, knocking the ashes out. "'Course, that's afore my time, but I remember my Pa talkin' 'bout it. Ta hear him tell it, them two sorry-assed cousins of mine were bang in the middle of 'er. Lotsa folks kilt and burned up."

I knew I couldn't sound too interested. I'd found you could shut a conversation off with these folks too easily — a wrong word or slight change in attitude was all it took. So, keeping as neutral a tone as I could, I said, "We had riots up north, too. Damn shame people can't get along." Then, "When did this one happen?"

Sticking his thumbs in his overall straps, he pondered a moment. "Ain't real positive," he said. "Like I said, afore my time. But I b'lieve it was somewhere 'round ten years afore th' turn of th' century. An' that's pretty much all I know 'bout it."

That final sentence indicated he was through with the topic, but there it was anyway. More proof of the Cleansing, an abomination that had happened a half-century ago this year.

We washed up at the pump and went in to eat. I guess I was so excited about another confirmation of the Cleansing that I got the blabber mouth and entertained those two old people with stories about life in the big twin cities of St. Paul and Minneapolis, which must've seemed as exotic to them as Cairo. They ate it up, and I ate up their food, which was some of the best I've ever put in my mouth. The squirrels were fork tender — we ate 'em with meat forks and our fingers — and those purple hull peas were seasoned with some kind of hot peppers Mrs. Gabber grew. I stuffed myself, and when we got through there were still three pieces of meat on the serving platter.

"You an' Pa finish up that food, now," said Mrs. Gabber, "or I'll have to throw it to th' hogs. I didn't cook my fingers to the bone so's you could go home hungry."

John, at that point I felt as fat as Roscoe Arbuckle. Still, Mr. Gabber and I obliged her – and then she went to the kitchen and brought out a pecan pie, slightly burned around the edge of the crust, just the way I like it.

When I finally lumbered out of their door, the sun had fallen behind some of those mountain ridges, so it was already dark in places. The moon was nearly full, though, so I had a lot of light on my way homeward. Still, of course, I had to use my headlight, and I was making pretty good time on a farm-to-market black-topped road I'd hit only about a mile from the Gabber place. "Pretty good time" at night on the big Indian means about thirty-five miles an hour, and I was doing every bit of that when, just as I got within sight of Mackaville's lights, I slowed to pass an old touring car I'd suddenly come up on. It was one of those old buses that have fallen out of favor now, a Studebaker Big Six from maybe the mid-'20s. The top was up so I couldn't see how many people were in it, but I figured the driver was ripped because the car kept swerving all over the road and going slower and slower. When it slowed to about 15 mph I gunned the bike and roared past.

Watching the Studebaker in my side mirror, I saw it pull to the side of the road. Then the lights darkened. And suddenly, my seventh sense went off, telling me something was dead wrong. But what?

I was still going pretty slow, maybe twenty-five, and the road was flat and empty as far ahead as I could see. The lights from town had grown brighter as I approached.

Then, in a heartbeat, I saw it coming.

No, I didn't see it, not really. I felt it coming – from the side of the road.

I responded by jerking open the throttle all the way, getting a sharp bark from the back tire as it took hold and I began to pick up speed. Then I saw it – a huge black shape, as big as the Indian, hurtling toward me from my left. I had the crazy panicked feeling it was Diffie's monster, and I hunched over the handlebars knowing it was a race for my life and the next couple of seconds would let me know who won.

Well, John, that big four-cylinder Indian saved my rear. As I gained speed, I could sense that the thing was right on my tail-light, though I dared not look back and take my eyes off the black top for even a moment. The next second or two stretched into infinity, hanging in the air as if all time had stopped and there was nothing in the world but the sound of the bike roaring through it. The speedometer began climbing, from 25 to 35 and then 45 miles an hour. When I hit 55 I knew, or at least thought, that I was safe. I kept it on 60 mph the rest of the way into town, half-expecting whatever it was to pop out at me again and wondering what in the hell that old touring car had to do with it.

When I pulled into the drive at Ma Stean's, there was Rennsdale, waiting for me, along with a couple of other cats I'd seen around. For no logical reason, I was very glad to see them all – even though Rennsdale kept staring at me with a weird look in her eye. I don't want to read too much into how she leveled her gaze at me, but I could have sworn she was scolding me for not taking her along.

A strange, spooky thing happened when I unlocked the door of the shed and started to push the bike in. Two of those cats got right in front of me, blocking the way, while Rennsdale zipped into the black interior and checked it out. I know how that sounds; I can only hope you're still suspending your disbelief when it comes to me and Mackaville.

As soon as Rennsdale came out, the other two cats melted away into the darkness, and I pushed the big Indian inside. I said something to Rennsdale and turned to pet her, but she'd disappeared, too. I'll tell you, John – that cat was put out with me.

I'd planned on writing up at least one of the stories I'd gotten, but the overeating coupled with the fading adrenaline whipped up by the "monster" attack conspired to take a little too much out of me. By the time I got up the stairs to my room – too late for dinner – I was barely able to get my clothes off before falling into dreamland. MacWhirtle stared at me like I was buggy, and when he saw I wasn't going to play he headed toward the door, not ready to call it a night. I was, though. After shutting the door behind him, I went out like a light.

Just got back from a few minutes of walking around with Mac outside, getting a little fresh air. I ought to go to bed, but since there's a lot more to tell you I'm going to try and get you completely caught up before I nod out – at least through Tuesday. So hold on. Here comes the rest of it.

The first thing Tuesday morning I called Sheriff Meagan and told him what had happened on the road. He was not pleased to get my call because whatever this thing was had also shown up at the Gabbers' houses and Old Man Black's place. They were screaming their heads off for him to do something, and now I'd been attacked, well south of the Gabbers and west of Black's home.

"You get a clear look at the thing?" he asked me brusquely.

"No, sir. It was too dark, and I was too busy making tracks to give it much of a gander."

He cursed at that. "That's just fuggin' dandy. Just dandy. No one's seen this thing. It smashed all the glass out of the windows in the back of both Gabber houses, and it broke out damn near every piece of glass at Black's place." Taking a breath, he added, "Shit, this is all I need. Some go'damn creature trying to get into people's houses. Old Man Black, who ain't scared of too much, has took up in the hotel here and he started packin' a gun everywhere he goes. So's them two idiot boys."

So Sam and Seth weren't gone after all. They were just keeping an uncustomarily low profile. That was disappointing. But I didn't say anything. I knew better to interrupt when the sheriff was in one of his rages.

"I can't have people walkin' around town like some kinda wild west gunslingers!" he bellowed, and I could hear him puffing madly on what I figured was his first rum-cured crook of the day. "Someone's gonna get shot. For the time bein', I've talked them Blacks out of carryin' for right now, but this whole burg's in an uproar."

With the Black twins still on my mind, I spoke before thinking my words through. "I guess this is a bad time to be asking, Sheriff," I said, "but can I wear my pistol once I get out of town?"

I was serious. With this heightened tension all around, I wanted to make sure I wouldn't get in any trouble with him. But I guess he thought I was being a smart ass. After a few moments of some really creative cussing, he shouted, "Hell, no, you can't wear your damn gun! Didn't you pay any attention to what I just said?" He paused, and in the background I heard a phone ring.

"Put it in your sidecar. That's the best I'll allow – and you'd better not pot anyone else."

I started to protest, for the tenth or twelfth time, about how I hadn't shot that naked dead guy he'd found up in the mountains. But the slam of the receiver on his end brought the conversation to a screeching halt.

I wandered into the dining room, where all three of the rails were eating – an unusual situation given the way their shifts were always getting moved around. Paul, his gangly body bent over the table like a vulture's, was gulping his breakfast and holding forth on the "monster" to Dave and Mister Clark. As he talked, I realized he wasn't going to work, but coming home from the midnight shift.

"Listen to this, Robert," he said as I sat down. "I was telling the fellers what I heard down at the shop this morning. "Robby Olson told me he heard this thing smashed out one of Old Man Black's windows Saturday morning, and when Ole Black let loose a coupla shotgun loads through the broken window, why, it was already on the other side of the house bustin' out more glass. Them two idiot boys of his kept trying to get a shot at it, but neither one of 'em saw anything at all to aim at."

He reached for the pitcher of milk and poured a glassful. I could see Ma in the kitchen doorway, acting like she wasn't listening.

"Ain't a window left at Black's house, Robby says. His cousin seen it."

"What'd you hear about the Gabber place?" I asked, spooning out some cream gravy onto one of Ma's big scratch biscuits.

"You knew about that?"

I nodded. "I hear things, too," I said. After these months, I still wasn't exactly sure what these guys thought about me, but I was pretty sure they thought I was a little unusual. It didn't hurt to keep up the mystery.

Paul looked at me for a moment, his big Adam's apple bobbing, and then he continued. "Well, you're right as rain. That thing got over the Gabbers' way, too, but by that time the sun was coming up and so it only knocked out a few windows before it disappeared. Gabbers boarded 'em up and they say they're staying and protecting their pigs. Whatever that thing is, it ain't been back yet."

Dave broke in, running his hand over his bald head. "You couldn't pay me enough to stay out there," he said. "It'll be back, and next time maybe it won't just be breakin' windows – it might be crackin' skulls!"

"You read too many mystery tales,"

harrumphed Mister Clark. "Give you funny ideas."

"It wasn't any idea that broke out those windows," Dave returned. He had a point there.

They batted the subject around a little more while I mostly listened and ate, figuring it was best not to share the story of my own attack and sneaking an occasional glance at Ma back in the kitchen. Our eyes met once, but I couldn't read anything in her face. After a few minutes, I got up to head out for more interviews – which were unexpectedly difficult. Most of the time, these old folks love to talk about their ancestors and tell old family yarns, etc., but word had traveled and all they wanted to know was if I'd heard anything more about the "monster." Then they'd tell me what they had heard, and it was awfully hard to get them back on track. Finally at around one p.m. I decided to say the hell with it and take the rest of the day off, or at least go back to Mackaville and try and get caught up on transcribing the stories, which were backing up on me.

Also, given what had happened the night before, I wasn't crazy about being out on those roads after dark, and night falls hard and fast in the mountains.

So I ate a quick meal at Castapolous's cafe. I could've gone back to Ma's and gotten something, but I wanted to eavesdrop on the lunchers – and I wasn't disappointed. A bunch of farmers at the table next to mine were loudly pondering the theory that the "monster" was a gorilla that had escaped from a carnival or circus, while on my other side a teenaged boy and girl were chuckling at them, the guy making monkey faces at his girlfriend.

Mr. Castapolous delivered my mortadella sandwich – one of his specialties, spicy and very flavorful, made with a special kind of sausage – and sat down with me.

"What do you think of all this 'monster' business?" I asked him softly, nodding toward the declaiming farmers next to us.

He shrugged. "Dunno," he said. "This country's kinda rough, lots of big animals around. Maybe, I think, a mountain lion. Or, hell, could be that skunk man s'posed to live around here."

I grinned at that remark.

"Sure. The skunk ape." He returned my grin. "I don't think I've told you, John, but there's a legend around here about a big, part-ape, part-human creature that smells like a skunk. Even though no one's actually seen it, it gets blamed for a lot of inexplicable things. Given what I've seen since hitting this burg, I'd be willing to consider anything, even the skunk man, but most of the folks around here consider it an imaginary bugaboo.

Still, it hadn't been any made-up creature

that had attacked me the night before. Whatever it was had been plenty real, even though I'd felt it more than seen it.

I didn't have much interest in going back to my room and working after the meal, so I guided the Indian over to Pete's Skelly and put in a few hours there, mounting and patching tires. We'd started selling a lot of tires. I'd come up with the idea to give a sales pitch to people about how the war might drive rubber prices up, and we'd sold about 20 in the past three weeks. Pete was thrilled. He gave me a buck commission on each one, and just about all my time at the station I was busy with tires. I don't suppose I'd been there more than a couple of hours when Old Man Black and the twins came by in his ancient truck, its bed full of something that was covered with a tarp and tied down. I felt a little warning bell go off when I saw them, but it dissipated before they'd even shut off their engine. Busy in one of the bays, fixing a tire, I saw Pete, out by the pumps tending to another auto, shoot me a glance as Diffie went out to take care of the Blacks.

Nodding back, I wondered if that sudden stab of pain in Old Man Black's chest a few days ago, after Ma had returned the doll to me, had been enough to dissuade him from dispatching any more fanged reptiles my way. I also wondered if he and his offspring were carrying guns, in spite of Sheriff Meghan.

And finally, I wondered why Seth and Sam hadn't tried to contact me. They had to know I was back in town, and had been for a couple of weeks.

I turned back to my task, but I can't say I was surprised when I felt a big hand drop onto my shoulder. One of the twins – Seth, the more verbal of the duo – stood there looking grim.

"You mighta been a little more..." I could tell he was searching for a word.

"More what?" I asked. "I told you I'd deal with him, and I appreciate you two leaving me alone while I'm doing it."

"He knows somethin's up. That's why we ain't come to see you." I saw him glance toward the truck and inch a little more inside the bay, where he couldn't be watched by his old man. I guess it was his version of discretion.

"But lissen," he added, dropping his voice even lower. "Just 'cause you dealin' with him don't mean you sic some booger on me an' Sam, too."

I nodded, not wanting to say the wrong thing and have a ham fist come crashing through my bridgework. On the other hand, I happened to be gripping a tire iron at the time, and I made no secret of it.

"I ain't sayin' it ain't workin'," he whispered. "But now, hell, he's ready to leave town an' go on down to Pasca-goola. He found one of th' letters our half-brother sent us, and he says we all oughta go. That'd ruin everything."

Then, his eyes narrowed. His voice still low, he said, "Thought you was gonna kill 'im, conjure man. Ain't you as good as your word?"

"I told you it would take some time."

"You said days," he returned. "I 'member. And hell, it's been weeks."

"It takes something big to get the job done," I said, thinking quickly. If he and his brother wanted to believe I'd called up a monster, then I might as well take advantage. "And when you turn something like that loose, it can be hard to control."

He swallowed, looking back toward the truck. "All right," he said. "Just kinda take it easy an' don't get us all, huh? Jest him'll be fine." Licking his lips, he departed.

The rest of the day passed uneventfully, and before I knew it night had fallen and the wind was up. No clouds though, and that bright moon shining in the sky.

I finished mounting a new tire on an old 1925 Dodge roadster before calling it a day. Pete and Diffie were already relaxing in the office when I came in and dug around in the pop box for my usual Cleo Cola.

"Hey, I've got an idea," Pete said. "Why don't you and Diffie take the motorcycle and go see if you can find that monster every-one's talkin' about? Bring it back alive, like Frank Buck. Or load up the shotgun with deer slugs and bring it back dead. Either way, you'd be big heroes."

Diffie jumped up from his seat on the counter. "I'd rather have a sister in a whore house," he said. "Y-you're plumb nuts!"

"And you're getting kidded, Diffie," I said, laughing as Pete grinned. "Besides, I've had all of that…whatever the hell it is, I want."

"You run into it?" he asked. "Really?"

"Didn't you hear yet? I'll tell the world I did. Just last night, up in the mountains."

He began peppering me with questions then, and after I told them both about my experience, Pete said, "Ain't you a little curious, though? I mean, since you never really saw it."

I thought a moment. "Sure, I guess. What are you proposing?"

"Want to run out that way tonight?" he asked. "In my auto, this time – and prepared? Butt me, will you?"

Diffie was looking from one to the other of us, his face a question mark, as I shook a coffin nail out of the pack of Spuds on the counter and Pete bent forward, taking it between his lips. Snapping a match with his thumbnail, he took a deep drag and continued. "You got any deer slugs?"

"In the sidecar," I said. "Four, along

with some triple-aught buck. You serious now? Because I am. I'd feel a hell of a lot safer in a car. I don't think that whatchamacallit could get into your Hudson, especially with a blast in its kisser."

Pete smoked thoughtfully. Finally, he broke the silence. "Okay. Sounds jake to me. I guess I'm game if you are." Turning to Diffie, he asked, "You wanna go too?"

But Diffie was already on his way to the door. Turning as he opened it, he said, "You two are strictly bughouse. I'm going home and breakin' open my piggy bank."

"Yeah?" Pete said. "Why?"

"So I'll have the money to send flowers to your d-double funeral," he stammered, shutting the door behind him and moving quickly out of our sight.

Pete and I both laughed, and when it died down, I said, "You're serious?"

"Uh-huh."

"All right. Let me bring the Indian in, and then I'll lock up the work bays."

While I did that, Pete shut the station lights off. I pulled the shotgun out from under the tarp in the sidecar and got my .45 and holster as well. Shucking the bird shot out of the shotgun, I slipped in the two deer shells, their big dimpled lead slugs bulging out of the front of the red paper cartridges. I felt that at close range they'd stop just about anything, which gave me confidence.

Pete was waiting in his Hudson, and I put

the shotgun in the back seat and laid the pistol and holster between us as I climbed in.

"All right, Robert," he said. "Where to?"

"How's about going by the Gabbers' houses? We could go out to Black's, but he's in town so the thing – whatever it is – might've given up on him."

Nodding agreement, Pete went through the gears and headed us out of town and up a mountain road. "Martin and Osa Johnson, on safari," I said with a laugh – although, truth to tell, I didn't feel much like laughing. The seventh sense had been creeping up on me ever since I'd climbed into Pete's car, and it was strengthening with every mile we drove.

"Which one of us is Osa?" he asked.

"Better make it Martin Johnson and Frank Buck."

He nodded agreement with a grin, and then we were climbing up the gravel roads, making good time and not passing another soul through all the twists and turns on the way to Witch Mountain and the Gabbers' farm. As we approached the place, a king-sized shudder went through me. I told myself I was just remembering the last time I was there, with the pigs and the snakes and my picking up Old Man Black's planted hatband that had damn near killed me.

Then, we were slowly driving past the place, its whitewashed fence dull in the moonlight. But back at both houses, the Gabbers had rigged up light bulbs on some kind of extension cords all around.

"Looks like a couple of damned Christmas trees," Pete snorted.

"Yeah. Or a two-bit carnival." We both chuckled, even though I didn't feel much like it.

About a quarter of a mile past the house, Pete coasted to a stop and pulled off the road beside a big rock outcropping. I reached over, got the shotgun, rolled the window down, and stuck the muzzle out. He killed the engine, and in the silence of the summer night we could hear frogs and crickets and night birds. We must've sat there for 20 minutes, smoking and saying nothing, when a sound snapped us both to attention. Somebody, some <u>thing</u>, was sawing wood up on that hillside.

You know the sound – "ah hah, ah hah, ah hah." Then it stopped all at once. "Who the shit would be working up there in the dark?" Pete whispered.

I started to whisper back, but stopped. The night had suddenly gone very quiet. No animal noises. No nothing but the moon shining down into the silence, throwing black shadows from every bush, shadows that to my straining eyes seemed to ebb and flow.

Then it happened. A long shriek of pure agony ripped apart the stillness, a sound that seemed to come straight out of Hell!

Immediately, other screams joined in, my seventh sense screaming right along with them.

The sound, I realized, wasn't human. It was animal. Pigs! Then, a crashing in the woods on the side of the hill, where the sawing noise had come from.

I looked over at Pete, the whites of his eyes wet and shiny in the darkness. His body jerked as he ground the starter hard and threw the Hudson in gear, spinning his tires and scattering gravel as we peeled out onto the road, headed away from the house. It wasn't any too soon, either. Just as we began to gather speed, we heard gunfire behind us.

Good place to stop, eh?

Your pal and faithful comrade,

Robert

August 18, 1939
Friday night

Dear John,

Well, I've had nearly two days of relative peace, knock on wood, and, since Pat is still in quarantine, I'm going to spend my Friday night writing you – even though you already know some of this because of the phone call and everything. But as I've been telling you, I want to have this all down just in case anything happens to me before I can get out of this place, which is still a distinct possibility, so pardon my repetition. Also, it's a hell of a yarn if nothing else, and who knows? If I survive, I might do something with it. And if I don't, you can, with my blessings. So, although I know you're doing it, please keep all these letters in a safe place.

As you know, we made it back fine Tuesday night, Pete roaring down the road like Barney Oldfield all the way into town. We both congratulated ourselves on getting out of there with haste, since we figured the Gabbers would likely be calling Sheriff Meagan and we didn't want to be around when he came out.

Still, it was a big mystery to us, especially what might have made that first terrible long scream we'd heard, and after I got back to the boarding house I laid in bed and thought about it for a long time.

The next morning I headed out early with both Rennsdale and my interview list and map in the sidecar (as well as my sawed-off shotgun, loaded with deer slugs, which I hope will at least slow down anything that gets after me). I've gotten pretty good at figuring out where these people live and doping out who's close to whom so I don't have to drive all over creation on any given day to get my interviewing done. The three old folks I got Wednesday all live around another Witch Mountain, not the Gabbers', and they were within a few miles of one another, which made it easy. One of them, an old guy named Page, was pretty windy, though, and it was almost 5 p.m. – suppertime – by the time I got back to Ma's. Mister Clark was the only absentee from the table; the others told me he was filling in on the second shift at the rail yard's head shed, which means he had to start at noon and wouldn't be off until eight.

"He left this for you, though," said Paul, reaching across the table with his rawboned hand and giving me a scrap of paper. I opened it and found a phone number, 678, which was unfamiliar to me. No name.

"Thanks," I said, sticking it in my front shirt pocket. "Pass the mashed potatoes, will you?"

I knew they were awfully curious about the

number, and so was Ma. So was I, for that matter. But something told me I'd be better off not making the call in front of them. I'd make it at the Skelly station instead, and then help Pete until closing time.

When I got there and explained to him that I wanted to make a call first, he nodded and said, "I'll make sure you got privacy." I guess he was referring to Diffie, who was giving him a hand on that day, too. Anyway, I was good and alone in his office when I got the operator and gave her the number. It rang three times and then twice, a party-line ring like all the others around here, and then a woman answered. She seemed a little browned off at the call, but when I identified myself, she told me to stay on the line.

I was totally flummoxed when a man angrily identifying himself as Jeb Gabber came on. "Lissen here," he said loudly, "I know it was you drove by my house last night. I'm warnin' you – call whatever the hell it is off us, or I'll send every damn boar we got after you! An' this time you ain't gonna be able to drive away!"

"Mr. Gabber," I said quickly. "It's not me. I don't–"

He cut me off, almost screaming: "Call it off!" And the receiver on his end slammed down hard.

I held onto Pete's phone, thinking. So maybe, I thought, what had chased me in the hills the other night was not any "monster," but a big boar hog. And that touring car? Had it been waiting for me, with the animal inside, or in the trunk?

I replaced the receiver in its cradle and went out, still pondering. It didn't much matter. If the Gabbers thought I was responsible for whatever attacked their houses, then I'd hardly be safe on the road. Hell, Black already had found out ways to get snakes to me. If this kept up, every damn animal in the mountains would be lining up to take their shot at Robert A. Brown.

And then there was the "monster." What was it? I had to try and find out, but I sure as hell didn't want to do it by myself. So, telling Pete (out of Diffie's earshot) about the one-sided conversation I'd just had, I managed to talk him into going back out a second night. I figured the Gabbers would be laying for us, so I thought we might pick up something by reconnoitering Old Man Black's. It wasn't much of a plan, but it was the only one I had.

Just at dusk, we left Diffie to close down and got away, drawing near to the Black house just as the moon was clearing the mountaintops, lighting everything up with its powdery pale glow. With the shotgun in the back seat and my pistol in the front between us, we coasted to a stop on a desolate dirt road just past the pitch-dark structure, knowing that he and his sons were still hunkered down in town. The empty house looked eerie in the moonlight, and my knowing there were probably snakes all around us didn't do anything to help my increasingly agitated state. Just like the night before, the old seventh sense had grabbed hold of me just as soon as we'd gotten into the car, and it wasn't about to let go.

We sat there maybe 10 minutes, me smoking a rum-cured crook, Pete firing up a couple of Spuds, one after the other, and then we heard that sawing noise again, this time from the vicinity of Black's house.

"What the hell?" Pete whispered.

"Yeah," I whispered back. "Same as last night."

It was that "ah hah, ah hah, ah hah," going on for about a half minute before abruptly stopping.

John, I don't know why I did what I did next. It was one of those almost instinctive things I've done all my life, like what I said the first time I met the Gabbers, and the seat-of-the-pants ritual I went through with David Jefferson. For whatever reason, I started imitating that sound, not matching the volume but getting pretty close.

"Shut the hell up!" Pete hissed, and I did, wondering what the hell had gotten into me and starting to make some sort of dumb joke when all of a sudden a soft thump came from the side of the car just below me and I became aware of a presence outside.

Something was leaning up against the side of his Hudson, right under my open window.

My head swiveling toward Pete, I saw him take a huge, sizzling drag on his smoke; the light from it winked ghostly pink on his face, his eyes gleaming and huge with fright as he looked past me.

Then, I turned. And like I told you, I was suddenly looking into the face of a demon. Two huge yellow eyes stared into mine. You know the expression "looked into your soul?" Now I know what that means.

I don't know how long those eyes held me. No more than a second or two, I'm sure. Then the face split into a mouth full of finger-long fangs, and I took a blast of fetid breath that seemed to spew from a sewer – or the grave. Then it was…gone. Just gone.

I was aware that Pete was frantically trying to get the Hudson started, although the noises seemed to be coming from someplace far away. We were moving before I even thought about the pistol, and as I grabbed it with one hand, I frantically cranked up the window with the other. I didn't have a chance to use it, and I wasn't at all sure it would've done any good anyway. Pete damn near wrecked us getting around the first turn, and he didn't slow down until we'd put a few miles between us and whatever had been back there.

When he finally did manage to gear it down

a little, he turned to me. "Well, now," he said. "Just what the hell was that?"

In those few minutes, I'd been thinking hard about it, and I'd drawn only one conclusion: I had to talk to you. You're the only guy I know with a degree in biology, even though you haven't used it too much except as a kind of hobby, and I just had a feeling, you know.

Sure you know. After all, I did talk to you.

Again, I apologize for waking you up. I actually feel worse about waking up Elaine, but she was gracious as usual, and while I could tell she didn't want to rouse you, she knew it was important and didn't waste any time.

I admit I felt just a little silly, sitting there in the dark office at Pete's Skelly station, Pete beside me, trying to re-create that sawing noise over the horn, adding my version of the shriek we'd heard the night before.

That should've awakened you good and proper, but you still sounded sleepy when you said, "I've got an idea, Robert, but it's a strange one. Give me a few minutes to get to my library and double-check. What's your number?"

After giving it to you, I stayed on the line and got the charges from the operator so I could pay Pete for the call. And I'll bet it wasn't 10 minutes, was it, before the telephone bell jangled sharply in the darkness.

I snatched it up, and I'll never forget your first word: "Leopard."

"What?" I said.

"It's a leopard," you said, not sounding sleepy anymore.

"John, that's nuts. There aren't any leopards in Arkansas."

"Seems to be at least one," you said. "The sounds you described – that's the only animal that makes 'em. They fit a leopard like a tailored suit."

Then, you remember, you read aloud from one of your zoology books, and I had to admit it all sounded exactly right. Somehow, there was an African or Indian leopard running around in the mountains outside of Mackaville, thousands of miles from where it should be.

I still think I should have paid for your return call, because I know it wasn't cheap, but you said you'd pick up the tab, and thanks again. You should know that after we hung up, Pete and I spent a good half-hour trying to figure what to do next. We even considered waking up the sheriff and telling him about what we'd seen. But finally, we decided to do nothing at all except say the hell with it and go to bed. Pete was nice enough to follow me to Ma's in his Hudson; with what had happened only an hour or two earlier, I was glad I didn't have to make that trip all by myself.

And now, I'm also glad things have been peaceful for a couple of days, even though I can't kid myself into thinking that it's going to last. Makes me glad I've got the good old seventh sense so that nothing will be able to catch me completely flat-footed.

Your pal and faithful comrade,
Robert

August 21, 1939
Monday evening

Dear John,

After that close shave Pete and I had Wednesday night, I knew all about Mackaville's "monster" that I wanted to know, so Thursday, Friday, Saturday, and Sunday nights found me staying close to home. I didn't go out after the panther again, and the panther returned the favor, which was jake with me. In fact, the "monster" seemed to stop going after anyone, from what I could hear. Forays to Foreman's Drug Store and the Castapolous Cafe, where I managed to listen to a lot of conversations without calling attention to myself, told me that the beast had apparently disappeared as quickly as it had shown up. It was just <u>gone</u>, and that was that. It was Mr. Foreman himself who told me that Black and his progeny had moved back home, boarding up the smashed windows until he could get someone out to replace them. The cheap old bastard probably got tired of paying for a hotel room.

I wasn't so sure the panther had taken a run-out powder, though – especially last night. I'd made my call to Patricia and was stretched out on the bed in my skivvies, MacWhirtle by my side, deep into the brand new <u>Spider</u> I'd bought from Mr. Foreman. It was a corker, too, all about this guy who's invented a spray that blows up people's eyeballs.

But the more I read, the more I found myself getting the creeps, and while the story was plenty gruesome it wasn't responsible for how I started feeling. For some reason, while I was right there relaxing with a pulp in my own little bed with my faithful watchdog beside me on a quiet Saturday night, the seventh sense had begun prodding me.

It was a hot and still night and I had the window open, so my first thought was that something might be out there – maybe Mackaville's "monster," paying me a return visit, or another of Black's serpentine buddies. The image of that giant reptile I'd encountered in the attic of the building at the Gabbers' plant suddenly flashed across my mind, tangling up with the image of the panther face staring into my soul out by Black's place. But when I walked over and tentatively stuck my head out, not only did I not see anything, I didn't feel any heightened sense of dread. So, leaving the window open, I went to the chest of drawers with the idea of getting my pistol. When I reached in under my socks, where I always kept it, I felt the edge of the ledger book, which I'd also stashed there – and I dug both items out.

I told you about that ledger book, I know, after I brought it down out of the mountains where it had been stashed. Names, including Gabber and Black, next to notations involving various amounts of money. Considering I'd found it in a hideout that belonged to some of Bloody Bill Anderson's ex-Rebel soldiers, and keeping in mind what David Jefferson had told me during our heart-to-heart in St. Louis, I knew this was a record of robbery and extortion and worse.

From time to time, I've pulled it out and looked it over, but I've never seen it as anything other than further documentation about the rotten part of Mackaville's foundations.

So I flipped through it again, noting the familiar and unfamiliar names, then I set it aside and, keeping the pistol with me, tried to settle back into Richard Wentworth's latest hair-raising adventure. I was doing a pretty good job of it when a knock at my door jolted me bolt upright.

"Robert?" asked the voice softly. It was Ma.

"Yeah, Ma."

"Saw your light on," she said. "How about a glass of milk?"

I wasn't all that interested in any milk, but something in her voice told me I'd better say yes.

"Sure. That sounds fine."

"C'm'on downstairs, then. I'll be in the kitchen."

I dressed quickly and descended the stairs, walking through the quiet dining room. Ma was dressed like she'd been out, and

I guessed she had, although I hadn't heard her car pull up. Old Grant Stockbridge, or whoever writes the Spider stories under that name, must have had me in more powerful of a grip than I'd thought.

Then I noticed that the seventh sense had, if not exactly dissipated, certainly gotten a lot less intense. A good thing, of course.

As it turned out, Ma had been to another board meeting that had me as one of its primary subjects, and while she soft-pedaled it, I could tell things had not been going well until she accused Black of sending the snake to her boarding house. As she explained to me, long ago when the board was first convened among the leaders of the town's various factions, Black's reputation was so bad that he'd had to swear not to send snakes to any of their houses for any reason. Ma wasn't on the board back then, but she and everybody else knew of the agreement.

"'Course, people don't have much regard for him anyway, but we gotta lissen to him on account of him bein' around so long," she said. "And the Gabbers – I don't have to tell you that they want you gone. Somehow, Jeb Gabber found out that his cousin said some things he shouldn't've to you the other day, and that just gave him another reason to say you knew too much and you needed to be, you know, put away."

Her eyes drifted away when she said those

last two words, and I was dead certain they were a euphemism for "murdered."

Still, my seventh sense had continued to ebb, so I felt pretty confident she hadn't gotten me down to the kitchen to tell my number was up.

"Anyhow, I ain't sayin' who voted your way an' who didn't. I'll just say it was plenty close before I told on Old Man Black. I think a couple of the folks voted your way just for spite after that, to show that ol' devil he ain't above our laws and regulations. But you're bein' watched awful close, Robert, an' they could call another meetin' any time."

"Thanks, Ma," I said. "I appreciate it. If they do, maybe there's some way for you to let them know that all I want to do is finish my work and go on to Washington, D.C. That's the gospel, Ma. There's no percentage in my spilling any of Mackaville's secrets."

She looked at me for a long count before responding. "I wanna believe you, Robert," she said. "I'm tryin' hard to. But like we was all sayin' tonight – we ain't none of us sure what your game is. Like a lotta little towns, I guess, we're naturally juberous of outsiders. But we've got some good reasons why. And you know about those reasons – most of 'em, anyway."

"I do. But that doesn't mean I feel compelled to share them with anyone else."

She gave me kind of a sad smile then. "I hope you don't, Robert. And I mean it."

I thanked her again, patted her on the shoulder, and climbed the stairs, grinning when I realized she hadn't even bothered to pour me a glass of milk. But at least I knew what that spell of seventh sense had been about: the meeting.

We ain't none of us sure what your game is, she'd said.

Well, I guess that's a good question. What is my game? At one point, it had something to do with getting to the bottom of the Cleansing and all these supernatural secrets swirling around me like phantoms. Now, well, my game is more along the lines of trying to get out of this valley alive, and of taking Patricia with me. I think about both of those things a lot these days. Too, I think that if I don't make it, I'll know that at least there'll always be these letters to document what I've been through.

I've decided to start going out a little earlier at least a couple of times a week in the hopes that I can maybe get an extra interview in and thereby get out of this burg a little more quickly. I also figure changing my schedule might throw Black and the Gabbers for a loop. On the days I get up and out early, I don't get to eat breakfast at Ma's, because I'm gone before she even starts cooking; however, as I wrote you before, Mr. Castapolous opens up around 4:30 every morning, and since I've got all this government money to burn, I can grab something from him and shoot the breeze a little before heading out. This morning, I put the log book in my front pocket before I left, intending to show it to Mr. Castapolous. I'd told him about it, but I hadn't ever shown it to him. Maybe, I thought, it was something he'd be interested in.

I was having ham and eggs with Mr. Castapolous around 5 a.m. when in came an older guy, heavily built and red-headed, his face wrinkled like a white freckled prune with blue marbles for eyes. When he sat down on the counter a few stools down from me and ordered coffee, I heard Mr. Castapolous call him "Mr. McDermott."

I knew the name, and when he started talking to Mr. Castapolous about the hot weather, I realized I knew the voice, too. It was one of those I'd heard that night when I'd eavesdropped on the meeting of the town's leaders. It seemed to me that Ma told me he'd been on my side, but I couldn't be sure.

What I could be sure of was that the McDermott name was one of those in my ledger book, the one I'd brought down out of the mountains.

Mr. Castapolous asked him if he was ready for school to start next month, and then I remembered that McDermott was the high school principal and, if memory served, a longtime history teacher. I vaguely recalled that Patricia had told me if I wanted to know anything about the town's history, Mr. Otis McDermott was the one who knew it all.

So, John, I thought: What the hell?

Although there were a few early risers at the tables in Mr. Castapolous's place, McDermott and I were the only ones at the bar. I swiveled around on my stool and said, "Mr. McDermott, I've been meaning to talk to you."

He turned toward me, his pale blue eyes narrowing.

"I'm Robert Brown," I said, by way of introduction, "and—"

"I know who you are," he said, cutting me off. "What can I do for you?"

"Since you know who I am, I'm sure you also know why I'm here." He nodded, so I continued. "I've only got a few names left on the list the WPA gave me, and I'm wondering if you might know of anybody else who might have a good folk tale I could record for posterity."

Unexpectedly, he grinned. "Well, I guess I could think of worse uses for government money," he said, and the way he said it made me think he approved. "You want to give me a list of the folks you've already talked to, I'll see if I can add anything."

"Thanks."

"So I guess your job here's about over?"

"Yessir. By early September, I'm thinking."

Then, John, I did one of those impulsive things I've been finding myself doing more and more lately. I said to Mr. McDermott, "I know you're the principal at the high school, but you're a history teacher and historian as well, aren't you?"

"That's right."

"Well," I returned, dipping a hand into my front pocket. "What do you make of this?"

I held up the log book, and, his watery blue eyes widening, he moved down with his coffee cup until he was on the stool next to me. I put the book in his hand.

"It's from the War between the States, I think. Got one of your ancestors' names in it, or at least someone named McDermott."

Mr. Castapolous, wrapping silverware in paper napkins behind the bar, had edged in a little closer, but McDermott didn't appear to notice him.

"I don't know all that much about it," I said, as he carefully opened it and looked down at the first page. "It's some sort of ledger. Could be something benign, like bank accounts. But the place I found it was a hideout for Civil War renegades, so I think it's something more."

He stopped looking at the book then, and his eyes glanced up at me. "Like what, Mr. Brown?" he asked.

"Correct me if I'm wrong, but didn't a lot of those ex-Rebel renegades who took up residence around here make money catching runaway slaves from Indian Territory and selling them back to their respective tribes?"

"So you're a historian, too," he said flatly.

"Not really. But enough to know that a lot of these bushwhackers were hunted down and exterminated. But before that, there was a lot of killing."

He was looking hard at me now.

"But," I added with a shrug, "that's all ancient history now. I guess Civil War scholars are the only people who care about it anymore."

Shaking his head, a ghost of a smile played across his seamed face. "I might disagree with that, Mr. Brown," he said. "A lot of the people around here still care about what happened during that terrible misfortune. Some care pretty deeply." Handing the ledger back to me, he drained his coffee and set the empty cup on the bar. "Nice to make your acquaintance," he said, fishing in his pocket for a dime to lay on the counter.

I knew that the next time the town leaders met, one vote might make all the difference.

So, milking the moment for all it was worth, I pretended to be giving something some hard thought. Then I said, "Mr. McDermott, you're a historian. If past truths always remained buried, for whatever reason, what kind of history would be left? Isn't truth an essential part of learning?"

He paused. "You seem like a well-read young man," he said. "I'm sure you're familiar with the idea that the truth can sometimes hurt the innocent as well as the guilty."

"Yessir," I said.

"Sometimes, it's best for some things to stay buried."

We stood there, looking at one another for a moment. To me, his message was inescapably personal and a lot like Ma's from the night before: Leave us alone, and don't spread our secrets.

It was probably that thought that prompted what I did next. "Here," I said, handing him the ledger book. "I think you should have this. It should stay here, in Mackaville."

He actually smiled as he took it. "Thank you, Mr. Brown," he said. "We will see that it is cared for." I knew he wasn't using the "we" accidentally. "And if you'd like to let me know the people you've interviewed, maybe I can find a couple you've missed."

I nodded, said thanks, and then he was gone, saying his goodbyes to Mr. Castapolous on the way out. I felt as though maybe I'd made an ally, although I'd learned that in this town you could never be sure.

After the door jangled shut, Mr. Castapolous grinned at me as he hurried over to wait on a couple of farmers who'd taken seats at the end of the bar. I knew he'd probably heard my whole exchange with McDermott and would have something to say about it, but it was getting light out and I had to get on my way. I slapped a quarter and a dime down on the marble-topped counter, gulped the last of my now-tepid coffee, and headed out. At the front counter, an announcer with war news was talking over Castapolous's table-model radio. I could barely hear it over the rumble of conversation in the cafe, but the gist of it seemed to be that Soviet Russia and Nazi Germany were getting chummy enough to forge a trade pact with one another. I don't trust Hitler or Stalin, and I was still pondering the implications of their deal when I kicked the big Indian into gear and headed for the hills, Rennsdale hunkering down in the sidecar, where she'd been since before dawn.

A few minutes later, we were cruising along in the early half-light when I felt Rennsdale's little claws prick my leg through my khakis, just above the knee. It didn't hurt, but it got my attention, and when I turned I saw that her eyes were looking past me, over my shoulder to a grassy field beyond. I turned just in time to see six or seven large hogs, at least half of them razorbacks, racing toward me.

"Not this time, boys!" I shouted as I gunned the engine and roared past. Looking back, I saw a couple making a half-hearted attempt to chase me.

"Thanks," I said, nodding at Rennsdale. Hell, John, I half-expected her to say, "You're welcome," but she didn't. Instead, she stretched and then settled into the folded-up tarp, blinking.

Had that been a Gabber attack, foiled by my early arrival at the spot where the hogs were waiting? What do you think?

Folks in these hills rise early, so the Logan family was already deep into their biscuits and sidemeat by the time I showed up and "hallooed the house." The first one to peer out at me from the doorway was the old grandpa I was supposed to interview. I know I've also explained to you that the WPA sent letters to all my potential interviewees back before I even got to town, telling them to expect me sometime in the next several weeks. Sometimes that didn't mean a lot to the recipients. I've run into whole families that can't read, for instance. And since phone service is still almost non-existent in the hills, I haven't been able to follow up with a call to most of the names on my list. What that means is a lot of the people have either forgotten about the government letter, didn't know what it meant, or simply have no idea I'm coming.

Still, most of them greet me, if not warmly, then at least openly. I think what I wear helps – the CCC uniforms (which are becoming increasingly threadbare, even though the local laundry is careful with them) hint that I have some sort of government function, while the newsboy cap indicates that I'm not there to be intimidating. At least that's what I hope.

Anyway, these folks were fine, and the old man had a couple of good stories about being raised dirt-ass poor, variations on a theme I hear again and again out here. But still, mine is not to reason why…

I managed to get a couple more interviews knocked out within the same 10-mile or so area, and so my day's work was done by mid-afternoon. After finishing the last one, I flipped a coin to determine which road I'd take out of the mountains, and the one going south won. I had the routes down well enough by now to know that this particular stretch would take me about three miles out of the way, but I figured no one could ambush me if they didn't know for sure which way I was headed, and I hadn't even known until I flipped that quarter.

Still, I made it my business to listen hard for any stirrings of the seventh sense as Rennsdale and I rode back toward home. The route took us past the back side of Old Man Black's land, and sure enough a big fat rattler came wriggling out of the weeds beside the road just as I passed. But I had no trouble avoiding it; in the heat of the afternoon, it seemed sluggish and uninterested. I don't even think it rattled at me. Hell, now that I think about it, it may not have even been a rattlesnake at all.

It did, however, get me to thinking about

Black, and just how many snakes there were on his property. I wondered if he kept any of 'em in his house. And if he did, I wondered if that was one of the reasons my buddies Seth and Sam wanted to swap life with their old man for an exciting life in the Mississippi shipyards.

With those thoughts as company, your faithful correspondent rolled down out of the mountains with his loyal feline sidekick, arriving without incident (for a change) and enjoying a good home-cooked meal with his companions. I wish every day in Mackaville could be like this one.

Your pal always,
Robert

August 25, 1939

Friday, late afternoon

Dear John,

I've been a little lax in my flow of letters because my life has, for the most part, been blessedly free from daily perils and hair-breadth escapes. However, taken as a whole, the last few days have yielded a couple of incidents worth recounting, so I'll go over 'em for you.

Wednesday, I headed off another pig attack. For the second time, Rennsdale alerted me with a tightening of her claws on my leg just as I saw them coming from two or three hundred yards away, thundering across a fenced grassy plain to my right. I shot the juice to the bike and roared past well before they got to the road. I didn't even bother to look back.

I guess I'm getting used to this crap. That "attack" didn't even rate my getting in a lather. I toyed with the idea of circling back and giving them a dose of deer slugs, but rejected that idea. The last time I'd shot up a bunch of pigs, Sheriff Meagan had ended up hauling my ass on the carpet and all but accusing me of murder. We were on good terms now, me and the sheriff, and I kind of liked it that way. Besides, if I've learned anything in this place, I've learned that when you think you're dealing with pigs you might also be dealing with people.

That was about it until a couple of hours ago. Coming in from the hills after notching three more interviews on my belt, I decided to stop in at Mr. Castapolous's place for one of his greasy hamburgers, which I love. It was a little after one p.m. with maybe a half-dozen people in the place, and I worked my way through to take a seat at a small table in the back of the room by his little showcase, where he displays all kinds of stuff, including Italian food and wine. Mr. Castapolous had just brought me my hamburger when the front door opened. A bulky guy in a dress jacket and tie stood there in the doorway, the glare of the sun behind him making him into a kind of silhouette.

I'd never seen him before. Judging from his soft utterance – "Well, who the hell's that?" – Mr. Castapolous hadn't either.

He gazed around the place, blinking, and I got just enough of a sudden sense to know he was looking for me. Of course, in my CCC duds, I wasn't hard to spot. He shut the door and started walking my way, and I watched him until he got there. Then, I turned my attention to opening the glassine bag of peanuts by my plate and slowly pouring them on top of the hamburger patty. I could feel him standing over my table.

"Your name Brown?" came the voice.

I looked up. He was thick, all right, and

it seemed to be mostly muscle. A flat nose, eyes set too close together on either side of it. A tough guy with a sneer in his voice and three palm trees on his tie.

"It might be," I said. "What's your name?"

I could tell he didn't like that.

"I want to talk to you," he said in the same menacing tone.

The choice was clear, John. I could smart-ass him around a little and see what happened, or I could take the more complaisant route, at least until I found out why he was looking for me. I decided to lead with the latter and, in a more friendly voice, said, "Sure. Sit down and I'll buy you a cup of coffee."

He didn't move an inch, and his face didn't change. "No. Let's you and me step outside and talk."

Suddenly, I didn't feel so agreeable anymore. I took a big bite of my hamburger, chewing slowly, crunching the peanuts, and even in the relative darkness of the cafe I could see his face was reddening. I let him stew a little more, then I said, "I'm eating right now. If you want to wait until I'm done, I'll be glad to go outside with you. But I hate cold hamburgers, even when they're as superior as this one."

Standing beside me and watching the proceedings, Mr. Castapolous nodded with pride.

The gee went for his inside jacket pocket

then, and for a split-second I was afraid he had a rod. Instead he whipped out a buzzer and some kind of identification card, flashed it at me, and pocketed it again.

"Huh-uh," I told him. "Too fast. If you want me to be impressed, you're going to have to give me time to read the badge. You might've gotten it at the bottom of a box of Cracker Jack."

He started to really bull up at that, but then Mr. Castapolous said, "Take it easy, mister. That sounds reasonable to me. We don't know you from Adam's off ox."

The guy gave Mr. Castapolous what I guess was meant to be a withering stare, but it got a lot less intimidating when he looked around to see a few other patrons staring at him, their expressions not particularly friendly.

"All right," he said, and showed me both pieces. They identified him as a member of the Railroad Police for the Rock Island Line. The gold badge was pretty impressive, with a big star in the middle and an "R.I." above the initials "RR."

"Satisfied?" he asked, but most of the bluster had left his voice.

"Sure. You're a cinder dick named Leviticus Allen."

Once again stashing the badge and card, he said, "That's it."

"What does a rail cop want with me?"

"You jumped one of our freights the other night."

I grinned and took another bite of my hamburger. "You got your wires crossed, Mr. Allen. When I ride the Rock Island, I buy a ticket."

"Not out of the Gabbers' packing plant you don't." A little bit of the meanness had returned to his voice. "Some men chased you out of there the other night, and they said you hopped one of our freights to get away."

So <u>that</u> was it.

"Sorry," I told him, chewing slowly. "I don't jump trains. I get around on a motorcycle." Gesturing with my thumb toward Mr. Castapolous, I added, "Ask this man. He owns this place."

As I spoke, I was trying to put it all together. I hadn't been wearing my usual CCC garb that night because I didn't want to stand out, and I didn't think anyone had gotten close enough to see my face. So how did this guy know about it?

"That's what <u>you</u> say."

Well, John, you know me. I'm a big believer in the best defense sometimes being a good offense. So just as he started to say something else, I jumped up, knocking my chair over for effect.

"You damn bet that's what I say!" I half-shouted. "And I also say that you're not on railroad property now so you don't have a bit of authority here! Not a <u>bit</u>!"

As you know, <u>Railroad Stories</u> isn't my favorite pulp, but I was glad then that I'd read a few copies and knew a little something about cinder dicks. "Look – take it easy," he began, but I interrupted him.

"Take it easy my ass," I said. "You're coming in here and interrupting my lunch and trying to push me around, and you and I both know that the Gabbers put you up to this. They're trying to get rid of me, and they'll do anything they think might cause me grief."

He started to speak again, but this time Mr. Castapolous stopped him. "This man is right," he said quietly. "You have no power here." While he was formulating a response to that, I kept up the pressure.

"Here's what you should do, Mister Allen," I said. "The sheriff's office is just down the street. Anyone in here can show you where. I'll be glad to point it out to you myself. You go tell Sheriff Meagan what you want with me and see what he has to say. If he wants me to answer your questions, I will."

That caught him off guard. "The sheriff," he said. "Oh, yeah. Sure." But there was no power or even anger behind his words. He was caught doing something he had no business doing and he knew it. Rail cops are tough birds, but they're human underneath like everyone else.

He stood there a minute, his bluff called, and I could see the indecision in his eyes.

Should he just leave and say to hell with it? He knew the Gabbers wouldn't like that.

But I knew he wasn't about to brace Sheriff Meagan, either. So I softened my tone.

"Look," I said. "I didn't jump your train. If it was stopped, these so-called witnesses of yours would've caught me. And if it was moving – well, I'm no 'bo. I can't jump trains. Never tried. So this is a mistake – if it's not pure-dee malice. The Gabbers are trying to use you, and I know they're big customers of the Rock Island, so your bosses hung the assignment on you. But this is a frame, pure and simple."

He swallowed, and I knew I had him.

"Sit down, Mr. Allen," I said solicitously. "I'll buy you that cup of coffee and answer any questions you have. Then you can file a report and we'll both be in the clear."

Well, John, that's what he did. I'm sure my apparent familiarity with Sheriff Meagan turned the confrontation to my advantage, and of course I lied like a rug when I answered his questions, but by the end he was almost congenial.

The Gabbers wouldn't be happy, of course. And I took delight in that fact. I can smell pork chops from downstairs, so it's time for me to sign off.

Your pal and faithful comrade,

Robert

August 29, 1939
Tuesday night

Dear John,

Just finished listening to Lowell Thomas's program with Ma and the other boarders, who have all three been on normal shifts for a change. I guess the news got me down a little. Mister Clark keeps talking about how there's going to be a war any day now, and sure enough it looks like the old bastard is right. We heard this evening how Henderson, the British diplomat to Germany, just told Hitler he has to choose between having a war with Poland and a friendship with Britain, and I can't think that the little dictator's going to go the pally route. Hell, by this time tomorrow bombs could be dropping in Europe.

It's a damned mess.

I've been a little lax about writing because, well, I guess it's true that you just get used to things. Between my seventh sense and Rennsdale's vigilance, I've dodged a couple more pig attacks, and there's been at least one bit of evidence, which I'll get to in just a minute, that Old Man Black is still seeking my demise, even though my little effigy and me have the Indian sign on him. Some of these incidents would've scared the liver out of me a few months ago; now, well, it's just another day at the office.

Let me go back to last Friday night, just after I wrote you. As we devoured our pork chops and greens and gravy, I told my fellow boarders about the encounter with Leviticus Allen, the cinder dick. With them being rails and all, I guess I figured they might take Allen's side, so I was surprised when they all came out for me.

"That packing-plant crowd," Mister Clark said, snorting in derision. "Every time they belch they expect us to pat them on the back and cut our rates. I'm awful sick of the arrogant bas—" Glancing up at Ma, who was hovering over us with a milk pitcher, he cut himself off just in time. Ma doesn't allow any bad language at her table (which makes her outburst about Black and the snake a couple of weeks ago seem even funnier).

He cleared his throat. "Anyway, they act like the Rock Island is their private railroad and we're all expected to jig to their tune." Anger animated his face, even as Paul and Dave nodded in agreement. "This Allen — he's from Little Rock, and he never even cleared himself through our office, like they're all supposed to do."

"Well, Mister Clark, I didn't give him anything to write home about," I said. "We parted on good enough terms."

"Very well, Robert. I'm sure your handling of this farce does you credit." He took a noisy drink of ice water. "Still, I'll send a letter to the main office reporting the incident and requesting in the future that they avoid such public humiliation of a railroad employee by clearing the matter first with our office here in Mackaville."

I realized then it wasn't me getting picked on that irked him; it was his resentment of the power the Gabbers had over his bosses – and, by extension, over him. But if he wanted to shoot a rocket up their collective pants leg, that was fine with me.

"Thank you, Mister Clark," I said. "I'd appreciate whatever you deem best."

"Happy to do it," he harrumphed, and that was that.

I wrote you earlier that I've been going out early to confuse anyone that might be on my trail. Well, now I've started mixing things up. Sometimes I'll still leave around dawn, and other times I won't head out of town until late morning. Yesterday was one of the latter, with Rennsdale and me not getting back to town until dark. I'd fought a hot, stiff crosswind all the way down the hills, and it was still howling at me when I pulled up in front of Ma's shed.

As I slowed, the beam of the Indian caught the figures of three cats staring back at me from the path just in front of the shed's closed doors. That's when the seventh sense kicked in. John, I've never been much of a cat lover, as you know, so I couldn't really tell you whether I'd seen these particular felines before or not. They may have included the ones I encountered a couple of weeks ago in this same place. Remember? I think I wrote you how it felt like those animals and Rennsdale were actually checking out the inside of the shed for me?

Leaving the bike idling on its kickstand, I went to the doors and opened them. They're corrugated tin, and they open out like bat wings. The cats moved out of the way, but this time they didn't go in. Rennsdale jumped down and took a place beside them as they all kept their eyes on me, tails flicking slowly, as I went to the bike. Then, Rennsdale jumped up with a little mewling sound and with two hops planted herself just in front of the dark shed.

My seventh sense told me it was a warning. So did her shining eyes, fixed on mine.

Since the bike was still running, I rolled it up closer to the open doorway and turned the beam of the headlight into it. I ran over every inch, but I couldn't see anything the least bit unusual. All the tools were hung in their places, the ground under the shed was clear, no surprises rested on the work benches. There wasn't a sign of a snake – which I'd first suspected – or anything else untoward.

I looked down at Rennsdale. "I don't see a thing, little girl," I told her – again, half-expecting her to reply. But between the unmoving cats and the alarm bells ringing inside me, I knew <u>something</u> had to be in there.

Then I thought, <u>the rafters</u>. Wheeling the bike just inside the door, I horsed it around until the beam was pointing at the ceiling and moved it around. Still no cigar.

Then it hit me. The ledge over the door – just above my neck. I backed out fast into the howling wind, pulling the bike along with me, trying to shake the image of a snake plopping down my collar. Standing there, I let several seconds pass while I tried to figure out what to do. All the while, the cats watched me, silently.

Finally, I dug around in my pockets until I found my handkerchief. Opening it up and shaking it out, I calculated that it was big enough for what I had in mind. The next part was going to be a little tricky, because what I wanted was in that shed. So I sent the beam from my still-running bike into a far corner, put it up on its kickstand again, and crept away from it to the other side of the open doorway. Just inside, I knew, stood a jumble of hoes and rakes and shovels. Slowly moving my arm through, and trying not to think of the snake I was sure lay above it, I grabbed the first wooden handle I touched and jerked it up and out. It turned out to be a busted-up old rake, with the tines all bent up and sticking out at odd angles. The handle, though, was still strong and stout. That was all I needed.

Twisting the handkerchief until I had it in a loose knot with a little tail sticking out, I took the cap off the Indian's gas tank and stuck the cloth into it for a couple of seconds. Then I wrapped it around the bent-up head of the rake, working fast to keep the gasoline from completely evaporating. My sawed-off Remington 12-gauge was in the sidecar, and I peeled away the oilcloth around it, checked the shells, and tucked it under my arm.

Despite the wind, the rag flared into flame with my third match. Taking a quick deep breath, squeezing the shotgun against my side with my left arm, I yelled, "Look out, Rennsdale," ran into the shed and thrust my makeshift torch into the space just above the upper ledge of the shed – hoping, with all the rain we'd had recently, that I wouldn't accidentally set fire to the shed. A flash in the corner of my eye told me Rennsdale had blown.

Then, head first, twisting and turning, a six-foot-long rattler uncoiled over that ledge, landing hard on the dirt floor. Dropping the torch, I whipped up the shotgun and blasted him into bloody tatters. Of course, that explosion brought out everyone in the house, where I guessed, from the sight of Paul with his napkin still tucked into his shirt, they'd been having supper. I was stomping out the torch when they arrived, and even though they may not have been able to see much outside the beam of the Indian, I don't imagine the sight of that bloody demolished snake did anything for their appetites. It did, however, enable them to understand the reason for the blast.

Just as they arrived, a yapping MacWhirtle at Ma's heels, I was cutting up the dead snake with the bolo knife I'd used on the copperhead a couple of weeks ago. The cats, including Rennsdale, still looked on, implacable.

"Why, that old—" Ma started, then stopped, realizing she was about to violate her own rules about cussing. "Another one from Black, eh?" she added more softly. I barely heard her.

The wind was blowing so hard that her words were lost to the other boarders.

"Yeah," I said, using a shovel to pick up the remains. "Sorry about the mess. I'll clean it up."

"It's all right," she returned. "I'll keep your supper warm for you."

She turned around and went back in, the others following. Even the cats dispersed, except for Rennsdale. I wouldn't say that she and MacWhirtle were exactly palsy-walsy, but he didn't pay much attention to her, instead sniffing around all over the ground where the reptile had met his maker. He even peed once, right in the doorway where the snake had been.

When I finished up and had dropped all the

remains I could scoop up in the burn barrel, I went inside to eat. The others were done and lounging around listening to the radio in the living room – all of them, that is, except for Ma, who was on the phone. She gestured me toward the dining table, and I went in to find my plate heaped full. I figured she was telling someone about what had happened out in the shed, but I couldn't tell who, because Dave came in right after I got seated and started asking questions, making the observation that snakes sure as shootin' seem to want to take a bite out of me.

Between the cats and the seventh sense, I'd jumped slick once again. But a few hours ago, I was sure the latter had deserted me.

I finished up around dusk today and got to Ma's in time for supper. Halfway through, Pete called to ask if I could come by the station when I was done. I found that kind of curious – I don't think he'd ever done it before – but I just figured he needed me, so I hotfooted on out without waiting for dessert.

When I got there, I saw no sign of Diffie, and Pete had two cars going at the pumps. He motioned me inside with a nod of his head. I took that to mean there were some tires to mount or fix, so I went on in and stepped through the office into the first bay.

I hadn't taken more than three steps when I heard what I'd call evil laughter behind me. When I turned around, the two hulking Black twins stood there, each one with a tire iron in his meaty paw.

That's your cliffhanger for this time around, chum. How did your hero get out of this one? All will be revealed in my next letter.

Your pal and faithful comrade,
Robert

September 2, 1939
Saturday afternoon

Dear John,

I apologize for taking so long to get back to you, but I have been busy.

Ok, I lie; I wanted you to squirm a little, wondering what happened to me at Pete's after those two palookas cornered me in the grease bay, tire irons in their ham fists.

Oddly enough, as I wrote you a few days ago, there had been no foreshadowing of any of this with me, not even a twinge of the seventh sense. And now here I was, suddenly in very deep shit.

So I started trying to talk my way out.

"Listen, fellas, I've told you I can't just kill your old man all at once," I said. "Honest. Even a conjure man has to have a little time."

"You think that crap's gonna fly with us?" Seth asked, and God help me I realized then I could tell them apart. "What <u>you</u> think, Bubba?" he asked, turning to his brother.

Sam gave out a pig-like grunt. "Don't think so. I say we split his lyin' skull."

I swallowed hard as they both took a step toward me. John, there wasn't any place for me to go. My back was against the grease ramp, and I knew they were too close for me to turn and dive under the metal channel we used to elevate the cars for grease jobs and oil changes. Other than that, there was no place for me to flee.

"I did my best," I managed to croak out, as they took another step toward me, both slapping the tire tools against their palms. My words sounded more desperate than I'd intended.

Then, Seth threw his tire iron down. And, in a moment, so did Sam. As their weapons clattered on the concrete floor, I wondered what now? Had they just decided to work me over with their fists? Well, I'd taken them on before and done all right – but one of them had been crippled up. They were hale and hearty now – and within reach of weapons that would put me at even more of a disadvantage.

Suddenly, both of them began guffawing. Literally. They were braying like donkeys.

Turning to his brother and speaking through gasps of laughter, Seth said, "You see…his face?"

"Shee-it!" returned Sam with the same breathless amusement. "He thought he…he was a dead sumbitch."

They both broke out in fresh spasms of laughter, leaving me to try to figure out just exactly what in hell was going on. After a moment, wiping tears from his eyes, Seth stepped up to me, stuck out his big hand, and said, "Put 'er there, conjure man!"

I still wasn't convinced I wasn't going to get murdered, and they were just toying with me before the kill. But I stuck out my mitt anyway and it disappeared in his big hand as he gave it a good shake. Then Sam stepped up and did the same. I guess my confusion must've been showing on my face, because they looked at me, looked at one another, and started laughing all over again, although the chortling wasn't quite as loud this time. I grinned, trying to get into the spirit of the thing, but I just couldn't make myself see the humor in it.

Finally, Seth told me, "We leavin' for Pasca-goola t'night on the eight o'clock, but we had to stop by and give you a little of the ol' razzberry first."

"Yeah," added his brother, "an' say thank-ya, too."

"Yup," Seth said. "You didn't kill th' old man, like you said you wuz gonna do, but you got him so flabberated he don't know which way's up. He says to us last night that we wuz 'cloudin' his spells' – whatever in hell thet means. It don't matter. We free."

"We goin' 'fore he changes his damned ol' mind," said Sam.

John, if you'll recall, the night before this happened was Monday, when I fended off the latest snake attack. Maybe Old Man Black thought these two clodhoppers were somehow getting in the way and that's why his snakes couldn't get to me.

From the beginning, something had been bugging me about their appearance that I couldn't put my finger on. Then I realized they were both dressed in stiff new white shirts and crisp blue jeans instead of their usual shapeless garb. Of course. They were all duded up for their big rail trip.

"Well, fellas," I said. "That's good news for you. Looks like you got your wish."

Seth grinned wide enough to display a couple of gaps where there should've been teeth. "Yeah. We snuck out and made us a call to our half-brother the other night, and he says with th' war goin' on an' all, over there in…" He paused.

"Germany," said Sam.

"Yeah. Germany. He says the U.S.A. is worried about it and so they're buildin' up their Navy and need workers down there in Pasca-goola, at a place called En-glass."

I knew he meant Ingalls.

"He says we'll start at the bottom," continued Seth. "But hell, we be makin' some real money."

"Yeah," echoed Sam. "Some real dough-re-mi."

Boy, they were excited, and so was I, mostly because I wasn't going to get beaten to death. While they were talking over one another telling about the assets of shipyard work, Pete came in, grinning like a possum eating wasps.

"What's going on back here?" he asked, but he knew full well what was going on. Hell, he'd been a party to the whole thing.

That prompted a fresh batch of guffaws.

"You shoulda seen 'im," Seth gasped out. "'Bout shit a brick."

They laughed some more, and I finally got to the point where I could laugh with them. We moved into the office and Pete stood them a going-away pop while they peppered me with questions about life in a city. What they wanted to know the most was where to pick up girls.

"Go to church," I told them, knowing how they'd take it. "Why, the Sunday school classes are just <u>full</u> of young women, ripe for the picking and looking for gentleman callers."

They fell all over themselves nixing that idea.

"Well then," I said, "You got the bars, but you'd better be careful. Pascagoula's a booming town, and some of the frills you'll meet in its taverns aren't exactly nice girls."

"We ain't lookin' for <u>nice</u> girls," Seth said. "We kinda lookin' for hoors."

He laughed then, slapping his brother on the shoulder. "C'mon, Bubba," he said. "Let's commence to lookin'."

They both got up, retrieving their new cardboard suitcases from behind Pete's counter.

They'd hidden them there so I'd have no inkling anyone else was on the premises. Then they did a funny thing. Setting the suitcases down beside them, they came over and each gave me a bone-crushing hug. I guess it was a nice thing to do, but it made me think that whatever girls they set their caps for better not be too particular about B.O.

Then, with a tinkle of the bell atop Pete's door, they were gone, heading in a trot toward the depot. After they were out of sight, I turned my attention to Pete, who, grinning, held up his hand.

"Now don't start," he said. "It was funny, and you know it. Besides, I've never seen those two lugs so happy in all the years I've been around 'em. They came by looking for you, and I couldn't turn 'em down."

"You set the whole thing up, didn't you? Those boys don't have the brain power. They couldn't have dreamed up a routine like that."

He shrugged, still grinning.

"You dirty rat," I added. "I've aged ten years."

"I'll bet you about wet yourself, didn't you?"

"Hell, no," I returned. "I was so knotted up I couldn't even spit."

He laughed at that, and I laughed too, and then a car came along and pulled up to the pumps. He went out to wait on the customer, and I headed back into the bay that, only a few minutes ago, I had been certain would be the scene of my demise.

As I mounted a couple of new tires on the

front of a Packard 120, I went back through what had just happened, thinking that yes, it had been funny, but at the same time trying to forestall a sense of gloom that had begun creeping over me. There hadn't been any activation of my seventh sense because I hadn't been in danger from the Black twins – appearances to the contrary. But I found myself wondering about Old Man Black and the whole "clouding his spells" bit. That had to mean he planned more spells – more attacks – on me, which in turn meant that I not only had to watch myself but also had to maybe revisit that little effigy in my chest of drawers and let him know I could still cause him plenty of pain if he pissed me off.

But it wasn't just the thought of a fresh round of attacks from Black that was getting me down. The twins had talked about how the war in Europe was affecting the ship yard, and I knew that was true. Very soon we're going to be in a war, John, and that's going to make my struggles in this crazy place look like a Warner Brothers cartoon. If I manage to get out of here, am I just going to be moving to a place where the stakes aren't only my life, but the lives of millions? I feel like I'm caught, like an insect in a jar. I feel like maybe we <u>all</u> are.

With that jolly thought in mind, I'll close by telling you nothing much new has happened since my Tuesday surprise. Mrs. Davis is finally getting better, and it won't be long before I'll be able to see Patricia again, which is something I'm sure looking forward to.

I wouldn't mind seeing <u>you</u> again, either, old pal.

Your faithful correspondent,
Robert

September 4, 1939
Monday night

Dear John,

Well, I know you've heard: Sunday, Britain, France, Australia, and New Zealand declared war on the little Heinie dictator. When I wrote you last, I told you I knew a war was on the way. I just didn't figure it would begin this quickly.

I got the news from the radio yesterday evening, when it was just Mister Clark and me.

Like me, Ma Stean likes the broadcasts of Lowell Thomas best, but since she was out somewhere, Mister Clark asked if we could switch to the Mutual Network for Gabriel Heatter. Mister Clark's a contrary old guy, as you may have gathered, but it didn't make that much difference to me and I said sure. That's where we got the war bulletin.

Mister Clark says that FDR won't keep us neutral for long, and never mind what the politicians and even a hero like Charles Lindbergh might say about our staying out of Europe's business. I'm not so sure we'll be able to do that either. And I'm not sure we should.

With all that going on, talking about myself and my own problems seems awfully self-centered. Still, I have to tell you these last two days have not been the best of my life. I'm sure the war news has something to do with my mood, but the feeling of menace and doom that hangs over me in this town has gotten stronger again – it seems to go in waves – and I find myself wondering once more whether I'll ever make it out other than feet first. Right now I feel like grabbing Patricia, scarlet fever or no scarlet fever, and hustling us both aboard the next train to D.C. Given the world situation, I might be headed into even more trouble, but at least it would be something I understood, something that didn't make me think I'm living in some sort of nightmare with no waking in sight.

I don't know. I'm kind of mixed up. I guess I should've laid off this jar of Dill Jolley's 'shine after the first sip, but it's still sitting here and now I realize the level of liquid has gone down impressively. I thought it'd do me some good, but instead it's gotten me to brooding about a lot of things, including a phone call I got only a couple of hours ago. Hell, now that I think of it, that may be what started me on this little jag in the first place.

Ma's been real good about letting me use her phone in the evenings, so that I can talk to Pat and find out how she and her grandmother are doing. A day or two ago, Mrs. Davis's fever broke, so I'm sure they're through the worst of it now.

Anyway, Patricia and I went through the usual topic Sunday night – how much I miss her, how much she misses me, how glad we'll both be when Doc Chavez lifts the quarantine and we can go to the movies again, etc. – and then a funny thing happened. I think it was funny – odd – to Patricia, too, because of the way she said, "Before you hang up, Robert, Grandma would like to have a word with you."

"Sure," I said. "Put her on." I almost said something about how I loved her before she got off the phone, but neither one of us says that yet – even though I think we both feel it.

Sorry about the detour into romance-story cliché.

So Mrs. Davis said something I couldn't hear to Patricia – it sounded blurred, like she had her hand over the mouthpiece – and then she spoke to me. Her voice was a bit unsteady from her illness, but there was plenty of power behind it. And she didn't waste any time.

"Robert," she said, "I'll make this quick, because this is a party line and someone else might listen in. Be careful. You've lost a good degree of your protection."

"My protection?" I asked.

"We had a powerful ally, but they're searching the woods for him with hounds, and it was too dangerous to keep him around anymore."

All of a sudden, John, I knew exactly what she was talking about, and the knowledge came with a little electric crackling through my body.

"You're talking about the leopard," I said.

"Yes." I detected a note of surprise in her voice. "We've sent him back to the zoo in Oklahoma City."

"Oklahoma City?" I said. "Why, that's at least 300 miles from here, isn't it?"

There was almost a chuckle in her voice. "It took a little while," she said.

I had another question, but she answered it with her next statement.

"The big cats, like leopards, are kept in natural-looking pits at the zoo. If they want to put forth a lot of effort, they can get out, but why should they? They're fed, they have shelter, and they're cared for. Since he answered our call, he's had to live out in the wild, in the elements, and catch and kill his own food. I'm sure he enjoyed that last part, as well as scaring humans."

"He was good at that," I said, remembering the two nights in Pete's car.

This time, she actually chuckled. I was sure she knew just how I knew he was so good at it. "I know," she said. "But things were getting dangerous for him. It was only a matter of time before someone got up a hunting party and shot him, and we couldn't have that."

"I see," I returned. Then, after a moment, I added, "Well, what happens now? With this protection gone, I mean?"

"The Gabbers have called another board meeting for Saturday, the ninth. The voting on you was within a vote last time, and I have every reason to believe at least one and maybe two will swing their way and we'll be outvoted. There's some feeling that you had something to do with the panther, and I want to apologize for that. Making people more skittish about you wasn't our intention."

"Well, Mrs. Davis, thank you. But I guess I can take care of myself." The words sounded hollow to me, unconvincing. They didn't convince her, either.

"No, Robert," she said. "That's why I wanted to talk to you. You'd better think about leaving Mackaville, and soon. If the board goes against you Saturday, I don't think we can keep you safe. I'm sorry. That's all I have to tell you."

There was a click at the other end, and that was that. As I hung up the receiver, I found myself wondering if Patricia had been listening in, at least to her grandmother's side of the conversation. My girlfriend, the woman I wanted to marry — how much did she know?

Monday, today, was stinking. A cool front came through, a heavy mist fell, and my interviews were brodies. I should have canceled them. My bad mood spoiled the rapport necessary to get these old people to open up, and I came home in disgust. I haven't even called Patricia yet. Maybe I won't. Hell, I don't know. I sit here typing this and wondering if I'll be able to send you any more letters, and I want you to know you've been the best pal a guy could ask for.

I'm having trouble focusing, so I'm going to return what's left in the jar to its hiding place and try to get some sleep. Wish me luck, but don't hold your breath.

Hope to write again.

Your pal and faithful comrade,

Robert

September 5, 1939
Tuesday night

Dear John,

I am going to write you every day. The axe could fall at any time and I want you to know as much as you can about this horror show. And while I'm writing you every day, please remember that I'm not mailing them every day, because I can't get over to Harrison more than twice a week. I haven't mailed any of my letters to you from Mackaville for a long time now. I know that Postmaster Gibson is not any too fond of me and even without the evidence he might've found if he'd intercepted the correspondence from my end, he will probably be one of the citizens voting for my demise Saturday. (And, again, I appreciate how general you are in your responses. You seem to have done that instinctively, before I even said anything. Maybe you've got a little of the seventh sense yourself.)

For a good while, I wasn't even mailing my Folklore Project reports from Mackaville. But I've reconsidered that lately and started using the local p.o. again. I figure if Gibson opens and reads them before he sends them on, all he'll get is his old neighbors talking about old things that happened. Of course, if I get anything in an interview that might reflect on this town and its secrets, that report'll go with your letters down the road to Harrison.

Still mixing up my start times to try and keep my adversaries off-track, I didn't head out until mid-morning today – slowed, maybe, by a little bit of a moonshine hangover. As usual, Rennsdale was waiting by the shed for me and hopped up in the sidecar as soon as I started it up. But she seemed, I don't know, different this time. I haven't studied cats much, so I really can't speak about what causes their different behavior patterns, but as sure as I'd sleep with Jean Rogers, that little calico had a changed attitude this morning. If I had to put an adjective to it, I'd call it "defiant."

I knew I'd only be doing one interview that day because the subject – a 98-year-old Civil War widow named Summer Denright – lives in a place that's remote even by local standards, with no one around for quite a ways. I checked out her location this morning, and I've already interviewed everyone within five or ten miles of her. I have a few of these that I've been putting off because it's a lot of effort for just one interview; now, I know I'd better be getting them as quickly as I can so I can get finished and, if luck's with me, light a shuck out of this place, and soon.

I was hardly past the Mackaville city limits when something tripped my seventh sense. It took a few moments to pin it down, but finally I knew I was being tailed by someone in a new white Ford pick-up truck. It never got real close, but it followed me the whole way to Mrs. Denright's hilltop, driving past just as I got part way up the dirt path that led to her tar paper house. As it passed, I spied the initials painted in gold on the door. They were a G and an M, inter-twined. Those stood for "Gabber Meats."

For some reason, knowing that a show-down is imminent has had a positive effect on me. I was back to my charming self in the inter-view, and Mrs. Denright responded by giving me two good stories. One involved a witch's changeling being substituted for a baby, and it was pretty gruesome, with the parents drowning the changeling in a creek. Mrs. Denright told me it changed to a fox when it died. Just another one of the stories I've taken down that seem to be ripped from the pages of *Weird Tales*.

When I finished and got back to the Indian, I made a show of stowing my notebook away in the sidecar, fussing around with the ground sheet. Actually, what I was doing was unwrapping my sawed-off boom stick, checking to make sure one barrel had a deer slug and the other triple aught buck shot. Either of them would go through a car door at close range. I stuck its muzzle down beside the folded-up tarp so I could grab it. I didn't know what the Gabber toady in the pick-up might do, but at least I'd be ready for it.

Kicking the bike to life, I steered out onto the path and headed toward the road, sure that I'd see the truck and its driver again, and soon. I was right.

The pick-up sat just off the side of the road, maybe a couple of hundred yards from the end of the trail to Mrs. Denright's place, laying for me around the first bend. The driver knew I'd just be starting to accelerate then, but instead when I saw the truck I throttled the Indian back. As I got closer I could see through the windshield a guy in one of those big black hats that western-movie Indians sometimes wear, the shapeless brim shading his face. His hand went up slowly and something in it flashed in the rays of the sun.

I was almost on him now, going very slowly, and I reached over, flipped the shotgun up, and cradled it on my arm.

Even seen through a dusty windshield, the change in that bozo's face was impressive. His mouth fell open and his hands flew up in the air, a pistol dropping from his right. John, he may have been a homicidal idiot, but he wasn't a fool. He knew what a twelve-gauge could do at point-black range.

His passenger-side window was open, and as I rolled by it, I shouted, "I've got deer slugs in here, mister! So you'd better not try to back-shoot me!" Then, without waiting for an answer, I gunned the bike and left him in a shower of gravel and dirt. It didn't take long for him to fall in behind me again, but he hung further back and showed no inclination to inch up.

When he peeled away as I descended the road into town, the thought occurred to me that maybe he wasn't sent to kill me at all. Maybe the Gabbers didn't want me leaving town until the meeting had decided my fate. That was going to make it tough to get to Harrison and mail my letters to you.

By this time, it was about 2 p.m., the shank of a hot dog-day afternoon, so I pulled into the Castapolous Cafe, thinking Mr. Castapolous might be in there by himself after the lunchtime rush. Sure enough, when I opened the door and entered the cool darkness, there wasn't another paying customer to be seen. He looked up from behind the bar, where he was polishing glasses, and his broad face split into a grin.

"How you doing, Robert?" he called out.

I shook my head as I approached him and plopped down on one of the stools. "If you really want to know," I said, "it'd probably do me good to tell you."

So, while he fried me up a hamburger and I went through two Cleo Colas, I unburdened myself, knowing he was a man I could trust. He already knew about some of the things the Gabbers and Black had tried to do to me, and when I told him I'd heard they were having another meeting, and added the tale of the Gabber goon who'd trailed me to my interview, he shook his head.

"Robert," he said, "you move in here. We'll fix any *bastardo* who comes looking for you."

I could see he had gotten agitated, and I thanked him but told him the last thing I wanted to do was get him in any trouble. Echoing one of the first conversations I'd had with Sheriff Meagan, I told Mr. Castapolous that he had to live in this town and I didn't – that if by the grace of God I was able to survive long enough to complete my work, I could leave this town and never look back. And, I added, that was damn sure my plan.

"Robert," he said somberly, after I'd finished, "lissen to me. You gotta run for it, you run here. I've had a good life, a very good life. I'm not afraid. The *porca miserias* can *mangia merda* before I let them take you without a fight. These Gabbers and Black – they get you, I'll take that Mannlicher and blow their *brutto figlio di puttana bastardo* heads off. Me, I can still hit a hen's egg at five hundred yards."

I didn't ask for a translation, because I caught the gist of what he was saying. Grinning, I reached across the bar, grabbed his hand and pumped it, assuring him I'd fort up with him if it got to that.

"I sure appreciate it, Mr. Castapolous," I told him. "And thanks for letting me tell you the story. I feel better now."

"We're friends," he returned, still clutching my hand. "Friends do this."

I did feel better, too. Maybe there wasn't much either of us could do about the forces around us, but it was good to know I had someone else on my side.

Leaving the cafe with a full stomach and a better mood, I decided to head down to Pete's and put in some honest labor for a few hours. When I arrived, he had four new tires sitting out, ready to mount on a beat-to-hell Willys Whippet that looked as though it had come over on the Mayflower. Handing me four bucks, he said, "That line of gab you're shooting is sure selling rubber. I had to order twenty more tires. The jobber balked until I showed him the mazuma and paid him up front." Then, as I pocketed the ones, he added, "Sit down a minute," and gestured toward one of the office chairs.

That was unusual for Pete. He didn't encourage much sitting while the station was open; there was always something that needed doing.

"What's up?" I asked, taking a seat.

"You were followed today, weren't you?"

I let out a sigh. "How'd you know?"

"People come in here all the time, Robert." He said. "This is a small town.

There aren't many secrets in a place like this. People talk."

I knew that was all I was going to get regarding his sources, so I told him the whole story. When I finished, he shook his head.

"They don't want you leaving town," he said.

"That's kind of what I figured."

"They really don't want you leaving town. They got a gang of toughs hanging around the depot. I spotted a couple of 'em along the track a ways, too." He shook out a Spud from the pack on the counter. "Fag?" he asked.

"No, thanks," I said. "But as long as I stick to my business and don't try to ankle the premises, I don't think things will boil over until Saturday, when they have their board meeting."

He nodded, lighting up. "You're probably right." Then he half-grinned. "Gives you plenty of time to get your bags packed, don't it?"

Like a lot of what Pete says, it was kidding wrapped around truth. Just as I started to say something back, an old Locomobile pulled up in front and, leaving his butt in the ash tray, Pete headed out to take care of it. That was my own cue to get to work, so I did, mounting and balancing all four tires before heading out. He got busy, and we never returned to the topic of me and my woes.

Rennsdale got busy too, prowling around the station for mice while Pete and I worked.

I'd fixed it up with Pete to leave before it got dark enough for the street lights to come on, so about 5:45 I mounted up and headed for the boarding house. When I pulled in the drive and rolled up to the shed, Rennsdale hopped off and stood by the pathway, the only cat around.

That was funny. Usually, there had been at least a couple of others to greet us when we returned, even if all they did was stand and look at us and then wander off. Not this time, though. Just Rennsdale, eyeing me with that same mixture of pride and defiance I'd noticed this morning. Then I wondered if the lack of felines had anything to do with what Mrs. Davis had told me about how their powers were weakening. Was Rennsdale's changed attitude a part of all that?

Although I didn't feel the stirrings of any seventh sense, I did feel as though things had spun a little off-kilter.

Pushing the Indian into the shed, I thought about taking the shotgun with me to my room but chose to leave it and take the pistol instead. By the time I locked the bat wing doors, dusk had fallen – hard and fast, like it does every night in these mountains.

Then, just as I turned toward the boarding house, someone sprang out of the shadows. A hand slapped across my mouth and my arms were pinned by someone so strong that I couldn't move an inch. *This is it,* I thought, *you stupid cocky fool. Now you're going to die*!

I don't want to give anything away, but I didn't. Die, that is. More later.

Your pal and faithful comrade,

Robert

September 6, 1939

Wednesday night

Dear John,

While you know I love sending you cliffhanger endings, there was a logical reason for my stopping where I did on yesterday's letter. I had other demands on my time after being jumped there in the dusk, because my attacker turned out to be none other than David Jefferson.

I didn't know that for a few frenzied heartbeats, though – not until he whispered right in my ear, "Robert. It's David." Then he released me so suddenly I almost dropped to the ground.

The street lamp a few houses down had just come on, so I could see him, dressed in a well-cut black suit and wearing a dark shirt and tie.

"Damn, David!" I hissed. "You scared the hell out of me."

He grinned, whispering back, "Isn't that what a preacher's <u>supposed</u> to do? Besides, I didn't want you to shoot me, and I figured you had that little pistol with you. With what's been going on around here, I wouldn't blame you for being quick on the trigger."

"You know about all of that, then?"

"What I need to know," he said. "That's why I'm back. The time has arrived to settle accounts with my brothers. You've made it possible. I owe you a great debt, and I want to take care of you."

I wasn't entirely sure what he meant by that, but in the pale light his face reflected a grimness that didn't welcome questions.

"I owe it to you to bring the sword of the Lord down on their necks – and I need you to take me to their farm tomorrow."

"Of course, I will," I returned. "But they're watching every move I make now. How–"

He cut me off. "I'll handle that," he said. "But now, I crave rest. Do you know where I might find a comfortable place to sleep?"

I reached out and punched him lightly on the arm; it was like hitting a lamp post. "Why not bunk here, with me?" I said. "I've got a regular-sized bed. You don't mind sleeping with a dog, do you?"

He grinned again. "It would not be the first time. Thank you."

"We'll have to be quiet about it," I said. "Where's your bag?"

"I don't have one. I won't be here that long. If all goes according to plan, I train out for Saint Louis tomorrow."

We went in the back way, through the kitchen, and once he was settled I returned and fixed a couple of ham sandwiches for us. He seemed grateful, and I was hungry, too. So was MacWhirtle, who sniffed at David when we first came in but didn't bark. We showed our gratitude by feeding him pinches of ham while we ate.

Then David lay down, falling asleep almost immediately. I wrote last night's letter to you and then turned in myself. It was the first time I'd ever shared a bed with a colored fellow, but neither Mac nor I had any problems. And unlike you, John, David does not pull covers.

The next thing I knew, I was being shaken awake in darkness. I heard David say, "Time for us to go, Robert," and before I was fully conscious, I was getting into my clothes. The radium-dial clock on my desk said it was a little after 5 a.m., and I knew the other occupants of the house were either still asleep or not yet off their rail shifts.

We both hit the bathroom and then we were off, easing down the staircase to the kitchen.

I unbolted the back door, and we slipped out undetected before I used my key to latch it. The screen door gave me an uneasy moment, squeaking as we exited, and I hoped like hell it didn't wake up Ma, whose bedroom was on the other side of the house.

I guess it didn't, because I looked back as David and I wheeled the big Indian out of the shed and no lights had come on. However, looking around I spotted another obstacle. Just down the street, another new Ford pick-up truck – or maybe the same one that had trailed me yesterday – sat at the side of the street, the fancy GM lettering on the side door indicating Gabber Meats. Even though it was away from the street light, I was sure I saw a head behind the windshield and an elbow resting beside it on the frame of the driver's side window.

"David," I whispered, turned toward him. "There's—"

The rest of the sentence died in my throat. He was nowhere to be seen.

Since I had no idea what to do next, I stood there in the darkness beside the motorcycle and kept my eye on the parked truck. Another heavy hot wind had come up, gusting noisily around me and then dying away. Within just a few moments, I saw an unmistakable bulk rise up beside the pick-up window and heard a strangled yelp. I had no idea how David had gotten there, but the next thing I knew, he'd jerked the driver out of the open window with one hand while he thumped him with the other. Then he raised the guy into the air, over his head, and he slammed him down into the truck's bed so hard that it sounded like an explosion, even in the middle of a sudden blast of wind. I flinched at the sound. Hustling around from the truck bed, David wrenched open the driver's-side door and dove in. I heard wrenching sounds and metallic whines coming from the cab's interior. Then he melted back into the darkness and almost before I knew it he'd materialized beside me.

"We can go now," he whispered, his hands full of wires.

"I'd think so," I returned. "Let's push the bike a little ways down the street before we start her."

With his help, the uphill push was nothing, and as we passed a neighbor's trash can a few doors away, he stepped over, lifted the lid, and dropped his load of wiring in. So far, the noise hadn't raised anyone. The intermittently howling wind had helped mute the noise of David's savage attack.

About a block and a half away, I kicked the Indian to life, and David climbed into the sidecar, pushing aside the ground sheet, my cloth-wrapped shotgun, and the other stuff until he could fit relatively comfortably inside.

I'd strapped on my H&R break-over .22 pistol that morning, taking a chance that I wouldn't meet Sheriff Meagan or any law officers in town. Luckily, I didn't, and soon we were motoring through the hills, on the way to the Gabbers'.

About a quarter of a mile before we reached their farm, David laid a hand on my arm and said, "Let's stop here and wait for the sun to rise. I want them up and dressed."

Off in the distance, I could see the two Gabber homes, still strung up with the lights they'd used to ward off the "monster." A pang of doubt gripped me then, something similar to what I'd felt after I'd agreed to kill Old

Man Black and set his boys free. It was pretty damn clear to me that David was going to murder both of them in cold blood. Even with all that they'd done, and tried to do, to me, I wasn't at all sure I wanted to be a part of that. I knew David's story. I knew he had every reason to kill them. And now, I thought with a start, he has a practical reason to do it: they want to kill his friend, the man who brought him out of Hell. In other words, I'm his excuse for murder.

As I pondered this idea, we sat down together on a little outcropping and watched the houses, hearing nothing but the sounds of frogs and crickets and the rattling ebb and flow of the hot wind. Then a rooster crowed, joined by another in the distance. The deeper darkness that followed the false dawn slowly gave way to a faint glow, as the sun began to rise over the top of the surrounding mountains.

I glanced over at David. In the dawn's orange light his eyes gleamed red. In that moment, I knew he was capable of just about anything, and whatever he was going to do, I was glad he was going to do it to the Gabbers and not me.

But then, I wasn't kidding myself. I knew what he was going to do. And I was, as he'd said last night, "the one who'd made it possible." I suppose his morality, which in this situation was more Old Testament than New, wouldn't allow him to seek revenge for his own satisfaction. But to save the life of a friend – well, that was a different story.

I was so lost in these thoughts that his sudden words shocked me. "Won't be long," he said in a low voice. "They'll be up now, and having their last breakfast." The wind kicked up then, swirling his dispassionate words away like so much dust, as I checked my strap watch. 6:23 a.m.

We sat together in the wind and the heat, both wrapped in our own thoughts, until the sun had risen completely above the eastern peaks of the mountains. Then David said, "Give me about twenty minutes, then drive on up."

"What about the pigs, David?" I asked, speaking above the gusting wind.

He smiled. "The pigs won't bother us. They're uphill in the woods. Don't worry about them." Before I could respond, he took off down the road, walking almost leisurely toward the Gabbers. I watched as the wind whipped his dark suit around him. He looked like some sort of phantom: a scythe-less Grim Reaper.

He walked up to the back gate of the picket fence, fooled with it a couple of moments, and slipped inside. Then he was at the back door of Jube's place, and, as far away as I stood and as windy as it was, I could still hear the splintering noise when he threw his body against it.

That was my cue to start up the Indian.

With the rending of that door, our silence wasn't too important anymore. I knew it hadn't been anything like twenty minutes yet, but what the hell? Among other things, I was damned curious about what he was going to do – curious and apprehensive, at the same time.

As I motored slowly down the road past the house, I stared over the points of the white-washed fence, trying to see what was going on. Suddenly, I saw the top of David's head as he slammed out of the front door, hauling Jube Gabber on his shoulder like a sack of wet cement. The part of Jube I could see was writhing slowly, as though he was stunned and hurt but still trying to get away. I had to get off the Indian to unlatch the front gate, and as I started my drive down the long path toward the houses I spotted Jube Gabber on the ground not far from his front porch, trying to get up and falling back down again. Then David marched out onto the porch of Jeb's house, carrying Jeb himself and dropping him next to his brother. Both of the Gabbers seemed to be in the same stunned state.

I was maybe 50 feet from where they lay when David, standing and looking over them, raised his head and looked at me.

"Dammit!" He shouted, his face contorted. "I said twenty minutes, Robert!"

I stopped then, confused. David seemed enraged.

He took a couple of steps toward me, and shouted again.

"Go back until our agreed-upon time!" he said. "I do not want you to see this!"

Well, John, I wasn't sure what to do. Like I said, I was curious as all hell. On the other hand, I didn't want David Jefferson mad at me.

I looked at him, the bike idling under me, and he glared back. Maybe that would've gone on for a long time, but something stirred behind David and I saw Jube Gabber struggle to his feet beside the inert body of his brother and start awkwardly clambering away. David's head whipped around and he bounded toward the man, striking him on the back of the neck with both fists.

Jube Gabber went down hard, and David scooped him up and hauled him back under one arm. Then he picked up the still-dazed Jeb and, hefting him with his other arm, began dragging them away from me toward the back gate. He looked back at me only once, but there was a clear warning in that steely gaze: Don't follow me, it said.

Then I heard the slam of a screen door, and Mrs. Jube Gabber stepped out onto the porch. She had a shotgun, and it was pointed right at me.

Maybe it was born of desperation, but I got another of those flashes of insight, just like the one that had come to me when I'd first met the Gabbers at that still. I'd had a weapon pointed at me then, too.

I was far enough away that I had to shout to make myself heard over the rumbling of the Indian and the swirling winds.

"Mrs. Gabber," I hollered. "You are about to become a very wealthy woman."

She stared at me over the barrel, the shotgun not wavering a fraction of an inch, for what seemed like a long time. Then she slowly smiled, turned, and went back inside. I only realized then that I'd been holding my breath.

In a moment, she returned. The gun was gone. Not even glancing my way, she sat down in a rocking chair and began rocking slowly. Silver-haired and dressed in a loose-fitting faded print dress, she seemed the very portrait of a rural matron relaxing on her porch – not a woman whose husband had just been carried off to what seemed certain death. There even seemed to be something patrician in her look then, a kind of stoic nobility. After watching her for a few moments, I realized she no longer had any interest in picking me off, so I killed the motor, put the bike on its stand, and walked to the side of the picket fence that bordered the hills, where I figured David had gone with the two Gabbers.

I spotted him about 100 yards away, up on the gently sloping side of a mountain beside an old fallen tree on the edge of a wooded stretch. He'd leaned the two still-dazed Gabbers against it, and what he did next scared me stiff. Throwing his head back, he began making loud animal noises, squeals and grunts – and almost immediately I spotted movement in the woods around him. It was as though the ground itself were coming to life. That black boar I remembered from my visit to the Gabbers – or one damn sure like it – was the first to crash through the brush, but the movement behind him showed me he wouldn't be the last.

David lowered his head, and I dropped mine behind the fence as well. I didn't want him seeing me and knowing that I'd disobeyed his order. In his bestial state, I wasn't sure what he was capable of doing – maybe even to me. When I ducked, though, I saw a knothole that had been knocked out of the fence, about on a level with the last button of my shirt. Glancing back at Mrs. Gabber, who sat rocking as though nothing out of the ordinary were going on, I dropped to my knees and peeked through the hole, just in time to see that huge black hog rip into Jeb. Jube screamed then and struggled to stand, but the pig spun around and cut Jube's legs out from under him with a maneuver that was almost surgical. Then other hogs stampeded in – a couple of razor-backs, others that looked domesticated – and jumped into the fray, the shrieks of the Gabbers mingling with the frenzied squealing of the pigs and the unholy sounds of ripping flesh.

I had to look away. When I put my eye to the knothole again, one of the razorbacks was scurrying off into the brush with a string of intestines. Blood and saliva sprayed through the air, and still the Gabbers screamed and the hogs rooted and squealed and – well, John, I'm not proud of it, but suddenly my insides churned and I threw up, hard.

Wiping my mouth with my sleeve, I shot a glance at Mrs. Gabber, who looked down at me implacably. Then, slowly, she stood up and left the porch, walking to me.

The noise of the slaughter was dying away as I got to my feet. I didn't want to look anymore, but I guess she did, because even as she spoke she was looking over my shoulder, toward the mountain.

"I have some castor oil, in case you need it," she said.

"No, thanks. I'm all right now," I said.

She nodded. "You wouldn't be doing any heaving, young man, if you'd just been released from thirty years of hell like I have." A long, futile shrieking wound through the air, the wind whipping it away. She smiled a little.

"Thirty years. That's how long I've waited for this to happen." She still wasn't looking at me, but toward the carnage David had created, as though it was something she wanted to remember forever.

"Oh, I was smart," she added. "Before I… married those two animals, I made them sign a will, a legal will, leaving everything to me if they died first."

Those two animals? I thought. She was married to them both? How could that—

"It took me a while to understand they figured on living at least fifty years longer than me, so making out a will like that was no skin off their noses."

Another, weaker scream bubbled up from the side of the mountain.

"I've won now," she said softly. "They'll be burning in Hell directly – like two June bugs in a fire – and things are going to change. I'm getting out of these godforsaken shacks and moving to town. I'm gonna spend some of this money they've squirreled away instead of living here like a God-damned flat-broke Arky, like I don't have two nickels to rub together. And I'm gonna take over the running of that plant, too. You see if I don't."

The wind picked up again, and I was glad of it. It covered up, if only for a moment, some of the obscene rooting noises 100 yards up the hill.

She turned to me then, gazing at me with her pale blue eyes. "You cannot imagine the degradations those two demons put me through, young man. But it's all mine now – the money, the plant. These here houses, this farm, all of it can go to blazes. I'll give it away to somebody. You want it?"

I swallowed. "No, ma'am. I'm no farmer. But thank you," I added quickly.

She nodded. "Someone'll take it. And be happy to get it."

Just then, David appeared from behind the house, his suit, tie, and shirt spattered with blood. There was an eerie calmness around him now, and I knew I didn't need to be afraid.

When he reached us, he turned toward Mrs. Gabber and bowed.

"I didn't have time to properly introduce myself this morning, Miz Gabber," he said. "My name is David Jefferson."

"I know who you are," she said, a hint of sharpness in her voice. "They'd been living in pure terror since they figured out you were free." Then she smiled. "Made my heart sing, Mr. Jefferson. It surely did."

David bowed again, as I tried to block out the muted but still audible grunts and groans from outside the fence and force myself to figure out just what the hell was going on.

"You two had better go on now," she added in near-motherly tones. "I'm going to go in and have a nice long breakfast. Then I'm gonna call a good lawyer, and after that I'll give the sheriff a ring. I reckon it'll take me 'bout four hours to get all that done. You all oughta be well away from these parts by that time; 'course, far as I'm concerned you ain't been here at all.

"Now git. And, Mr. David Jefferson, thank you. Thank you from the bottom of my heart."

David bowed a third time and then we were off. Silently we rode back to town, with the noises – the motor and the whirling of the wind in my ears – competing for space in my head with the unforgettably sinister sounds of the attacking hogs and the screams of their victims.

David's swords of the Lord, I thought, had been the tusks of wild pigs. I almost got sick again at the thought and the images it evoked.

By this time it was mid-morning, and, taking less-traveled roads into town, I pulled into the alley behind Mr. Castapolous's place and killed the Indian.

"Tell Mr. Castapolous you're with me and you need a place to clean up," I said. It was the first time either of us had spoken since we'd gotten on the bike. "He's a good man. You're safe with him. I'm going to pull around and go in the front way."

His eyebrows raised at that.

"I'm being watched," I explained. "Now that the Gabbers are…gone, that's likely going to change somewhat, but for right now it's best if you and I aren't seen palling around together."

"All right, Robert," he said. The words

hung in the humid air as he looked at me expectantly.

Then I knew. Given the ferocity of what I'd seen, it was hard for me to say it, because by saying it I would implicate me forever, if only in my own mind.

I said it anyway.

"Thank you, David," I told him, gripping his hand. "It's very likely you have saved my life."

"The Lord says that vengeance is his," he returned. "Deuteronomy 32, verse 35. I've looked into my own soul, and I pray what I did was not for vengeance, but to spare the life of a friend. A good friend."

I nodded. "I'm grateful," I said. But the image of a squealing razorback dragging intestines through the brush still haunted my mind.

David came out of the living quarters in the back of the cafe while I was sitting at the counter talking with Mr. Castapolous. It was midmorning, and there were only two other patrons – both overall-wearing farmers who were unfamiliar to me – in the place. They were drinking coffee at a table about as far away from the bar as you could get, so I could've told Mr. Castapolous all about everything without any fear of being overheard. Still, as much as I knew he was my friend and ally, someone I could count on, I couldn't bring myself to tell him about what had happened up in those hills. It was guilt, maybe – guilt by association. I'm sure he knew there was something askew with me, but he didn't say anything. David had managed to clean most of the blood off his dark suit and tie with scrubbing and water from Mr. Castapolous's private sink, and while his shirt was still spattered with tiny rust-colored stains, those weren't likely to attract much attention.

"My train will be here soon, so I must go," he said as he approached us. Turning to Mr. Castapolous, he stuck out his hand. "Thank you," he said.

"You're welcome. Come back anytime."

David nodded. "And you," he said to me. "I'm happy to have been able to pay my debt to you."

"There was no debt, David," I said.

"Oh, yes," he returned. "Yes." He shook my hand and then walked away, going out the back door. We watched as the door shut behind him.

Then, I said, "Mr. Castapolous. I know it's early. But I need a drink."

Your pal and faithful correspondent,
Robert

September 7, 1939
Thursday night

Dear John,

As you might have divined from my last letter, by noon yesterday I wasn't worth a tinker's dam. Although he didn't prod me for details, Mr. Castapolous knew I could use a dip in the waters of forgetfulness, so he broke out what I guess was some special giggle water. Ouzo, he called it. He even spelled it for me. After four shots of it, I couldn't spell my own name. Not even the roar of the wind and the heat that beat down on me as I steered the Indian home could sober me up.

I'd had the presence of mind to accept the Sen-Sen Mr. Castapolous offered me as I left, and that turned out to be a good idea, since Ma was bustling around in the kitchen when I tried to sneak in. I think I sold her on the idea that I was under the weather and my stomach was doing flip-flops, so I was going to go up to my room and go to bed. I don't want her to think she's got a lush on the premises.

Anyway, between the stress and the hootch I slept hard for most of the afternoon, waking up in a sweat from the heat at about 5:30 p.m. I was ok, though. In fact, I felt good enough to go down to dinner, where the removal of the Gabbers' truck and the ambulance transport of its driver to Dodd General Hospital in Harrison (my old stomping ground) were the topics du jour.

I'd tell you that the main course last night – baked ham – was ironic given what I'd seen that morning, but pork is a staple of Ma Stean's boarding house and, I imagine, Mackaville in general.

That doesn't mean I ate it. Still claiming a bad stomach, I drank a glass of milk, ate a couple of Ma's big dinner rolls, and then went back up to my room, stretched out, and read the latest Dime Detective. This issue has another story about that nutty detective Inspector Allhoff, who's addicted to coffee and spends a lot of time browbeating one of his assistants, who was responsible for Allhoff losing both of his legs in a hail of gangsters' bullets. After finishing that story, I wrote you, and now here I am again – with plenty more to relate.

Between sleeping off Mr. Castapolous's ouzo most of the day and the memories of what I'd seen happen on that mountainside, I didn't sleep a whole lot last night, so I was up and out before dawn. I'd gotten the idea to go out around the Gabber's place and pick up some of the people I hadn't interviewed yet. My list contained the names of four families who lived within a few miles of the Gabbers, but I hadn't talked to any of them because I hadn't wanted to risk another encounter with the Gabbers' murderous hogs, or with any other trap they might have laid for me.

John, I could've stayed at the boarding house reading pulps for all the good it did me. I went to all four of the places on my list and didn't get a single story. Every household — they each had at least two generations under a roof — was too worked up about the death of the Gabbers. I have no idea how the news traveled so fast in those hills; I didn't see a telephone in any of those homes. But they'd gotten the word, and no matter how I tried to turn the conversation back around to their reminiscences, they doggedly stuck to asking what I'd heard and telling me what they knew about the Gabbers' demise. I guess it's the biggest thing to happen around these parts in a long time. The best thing I could do, I figured, was to indulge them and then make appointments to come back later on, when the excitement has died down. As wild-eyed as they all seemed to be about the deaths, that may not be anytime soon.

By noon, I'd visited all four families and heard over and over about how the "hogs et" the Gabber brothers. At my last stop, one particularly vocal old lady, her eyes shining, told me how she'd happened to be riding back from town in a mule-drawn wagon when she was passed by an ambulance and three or four "highway-law cars." When they pulled into the Gabbers, she followed, getting there in time to see what was left of the men being loaded in the ambulance.

"The law had to fire their guns 'fore them hogs'd move offen the Gabbers," she said. "And when them pigs cleared out, what was left wouldn't hardly have made a grease spot in a fryin' pan."

The way the rest of her family bobbed their heads and grinned told me this wasn't the first time she'd related that tale. I knew it was far from the last, too. She'd enjoy her status as an eyewitness for a good long time.

Maybe because I hadn't had much to eat last night or this morning – I passed on the sidemeat Ma cooked up for breakfast – I found myself getting hungry, so I aimed the Indian toward Dill Jolley's Mercantile, where I knew I could buy a lunch that wouldn't include pork.

Of course, pudgy old Mr. Jolley and the Greek chorus of derelicts hanging around his store were full of excitement about the Gabbers, too, so before I could get out of there with my sardines, crackers, bottle of pop, and freshly sliced rat cheese, I had to hear about the Gabber massacre all over again.

It was finally a treat to get away from everyone, sit by myself in the shade of a big rock outcropping, and eat my lunch in peace. That lasted I guess about fifteen minutes, until I spotted a big rattler sliding around a pile of boulders that lay maybe twenty-five feet from me, up against the side of a mountain.

Damn that Old Man Black. With all the concentration on the Gabbers and their demise, I hadn't even thought about him and his snakes. And now, here was something that made me remember.

Honest, John, I would've let that reptile live if he'd just slithered off and let me alone. But no such luck. He headed right for me, rattlers going, and I had no choice but to unload the shotgun on him. It left a mess that reminded me of what the Gabbers had looked like when the pigs finished, and I pitched the rest of my tin of sardines into the gorge beside me. I blamed Old Man Black for contributing to my loss of appetite.

I got to Pete's Skelly around two p.m., and who should be pulling out but Ma in her big old Pontiac – with none other than Mrs. Gabber sitting beside her! The new widow looked about 20 years younger and a lot more dolled-up than she had yesterday, but it was sure enough the same woman, with the patrician air even more pronounced. Ma waved and shouted hello as I pulled past them on the Indian, but Mrs. Gabber played it cool and just kind of nodded. The look in her eyes, though, told me she'd recognized me but wasn't letting on. That was damn good of her.

Over the next few hours, I got the scoop from Pete in bits and pieces. Ma and Mrs.

Gabber – Mary Lou, to give you her proper name – have been friends for a long time, and Ma volunteered to drive her around town today.

"Mrs. Mary Lou Gabber sure ain't letting any grass grow under her feet," Pete said at one point. "Ma's taken her to the beauty parlor and the bank, where I hear she drew out a thousand simoleons. She's taken the best room at the hotel and paid cash money for a month's stay. And word has it that both them Gabbers left her everything they had." He raised his eyebrows. "Both of 'em."

Of course, John, you and I know she was "married" to the two of them, and she must've done some pretty fancy maneuvering to get them to leave her everything. Then again, maybe not. If there's truth in what I believe about the Gabbers, based on what she told me and David's words about their longevity, then they were sure they'd outlive her, anyway. She'd been a striking woman, Pete said, when she'd first gotten married: I guess between the two of them they'd squeezed all the beauty out of her, so it's probable her days would've been numbered if David hadn't put the quietus to the two. Maybe she knew that. And maybe she deserved what she was getting now. Living like a backwoods pauper, at the beck and call of whichever one wanted her – hell, she'd probably dreamed of this day, never expecting it would really happen.

And, by the way, according to the coroner

(again, this is from Pete), the Gabbers' kiss-off has been officially ruled "death by misadventure."

I heard more about Mary Lou Gabber that evening at supper. Mister Clark told us that the manager at Gabber Meats wanted to shut down the packing plant and cannery for a day to honor its fallen founders, but Mrs. Gabber said nothing doing.

"Rumor has it," said Mister Clark, spearing a piece of pork roast, "she put that manager on notice, too. Maybe now we'll get someone who'll treat us railroad boys with some decency." Ma, standing nearby, kept her own counsel.

That's about all for now. I listened to Rudy Vallee's show on the big radio in the living room, and it was just what I needed to relax and turn my mind to something else, if only for an hour. And now that I've finished this letter to you, I'm going to turn in. MacWhirtle is already chasing rabbits from his spot on the bed.

Your pal and faithful comrade,

Robert

September 9, 1939

<u>very</u> early Saturday morning

Dear John,

I know I have told you some things over the past several months that would be very hard for anyone to swallow. From the letters I've gotten back from you, I think you believe what I'm saying. Or if you don't, you respect me enough not to tell me it's all malarkey or you're worried for my sanity. (And once again, I appreciate the way you never get specific about what I've written, so if Barney Gibson or anyone else looks at your letters before I get 'em, they won't find anything to convict me. Kid, that's some of the best writing you've ever done!)

I write all of this because what I'm about to put down is really going to test the limits of your belief in what I'm saying. But I've thought it over, and I have no choice but to tell you. I don't know where you're storing these letters, but I hope they're in a very safe place and somewhere that no eyes but yours will be on them.

First of all, I woke up this morning convinced that Old Man Black is about to unleash a killer-diller – a real Jack Johnson, as Mr. Foreman down at the drug store would put it. I know this the way I've known a lot of things over my life, but especially since I landed here. My seventh sense tells me it's coming, but I haven't got a clue about how to face it. In an attempt to find out, I stuck my finger in the fire, even though I had a feeling that the process of finding out could be as dangerous to me as anything he unleashes. And I was right.

I'm also still worried about the board, which meets this evening, although I have reason to believe that I may be ok on that front for a while. Mrs. Gabber has wasted no time, canning the plant manager yesterday morning and picking a new one, which turns out to be Diffie's old man. Word is that she's calling all the shots now.

So the Gabber boys, who wanted me dead, are instead deceased themselves, and I get a feeling that Mrs. Gabber, who I assume will take both their places on the board, will be more sympathetic to me, if only because of her friendship with my apologist Ma Stean. But I don't know about the other members. Even with the coroner's "death by misadventure" ruling, I know there are a lot of people who believe I was the one who somehow did the Gabbers in. And while my hands aren't exactly clean – at the very least, I was a catalyst – I'm doing my best not to feel or act guilty. Maybe this suspicion about my involvement strengthens the case for my enemies on the board, or maybe it scares them. I don't know. All I know is that Mrs. Gabber knows who killed those two, and the only other people on earth with that knowledge are David Jefferson and myself. She probably thinks it was simple revenge; I can't imagine she sees it the way David justifies it, as being forced to kill in order to keep your friend safe.

This afternoon, I was helping Pete at the filling station when Diffie came by in his old Dodge Roadster with some papers his dad had left at home. He was going to the plant to deliver them and asked if I wanted to go with him. Well, the only other time I'd been at the plant I'd had to sneak around. It would be nice to be able to go in the front door. So, with Pete's blessing, I climbed in beside Diffie and we headed across town.

"Dad's in charge now," Diffie told me proudly as the wind whipped around us.

"Good for him," I said.

"Things are gonna be different now," he added. "You wait and see."

When we arrived, they passed us right on in. I just had a moment to gaze down past the loading docks at the building I'd scaled a few weeks earlier to listen in on the board meeting. The sight of it brought to mind the huge snake that had cut off my spying session, and that in turn made me think about Old Man Black.

Diffie marched us right straight through the front entrance, nodding importantly at a trim little secretary sitting at a desk and telling her, with a slightly haughty air I found amusing, "Mr. Gallagher to see Mr. Gallagher."

It struck me that in all these months of knowing Diffie I'd thought "Diffie" was his last name, not his first. Now, he was "Mr. Gallagher." Mr. Diffie Gallagher. Given his new taste of reflected glory, I wondered if I'd have to start calling him "mister," like we did Mister Clark back at the boarding house.

The young woman said pleasantly, "He's with Mrs. Gabber right now, Mr. Gallagher. Please have a seat."

Behind her was a long rectangular area lined with dark wood and glass bricks that led to several doors. We sat down in comfortable chairs beside a coffee table full of magazines, Diffie grinning as he picked them up one by one. "Look here, Robert," he said. "All the best ones. Life, Look, Liberty – even Popular Science."

"What kind of a place is this, anyway?" I returned. "They don't have a single issue of The Spider."

Before he could tell whether I was kidding or not, a door opened at the end of the hallway and out came a man with Mrs. Gabber. Both were grinning. The way Diffie got to his feet and stuck out his papers, I figured the man was his daddy, and I wasn't wrong, even though they didn't look a whole lot alike. I think I've told you that Diffie is pudgy and a little goofy-looking. His dad, though –

well, he reminds me of Warren William, the guy who played Perry Mason in the movies a few years ago. He's tall and slim, with a moustache and a cultured way of speaking. Even though Diffie has that coffee-and-cream coloration peculiar to most of the residents of Mackaville, his dad's a little blacker.

Anyway, Diffie introduced us all around, and Mrs. Gabber received me pleasantly, as though it were the first time we'd ever seen one another. She looked even classier than she had in Ma Stean's car just the day before. We made small talk for a few moments, and then the two excused themselves, with Mr. Gallagher suggesting to Diffie that he show me around the plant, something Diffie seemed excited to do. He almost pulled me down the outside hallway, past a switchboard operator and another secretary, to a big glass display case, which held examples of every tinned product the plant had ever made, all the way back to the Civil War. Through Diffie's chattering, I could pick up bits of the switchboard operator's conversations, and I got the idea that everyone who'd been with Gabber Meats for more than a year was in line for a dollar an hour raise. There was a new sheriff in town, and she had the whole atmosphere charged with electricity. All for the better, I suspect.

I now realize I've been writing about this pleasant visit to keep from getting to the material I warned you about at the first of this letter. Finding myself hesitant to begin, I guess the best way is just to plunge in and do it. So here goes.

Ever since you sent me those magic books from my library back home, I've been intermittently studying them. I've been very reluctant to put anything else I've learned into practice, however. For one thing, it's hard for me to completely believe in all of it, and for another, the effigy of Old Man Black I learned how to make seems to have worked almost too well. I realize there's a contradiction there. In a way, it's like what William James wrote about having faith in God – is a fear that we're wrong about it somehow better than a hope that we're right? That's not a bad way to put it, and it kind of sums up how I felt last night, when I decided to retrieve Black's hat – the one whose rattlesnake hatband had damn near killed me – from the deepest recesses of my closet and see if I could use it to divine what the old man might have in store for me.

So tonight after dinner, when everyone was gathered around the radio, I slipped outside in the darkness to Ma's storm cellar, whose door lay at an angle on a mound of earth against one side of the boarding house. The homes here in Arkansas don't have basements like we do in Minnesota, but a lot of them have these cellars people can get into in case of tornadoes. They also use 'em for other things, including storing jars of home-canned goods.

Truth to tell, one of the reasons I didn't want to get much deeper into the magic is because some of the rituals are very elaborate, and I didn't feel like my room was a private enough place to do them. It'd be damned difficult to explain all the candles and chanting and the pentagram drawn on the floor to one of my house mates who happened by while it was going on.

So while I'd been thinking about doing what I just did for some time, I couldn't figure out a safe place for it to happen. It wasn't until this morning, as I was leaving the shed with the Indian, that I looked over at the cellar and suddenly realized it could be perfect for my needs.

Later today, after I came in from the hills but before I headed for Pete's, I rode by the boarding house, saw Ma's car wasn't in the driveway, and took the opportunity to do a little reconnoitering. One of the things to remember about cellars is that they're sometimes snaky, so before using Ma's I wanted to take a good look around. Opening the slanted corrugated-metal door carefully, I shined my flash down the concrete steps, finding nothing but a bare floor with a couple of old wooden chairs, a cot, a couple of kerosene lamps, and a wall with jars of pickles and preserves and other things Ma had put up over the years. There was even a naked light bulb hanging from the middle of the ceiling with a chain attached, and it worked.

So now that I had my location, I had no more excuses. A few hours ago – hours that seem like days – I took that hat down into the cellar along with a paper sack full of stuff I'd gotten at Lowery's Five & Dime: candles, some small bowls, and a stick of blue chalk. Ma had a broom propped in one corner, and I used it to sweep some long-dead insects and a bit of other debris under the cot. Then I drew a pentagram, a five-pointed star, with the chalk. (One of the books you sent me from my home library, The Book of Black Magic and of Pacts by Arthur Edward Waite, from 1898, indicates that blue is a significant color in the occult.)

Leaving one side of the diagram open, or unfinished, I stepped across that side and placed Black's hat right in the middle of the pentagram. I also poured a little oil on it from one of the lamps, which I guess Ma Stean keeps down there in case the electricity goes out and leaves them without light.

After that, I put the little bowls in the vales – the areas below each point of the star – and set candles at the top of the points. Pouring a little water from my canteen in each dish, I pricked the end of my finger with my pocket knife and let a drop of blood fall in each of the five bowls. Then I lit the candles and the two kerosene lamps, stepped back outside the pentagram, and chalked a line across the place I'd left open, closing off the drawing.

What I hoped to accomplish was to see what Black had in mind – to enhance my seventh sense beyond simply "feeling" into knowledge. To do that, I had to open a way for forces I wasn't sure I could control – if, indeed, those forces existed. The pentagram, the little bowls of water topped with blood, the candles, were supposed to form a barrier that would keep anything I contacted from harming me.

As it turned out, John, the book gave me no idea of the forces I was about to unleash. Waite did talk about the magic of the North, of Europe, and how it compared with the ancient magic of the South, or Africa. In an abstract way, I saw the North as me and the South as Black. But tonight, the abstract turned deeply personal.

As the glow from the five candles and the two lamps wavered in the darkness, I reached up and clicked on the overhead light bulb, giving me plenty of light to see by. Sitting cross-legged on the floor outside the pentagram, I began to read aloud from an exhortation I'd written down, based on instructions given by Waite in his book. On one hand, I felt foolish. On the other, terrified.

Now, John, what I'm going to write here is not exactly what I read. I've thought a lot about this, and while I know you're keeping this letters in a very safe place, some day when we've both passed this could fall into someone's hands, and the results could be devastating. So I've changed around a couple of the critical phrases while still giving you the gist of what I said:

I conjure thee, O Guland, in the name of Satan, in the name of Beelzebub, in the name of Astaroth, and in the name of all other Spirits, to make haste and serve me. Come then, in the name of Satan and in the names of all other demons. Come to me, I command thee, in the name of the Most Holy Trinity. Come without inflicting any harm upon me, without injury to my body or soul, without maltreating anything which I use. I command thee to rend the walls of time and show unto me what mine enemies have planned or will do unto me. Then thou shall depart but in no wise until thee hath in all ways fulfilled my desire.

Then I waited, both skeptical and shaking in my boots. Remember I was doing this in kind of a "reverse" way. Instead of my being in the pentagram, I was calling forth the spirit to appear within it, hoping it would be unable to get out. The last thing I wanted to do was call up something that would be able to roam around Ma's boarding house doing God knows what.

I didn't have long to wait. Almost immediately, the candles dimmed, then flared into flames at least a foot high. I remember thinking, "Impossible!"

Then, in the center of my five-pointed blue star, Black's hat began to smoke. That may not be the right word. At first it looked like smoke, but then the vapor flattened and flowed until it had covered the drawing and the substance above the hat began condensing into a thick, dark ball. The ball began spinning — and then it happened, too fast for words.

All of a sudden, I was upstairs in the house, in my room, shaking from head to toe with naked terror. I "knew" something was coming down the hallway for me, and I knew I couldn't just wait for it to get me. I had to go meet it. Such was my mental state. So I grabbed my big flashlight off the bedside table and threw open the door, just as the hall light in front of me began to flash and dim and flash again. I think it finally went completely out, but I couldn't swear to that. I was too busy watching the top of the stairs some 20 or so feet away from me, where <u>something</u> had just poked its head into the beam of my flashlight. For a moment, I thought it was some sort of gigantic spider, about MacWhirtle's size. But the eyes were wrong. There were only two of them, glowing, and they weaved from side to side, trying to dodge the light. Then it threw a small skinny hand up in front of its face and hissed.

Yeah, a <u>hand</u>. It was some kind of a monkey — or so I thought at first. Then as it shambled a little closer and the flash's beam became stronger, I could see it was hairless and covered with scales. When that little hand dropped, I was gazing into the frigid eyes of a snake.

It hissed again, opening a mouth that revealed two huge fangs. Venom spewed from their tips, splattering the floor. Then it began bobbing and weaving, trying to dodge the light in earnest, scrambling up the door frame of David's room, leaping to the floor, and suddenly making for me with a horrifying burst of speed. Rooted to the spot, frozen with fear, I realized I had nothing but the flashlight for a weapon.

Then I was back in the cellar, shaking like I had the palsy and staring at the same creature, doing what seemed to be some sort of obscene dance. It would spring into the air, jump at me, and then roll back hard as though it had hit something solid. Getting more frenzied with every leap, it attacked again and again, only to be restrained by an invisible barrier, and I knew the incantation was working – so far.

Even as terrified as I was, I knew what I was supposed to do next. Pulling a book of matches and another sheet of paper from my shirt pocket, I opened the latter and began the finishing words of the "summonsing." I won't type it here, but it was short, and I made it even shorter by my hurried words. Then I lit the entire book of matches and, just as the creature leapt up again, I flipped it into the center of the pentagram onto Black's hat, which immediately burst into wild, crackling flames. The little beast, once again hitting the barrier, rolled back into it and was immediately consumed by the fire, letting loose a wild shriek I was sure would bring someone running from the house. As it burned, I chanted the final part of the incantation, ending with, "Send this spawn of the nether world back to its master, never to return!"

A final hot surge of flame erupted from the pentagram's center, and then, nothing. Not even a wisp of smoke. The candles and lanterns were all dark as well, suddenly snuffed.

If my studies had led to the right conclusion, the snake monkey had now returned to the person who had planned to sic it on me. This, of course, was Old Man Black, and I have to admit it gave me a great deal of pleasure to consider what the scene would be like when it materialized in Black's house. I figured it would be one pissed-off little demon.

All that I had left to do was get rid of the pentagram and its accoutrements, and I got a little too hasty about it, worrying that the shriek of the little beast might have drawn some unwanted attention from the boarders. So I reached for a bowl with my bare fingers and burned the holy crap out of myself. Those damn things were so hot they were almost glowing. Not only that, but the water, enhanced with a soupcon of Brown blood, had boiled away in every one of the five bowls, leaving no trace of anything.

Pulling out my bandana, I bent over to erase the pentagram with it, and when I first broke the border it made the noise you get when you open a can of coffee, like a vacuum popping. As I erased it, I used the bandana to slide the bowls out of the vales. Then, taking up the paper sack, I tossed in the candles and chalk and waited a couple of minutes, aware that I was still a bit shaky. Oddly enough, in that short time those bowls became cool to the touch, and I put them in the bag with the rest of the stuff.

Carefully pushing open the cellar door and closing it quietly behind me, I crept to Ma's trash barrel and stuck the bag in it down deep, underneath the ashes. It was only when I straightened up that I realized I was bathed in sweat, so I took off my shirt and flapped it a few times in the humid night air to at least partially dry it out. A sweat-soaked shirt could lead to some unwanted questions.

When I walked past the living room, Dave, Mister Clark, and Ma Stean were listening to Lowell Thomas, and I was glad for the newscaster's commanding voice – and, maybe, for Ma being a little hard of hearing. The loudness of the broadcast had likely covered up the scream of the apparition in the cellar.

Both of them were concentrating hard on what Thomas was saying, and I stopped long enough to hear him relate how the Heinies were fighting in Poland, and how the British and French navies were blockading Germany – with Roosevelt still proclaiming the neutrality of the U.S. I'd just started to turn away to go upstairs, when I became aware of the sounds of intertwined sirens outside. That got the attention of the two boarders and Ma, who turned down the broadcast so they could hear better. Dave went to the front door and opened it, listening.

"Sounds like two or three fire trucks," he called back.

In a moment, Ma and Mister Clark joined him, and I got up as well. "We only got three in all of Mackaville," Ma said, and then cocked her ear, listening. "Over on the other side of town. Hope nobody got hurt."

That baffled me. Old Man Black didn't live on the other side of town, but up in the hills. So if the fire was a result of my incantation, what was it doing flaring up in town?

"Some fool probably fell asleep smoking," opined Mister Clark. "Nasty habit. Can kill you any number of ways."

Although I was a little buffaloed, I took my leave and headed to my room, half-expecting to see the liquid poison from the fangs of the creature pooled on the wood of the hallway floor. Of course, it wasn't.

I tried to lie down and sleep, but it just wouldn't come. So after a while I got up and started this missive, which may be long, but it's just as long as it needs to be. And maybe, after unburdening myself on you with the details of this story, I can get some shut-eye now.

Your pal and faithful comrade,
Robert

September 9, 1939
Saturday evening

Dear John,

I am beat like a red-headed stepchild, but it's early enough that I can write you and then go to bed. I think I can sleep even though I know that at this very moment the town leaders are having a meeting at the Gabber Meats plant, with one of the agenda items having to do with whether I'll be able to exit this town with my carcass intact.

Maybe I'm kidding myself, but with the Gabber brothers out of the picture and Mrs. Mary Lou Gabber taking their place, I feel secure enough not to worry too much about it. What I'm worried more about is that I'll drop off before I finish this letter. That's how tired I am. I don't want someone coming in and finding me asleep on top of this half-written missive. It might fire up someone's curiosity. (Now that I think about it, though, I don't think Ma or any of the boarders would ever walk in on me. Still, Ma did "borrow" Old Man Black Jr. from my dresser drawer without my knowing it.)

Why am I so fagged, you ask? Well, not ten minutes after I wrote you all about the *incident* in the cellar I was unburdened and asleep, the letters to you, like always, stuck deep between the mattress and box springs. And not more than three hours after that, I was rudely brought back to consciousness by an insistent knocking on my door and the sound of my name being called.

It turned out to be Ma, telling me that Sheriff Meagan's secretary was on the line and insisting on speaking to me.

"Sorry, Robert," she said from outside my door, as I struggled into a shirt and trousers. "That old Miz Floyd's dogged as a door-to-door peddler; she said her orders was to talk to you, and she wasn't hanging up 'til she did."

As I shuffled barefooted down the stairs behind Ma, trying to clear my brain, I got a feeling – yeah, one of those – that this was about last night's fire.

She picked up the phone from the living room table and, after a cool, "Here he is," handed it over to me.

She may have been strident with Ma, but when she spoke to me, butter wouldn't have melted in her mouth.

"Mr. Brown," she said sweetly. "Sheriff Meagan wishes to see you as soon as you can get over here."

"All right," I told her. "Tell him I'll get dressed and be right there."

There was a prim, "Thank you," and then the click of the receiver. I turned away, and as my eyes swept across the room I noticed a couple of things: the grandfather clock in the corner read 7:43, and Mister Clark was sitting at the breakfast table, looking casually at me as he buttered one of Ma's buttermilk biscuits. Sheriff Megan and his employees punched the time clock early, even on Saturdays.

I went back upstairs, and as I was washing up in the communal bathroom, Ma knocked. "I left a glass of milk and a couple of biscuits and honey outside your door, Robert," she said through the door. "You hadn't oughtta go out without something in your stomach."

"You're aces, Ma. Thanks."

I was still chewing the second biscuit when I rolled the Indian out of the shed and fired it up. I thought about leaving the double-barreled Remington behind, given the sheriff's recent goosiness about firearms in town, but instead I just shoved it completely under the ground sheet in the sidecar, after first double-checking to see that it was loaded with No. 2 shot, not anything that could kill a man. Sheriff Meagan was already suspicious enough of me. I didn't need to give him any other reasons.

Old Mrs. Floyd – I hadn't known her name before this morning – barely looked up from her typing when I came through the door, but she did give me one of her skeletal grins.

"Just knock, Mr. Brown," she said. "He knows you're coming."

I did, and the growl from behind the door that told me to come in indicated I'd be getting the "shit" sheriff this morning, not the "sugar" version. He sat behind his desk, a dead crooked stogie clamped in his teeth, and he didn't get up when I came in. Not that I expected him to.

"Shut that damn door behind you," he snapped.

A smell of coffee wafted through the office, and I spotted the pot over in the corner, beside a little sink. Easing the door shut, I nodded toward it. "I came over here before I could get any coffee. Mind if—"

"Knock yourself out," he interrupted.

None of the three cups on the counter was anywhere near clean, so I grabbed one at random and poured the brew into it, wondering what I was about to hear from him. As I said, I had a suspicion about why I was there, but no clear idea.

Holding my steaming cup out and nodding my thanks, I started to take a seat in one of the battered chairs that faced his desk. But he stuck up a hand.

"Don't bother sittin' down," he said. "This ain't gonna take long."

Taking off my cap and sticking it in my back pocket, I blew on my coffee. "All right, sheriff. How can I help you?"

His face reddened and cuss words snapped out of him like firecrackers on a string. "Help me? Yeah. All right. I got a question to ask you, and I expect a God-damned straight answer – not that I'll get one from your sorry ass."

I shuffled my feet a little, sipped my coffee (which was hot enough to burn my tongue), and waited.

"Maybe you heard about the fire we had last night," he said, his eyes hard.

"I heard the sirens," I said, "along with everybody else in Ma's place."

"Yeah, you were at the boarding house. I know. That ain't the question." Taking the crook out of his mouth, he set it in the big green-glass ashtray atop his desk. Then he glared at me.

"This here's the question, Brown. You want to tell me why, when the fire boys got to Barney Gibson's place and hauled him and old man Black out of there just before it collapsed in flames, that Mackaville's post-master was screamin' about you and callin' you everything but white?"

Now, John, there was a shock. But it answered the question that had been rattling around in my skull ever since I'd first heard those fire trucks. Now I knew why the fire had been in town.

It was because Black had been in town.

While thinking this, I managed to stammer out, "I got no idea, sheriff. Like I say, I wasn't anywhere near there when it happened."

He gave me the fish-eye again. "Yeah. I get it. You've established your alibi." Suddenly, his fist thundered down on his desk. "But there's a reason. He didn't pull your name out of the fuggin' sky."

Then he relaxed a little. "The boys tell me Black shushed him up pretty quick. They asked Gibson how come he'd brought you into it, but he didn't say nothing after that. Neither did Black."

I made myself look innocent.

"Only thing I can think of is maybe he and Black were discussing me when the fire started and somehow he got everything all jumbled."

That sounded unconvincing even to me.

"Now look here, Brown," he said. "There's suddenly truck loads of shit bein' dumped all over this town, and you always seem to be the one pullin' the lever. I've been knowing about you and Black for a long time — no secret there. But now Gibson's in it. And I know you had somethin' to do with them Gabbers dyin' — 'death by misadventure' my sweet ass." His eyes narrowed again, but his voice turned surprisingly soft. "What do you suppose did happen to our two beloved town leaders?"

That caught me completely off base, and I suddenly realized that for all his bluster and unpredictability, Sheriff Arthur Meagan was no fool. Some of this had to be an act, designed to keep me off balance and maybe draw something out of me I didn't want to say. I saw him now for the clever man he was.

So, invited or not, I sat down, putting my

coffee cup on his desk. "Sheriff, did you ever see those Gabber brothers work their pigs?" I asked.

His expression told me nothing. So I plunged on.

"They had some weird way of communicating with 'em – I mean, beyond just a farmer-and-livestock connection. I saw it in action on more than one occasion. They actually had some sort of mental power over them."

He started to speak, but I hurried on.

"I think when Jube got sick with his mysterious ailment, the hold they had was weakened and the pigs attacked."

It was quiet in that office then, and for a few seconds all I could hear was the hum of the ceiling fan. Picking up his cigar, Sheriff Meagan took out a Zippo and lit the crook thoughtfully. Somehow, just when I figured he might explode again over the sheer incredibility of the theory I'd handed him, he'd become the "sugar" sheriff again.

Heartened, I continued. "I realize how crazy that sounds. But I'm not the only person to see them work their pigs the way they did. I believe they lost control, and that's what killed 'em."

Pursing his lips, he blew out a stream of iron-gray smoke. "There may be somethin' in what you say," he began. "I've seen 'em with the pigs, too. I couldn't never put my finger on it, but it just didn't seem natural." He shrugged and shook his head slowly. "Hell of a way to go, anyway," he added, looking down at the desk. "But the town's a damn sight better off without them two runnin' it."

Then his eyes snapped back to me. "All right. Get the hell out of here so's I can get some work done."

"All right, Sheriff," I said, rising. "Thanks for the coffee."

He grunted and nodded, and I left. Sorting out the new information in my mind, I tried to picture what I knew must have happened, with Black and Barney Gibson suddenly confronted by a creature that looked to be half-monkey and half-snake. It had to have been in flames and dying by the time it materialized there; otherwise, I reasoned, they'd both be dead now.

What did Black think about this latest development? Was it enough for him to lay off me? He knew I had the effigy again, and while he had the idea I might not be able to kill him with it – or, rather, that I might be reluctant to take someone's life, even his – I could sure make his life miserable. And now I'd struck again. If I'd indeed seen into an alternate future, and I believe I had, then he – and maybe Gibson too – had tried to use magic against me. But I'd been able to make it boomerang. Thank God (and you) for those magic books of mine.

Writing that last line just gave me the creeps. I know it wasn't God I was calling up last night.

Now, even though it's early, I'm going to try to get some sleep. I think I'll go to church tomorrow, too.

Your pal and faithful comrade,
Robert

September 11, 1939
Monday night

Dear John,

Once again there is plenty to write you about – so much, in fact, that it's hard for me to rewind my brain back to Sunday morning, the place I need to start. And, for reasons you'll soon see, this letter may be truncated because I'm not at 100 percent. I hope to get through it, though. We'll see.

Even though some disturbing dark shadows roamed and fluttered through my dreams, I got plenty of sleep Saturday night and was up early enough to partake of the breakfast Ma offers to all her good church-going boarders. I seemed to be the only partaker of the Sabbath yesterday morning, so after a fine meal I got in Ma's car and started to drive us off toward church. Even given everything that had been going on, my heart was somehow light. I think it was because Ma had informed me of a couple things at breakfast. First, she told me in a low voice, looking around to make sure none of my comrades had sneaked down to breakfast without her knowing, that I'd survived another meeting of the town elders.

"Please don't ask me no questions," she whispered. "Just know you got through ok."

Then she told me in a normal voice that

she thought Dr. Chavez would take Patricia and her grandmother off quarantine, maybe as soon as the next day.

You know I hadn't seen Pat for weeks. I'd only heard her voice on the phone. And this new development made me very happy, but also a little apprehensive. I was getting closer every minute to ankling Mackaville for Washington, D.C., and if I really thought I wanted to take Patricia along as my wife I'd better be asking her to marry me.

I'm sure I want her with me. I'm sure.

Anyway, as we pulled out Ma said we needed to go by the hotel and pick up Mary Lou Gabber. I was surprised by that, but then Ma volunteered, "She ain't been to church for a good long while, but it wasn't on account of her, if you get my drift."

I did. The Gabbers had forbidden her to go. "Didn't Jube Gabber go to any church, Ma?"

"Shoot, no," she said. "He wasn't no Christian a'tall. Neither was his brother. But they'll have 'em a big funeral at the Baptist church, the biggest church in town, and Ol' Brother Lewis'll talk about what wonderful fellas they was an' have his altar call just like he didn't know no better."

Mrs. Gabber came out the door of the hotel lobby just as we pulled up, looking like a million bucks. When I got out and opened the door for her, I got a little whiff of perfume that smelled so expensive I wondered where around here she could've gotten it.

Reverend Venable's sermon was about the land owner in the Bible who had a big harvest and built a bunch of new and bigger barns to store his bounty in, thinking he had plenty for the foreseeable future and now he could relax and eat and drink and be merry. But then he died, so having it all didn't do him a bit of good. The way I understood it, Jesus was telling people to seek God instead of earthly possessions.

As the reverend preached this message, I thought about my own earthly possessions, which mostly amount to books and pulps. You know any of them you want are yours if something happens to me. And I began to think that maybe seeking God a little more wasn't all that bad of an idea. After all, a few nights ago, I'd seen what could happen when you seek, well, some other power.

I still felt a little troubled about what I'd called up Saturday night, but then I told myself I really hadn't had any choice. I suppose I could've prayed about my situation and hoped for the best, but then I remembered "God helps those who help themselves" – not from the Bible, as a lot of people think, but from Poor Richard's Almanac – and knew that taking action was what I had to do.

Anyway, being in church felt good, and I got a surprise afterward when Mrs. Gabber asked Ma and me to come up to her place for lunch. I parked in front of the hotel, and we went in through the lobby to the elevator, which was being run by a really cute little trick in a green uniform. She was coffee-and-cream colored like most of the rest of Mackaville's people, with a mop of curly brown hair that'd make Shirley Temple envious. She gave me the once-over, surreptitiously, and when I winked at her I was rewarded with a very becoming blush. Ah, the joys of youth.

As we walked toward Mrs. Gabber's third-floor suite, I had a sudden premonition that the conversation among us wasn't going to be just the usual polite gum-bumping. There seemed to be something a little different in the demeanor of both women. I tried my best to sense more, but nothing came through. However, I felt, for lack of a better word, that I would be "safe" with them.

The room was far more opulent than any I expected to see in this burg. I mean, it wasn't the Ritz, but it wasn't because the management hadn't tried. Oriental carpeting, vases in the corners, sturdy and expensive-looking dark furniture, a big overstuffed davenport covered with pillows.

Saying she'd put on the coffee and make some sandwiches, Ma immediately exited to what I assumed was the kitchen. Then, arranging herself on the sofa, Mrs. Gabber asked me to pull up a chair. Looking at me, she cleared her throat and began.

"Robert," she said, "I want to tell you about the Cleansing. And the only reason I'm doing it is that I don't want you, or anyone else, to get killed by your efforts to find out what it was."

My first impulse was to tell her that I already knew about it, thanks to David Jefferson and the Gabber cousin I'd interviewed a couple of weeks ago, but I just held my tongue and nodded. Maybe she'd have something new to add.

"Thank you," I said.

"It was before my time, of course," she said, "but those two devil's brothers I was lashed to often spoke about it. In 1889, the first Mr. Gabber, who was running the plant and the town as well, made a rash decision. You have to understand that he'd always thought of himself as a white man, even though he had the same blood as many of the Negro people who worked for him – the blood that, as I'm sure you know, most of Mackaville has running through its veins. He's what the outside world calls high-yellow, and I suspect he'd passed in white society more than once, so that surely had something to do with his attitude."

She paused, watching me for a reaction. I nodded again.

"An evil man, just like the sons of his I lived with for thirty long years. He made the decision that Mackaville needed to change, from a small town built on tolerance and brotherhood to a company town where whites ran everything and the blacks were little better than slaves.

"He brought in a crowd he'd run with back east in Virginia, ex-Confederate soldiers and their families. Then he fired all the locals who'd been running the plant and the cannery and replaced them with these arrogant Rebs. After that he ran all the workers out of the company housing, where they'd been living almost rent-free, and turned it over to these new people.

Mackaville became just like any other Southern place, with whites on one side of town and blacks on the other, and those in-between – which was most of the people here – forced to choose sides."

She took a deep breath.

"The first Mr. Gabber thought he was God to the folks around here, so he didn't take into account the strange powers that many of our people have. I think you're aware of that."

Oh brother, am I! I thought, but simply said, "Yes, Mrs. Gabber. I'm aware."

"Those powers used to be even stronger. And please call me Miss Castle, my maiden name – or Mary Lou, if you want."

"Thank you," I said again.

"My former husbands loved to tell the story about how, on a given night, the white people my father had brought to town were set upon by snakes and hogs. Many died in those attacks. And then, in a second wave, a good number of the long-time townspeople rose up and struck the Rebs, and every last white newcomer died before the sun rose that morning. Men, women, children, even babies – all dead. There were fires. Some of the townspeople refused to join in the slaughter for reasons of faith or religion, like the preacher David Jefferson, my liberator. I imagine you know he is a half-brother to my late husbands."

"Yes. I know."

"Those like David were either slaughtered out of hand or disappeared forever. As men, that is. Mr. Jefferson's the only one to come back." She was silent for a moment, and then turned her eyes toward me. There was pain in them, but also a kind of resolve. "That's all I can tell you. That's all they told me. But it was a night of horror and death, and it came to be known as the Cleansing. Because it's the town's darkest secret, and it could still tear us wide open, some people will go to great lengths not to let it get out. Do you understand?"

I did, but at that moment I wasn't quite sure how to respond. So, as sometimes happens, I just opened my mouth to see what would come out. So far in this town, that approach has served me well.

"Mrs. Gab – Miss Castle," I began, "I

appreciate the courage it took to tell me this, not knowing for sure whether you can trust me to keep it a secret. But I will. I believe it needs to remain buried, fifty years in the past, and that's where I'm going to leave it."

I could see the tightness in her face relax then, and she even managed something that looked like a smile.

"I'm glad," she said. "The whole town will be, too."

I smiled back. "I don't know a lot about what you're doing with the packing plant, but it seems to me you want to create more opportunity with it, maybe help keep the young people around instead of having to move away to get work. I think that's grand of you."

Suddenly, I realized Ma had arrived with the coffee and a tray of what looked to be deviled-ham sandwiches. Had she been staying discreetly out of the picture to give her friend time to tell me the story? It was a good bet. That way, if I pressed Ma for any more details on the Cleansing, she could claim ignorance.

For the second time that weekend, I understood that some of the folks in Mackaville were a little brighter than I'd thought.

We chatted and ate for a good half-hour, Miss Castle (hard to get used to calling her that) telling about her ideas for expanding Gabber Meats and providing more jobs. It all sounded pretty swell to me, even the part where she said she was going to change the name to Castle Foods.

Then the conversation wound down, and Ma and I took our leave. As soon as we said our goodbyes, I was seized by uneasiness, and I started thinking so hard that I didn't even realize I hadn't flirted again with the little elevator girl until we were out in the street. I couldn't even remember seeing her, but I know I must have.

My intense cogitation had to do with what I'd told Mary Lou Castle. I'd all but sworn that I wouldn't tell anyone else about the Cleansing, yet at the same time I knew I'd be writing you about it. Of course, I know I can trust you, but what if this information was to fall into other hands? And even more to the point, if I knew all along I was going to put it down on paper, had I willfully lied to the woman? What kind of a jerk was I becoming?

John, this all really troubled me, to the point that I told Ma I'd walk back to her place, muttering something about needed the exercise. What I really wanted was to be alone, just to walk and think and try to shake this feeling of distress that had settled over me and seemed to be getting stronger.

Too late, I understood what the seventh sense had been trying to tell me. As I reached the corner of the hotel and started to pass in front of the alley that separated it from the next building, a guy's heavy grabber landed on my shoulder, and I felt a sharp blade poke through my shirt and at least the first two layers of skin next to my spine.

"Turn into that alley, shit head," a voice hissed. "Don't make a peep or you'll get it right here."

There wasn't anything else I could do. I stepped sideways into the dark mouth of the alley and felt rather than saw someone make a threatening motion above my head. Something slammed into the side of my skull, and as I went down I felt that knife tear into the muscles of my back.

My last memory before oblivion was hearing someone scream. Then I died.

No. Just kidding. But I was sure out, and when I started coming to, I didn't know if I'd been under for a second or a week. My head was one giant throbbing ache, so overpowering that I found it impossible at first to focus my eyes.

You can excuse me if I thought I'd cashed in. Because when I did manage to see something clearly, it was Pat's beautiful, concerned face, coming into focus as it would have in an especially vivid dream. I tried to hold the vision, but I couldn't, and darkness rolled in again.

The next thing I knew I was in Dr. Chavez's office with an ice bag on the side of my head and a nasty bitter taste in my mouth. The doc was trying to pour some sort of noxious liquid down my throat, and I was sputtering like Daffy Duck, conscious of various pains echoing through my body.

"Swallow it, Robert," said a voice like an angel's. "It'll help you."

I knew it was Pat, but I was still in a fog and couldn't see her. I tried to sit up and look, but strong hands pushed me back down.

"Hold it," said a voice. "Take it easy for a minute, now." It was Dr. Chavez, talking to me in that "soothing" voice that doctors in the movies use when their patient is about to croak. It didn't comfort me much. When I tried to speak, the words didn't come out like I'd planned.

Instead, I asked something like, "How cut up my back I am?"

The heartless S.O.B. actually laughed. Imagine that. Here I was dying and he was giving me the horse laugh.

"You, Mr. Brown, are the luckiest man I have ever met."

Then he gently helped me to a sitting position, easing me up by my shoulder and back. I was still foggy, and I kept blinking my eyes at the stabs of pain, hoping to bring everything into focus. All I could see at the moment was a vague outline of the doc's rounded face, with an impression of horn-rimmed glasses.

"When that thug sapped you, you must've

twisted as you fell," he was saying. "You're cut from your spine around the side to your belly button, but it's only skin deep." He chuckled. The bastard.

"You bled a river. But you're a red head, and you people bleed like that."

He guided my right hand to my midsection, where I felt the rough surface of a bandage. "You didn't need stitches, just some tape and gauze," he continued. "Give it a few days and you'll be fine. I'm more worried about your head."

Automatically, I reached up to touch my temple, but he put his hand over mine.

"Just leave it alone, if you can," he said. "I think you have a mild concussion – mild to me, that is. Not to you." Again, he chuckled.

"I am sending you back with Mrs. Stean. I've given her some powders for your pain, and she'll mix a dose up in water for you when you get home. I know it tastes terrible, but drink it all down and then go to bed. It'll help you sleep. Tomorrow morning you'll feel so bad you won't want to get up, so don't. Stay down. By the afternoon you should be ok. If you're not, I'll send you to back to Dodd General."

The name brought back all the pain and fear that had come along with that rattlesnake bite back in June, the one that had nearly put me under the ground for good.

They'd pulled me through up there, but that didn't mean I had any interest in returning.

I started to shake my head to try and clear it, but stopped at the first shock of pain. Squeezing my eyes together tightly, I felt another, lighter, touch on my shoulder and when I looked I could see Patricia's face, again as clear as a snapshot. Behind her, I glimpsed a pair of other faces: Ma Stean's and Sheriff Meagan's.

But it was Patricia's I was interested in.

"Pat," I whispered, reaching for her. But the doc stepped in.

"Take it easy, Mr. Brown," he said. "No sudden moves."

"But…" I started, and then the words got all jumbled in my mind as Patricia took my hand and squeezed it. Her eyes were moist.

"I was coming to tell you that I was out of quarantine," she said softly. "It was only a few hours ago that Doctor Chavez told me I wasn't quarantined anymore. It was too late for church, but I went to Ma's and waited for you to come back. When she came in by herself, she told me where you were, and I got in the car and drove over to the hotel, looking for you along the way. They…they must've only had you for a few seconds when I reached the alley."

"She saved your bacon, Brown," said the sheriff. "When she screamed, a couple of men bolted around the corner and the bums who nabbed you scattered like quail."

"It was…awful, Robert," she said, squeezing my hand in hers. Her voice trembled. "Blood. All over. Your blood." Ma reached for her then, and Patricia turned her face away, burying it in Ma's ample bosom.

"She says there was two of 'em," said Chief Lawson. "Any idea who they were?"

"Nossir. I didn't even really see their faces." I was starting to fade out again, but I fought it. Turning to Doc Chavez, I asked, "What time is it? How long was I out?"

It was Sheriff Meagan who spoke up. "We brought you in about two thirty. It's a little after three now."

I started to nod, but the pain stopped me. "Ok," I said. "Thanks."

"You feel like you can walk?" asked the doc.

"I'll try."

He and Pat eased me off the examination table, and Ma brought me my shirt and undershirt. That's when I realized I was barechested, and it's funny how that made me a little embarrassed, being in front of those women dressed like Tarzan.

It took me no short while to get into my clothes, and then Doc Chavez and Pat, with Ma assisting, eased me to my feet. I wobbled and started to go down, falling against Pat as my knees buckled.

"Here, fella," said Sheriff Meagan, grabbing me none-too-gently under the armpits.

"You're too heavy for a little thing like her. Let me help."

As the three of them started moving me slowly across the room toward the door, I turned to the doc.

"How much do I owe you?" I asked, and actually fumbled for my wallet. It's funny the dumb things you do in situations like that.

He laughed. It seemed like he'd been doing a lot of that. "I'll send you a bill. You've turned into such a regular customer that I'll have to figure in a discount."

From the amused look on his face, I got the idea there might not even be a bill.

They somehow got me into the back seat of Ma's Pontiac, and by this time I was becoming more and more conscious of the pain that ran like hot wiring halfway around my girth and echoed like the flash of a lighthouse beam in my head. We couldn't get to the boarding house fast enough to suit me, so Ma could mix me up something for all the aching and throbbing.

Then again, I had Pat beside me once more, and just feeling the warmth of her body as I half-sat, half-lay against her made me feel considerably better. It also made me realize how much I'd been missing her.

Hell, John, I almost proposed right then. Instead, I smiled at her with what I hoped looked like a brave little smile, something like Errol Flynn or John Carroll might do in the situation. She looked back at me with concern.

"Do you hurt very much?" she asked.

"Not as long as I can look at you," I returned.

It sounded like a line from a movie. Rolling her eyes, she smiled and softly stroked my head.

When we got to the boarding house, Ma went in and roused little Dave and tall Paul, and the four of them managed to get me up the stairs to my room. I saw MacWhirtle at my feet, sniffing and looking up at me, trying to figure out what had happened to his chum.

When Ma left to mix up the powder and water, I realized how badly I had to pee, so Dave and Paul (and MacWhirtle, kind of) helped me to the bathroom and stood there holding me up. As you know, I've got a kind of phobia about taking a whiz in front of other people, but the need to relieve myself was so urgent that it didn't stop me. I felt like I stood there chipping porcelain for a good five minutes before I was finally done. Then they half-dragged me back to my room and Ma handed me a tumbler full of the same vile-tasting stuff I'd had at Doc Chavez's. I drank it down, and before I knew it I was in bed with a sheet over me, stripped to my underwear, feeling the breeze kicked up by my little fan. I remember thinking how hot it was and then dropping down into warm darkness as though I were being pulled into an abyss by unseen hands.

When I woke up it was cooler and the light from outside was dim, almost dark. I could make out MacWhirtle, curled up beside me. As I lay there, figuring it was dusk, the grumble in my stomach, under the bandage, told me it must be morning. So did the birds that started up their calls in the trees outside my window.

My wound still hurt, and when I tried to raise my head the pain came sharply and immediately, and I thought I was going to throw up. I must've grunted or jerked or something, because MacWhirtle jumped and then eyed me suspiciously. But after giving myself a couple of minutes, I maneuvered very slowly until I could push myself up with my forearms against the mattress, and that worked a lot better.

I was still experimenting with what I could and couldn't do when I heard a soft knock at the door. It turned out to be Ma with a plate of biscuits, eggs, and gravy. She'd mixed up another glass of the doc's poisonous-tasting elixir and had a tin of Bayer aspirin sitting beside it, along with a tumbler full of milk.

"Feel like eatin' anything?" she asked solicitously.

"You bet, Ma," I said, inching my back up the headboard. "Just give me a minute to sit up."

She stood silently as I moved by degrees until I was in more or less of a sitting position. Then she set the tray down in my lap. My body was warning me that I'd regret any wrong move, so everything thing I did was in slow motion. That seemed to work, and the food, once I was able to get the first forkful in my mouth, tasted great.

Watching me eat, Ma said, "I'm s'posed to call Doc Chavez and Patricia and tell 'em how you are. Her grandma's still a little sick and can't quite do for herself yet; otherwise, Patricia'd be here right now. I think she'd want you to know that."

"Thank you, Ma. I understand," I said. Then, reaching for the prescribed drink, I added, "Well, here goes," and slowly tilted my head back and drank. It was just as bad as I remembered.

"Doc says take two of them aspirin every four hours and try to get more sleep."

"I will."

"If you ain't asleep, I'll bring you your lunch. But I ain't s'posed to wake you up."

"You're an angel, Ma."

"I need to keep Mac outta here?"

"No," I said. "He's fine." From the floor, he looked up at me, hoping for something off my plate, but I thought it might not be good to slip him something right in front of Ma's eyes.

I ate a few more bites, maybe finishing half of what she'd brought, and then I said,

"It's awfully good, but I think that's all I can do." I swallowed the aspirin, washing them down with milk, and then she took the tray away and said she'd check in on me every couple of hours if I didn't mind leaving the door cracked.

By this time Doc Chavez's powder was already working its magic, and I passed out again, this time with a full stomach. When I awakened, the clock on my desk read 2:48. It was hotter than the hinges of hell, that stifling mid-afternoon heat, and the fan wasn't doing much to cool me off. But when I tentatively began raising myself up, I found that both the upper and lower pains had abated. I actually got my feet on the floor without more than a couple of minor twinges. At some point, MacWhirtle had exited out the partially opened door.

Nature was calling, and, even given my weakened condition, it wasn't going to take "no" for an answer.

I didn't want to embarrass Ma if I happened to run into her, but the urgency of my situation, plus the physical shape I was in, didn't allow me time to pull on any pants. So, clad in only undershirt and shorts, I wove my way to the bathroom and, a few minutes later, wove my way back – just in time to see Ma and Patricia standing outside my door at the end of the hall. Sheriff Meagan stood behind them in his khaki uniform, looking solemn.

We all saw one another at about the same time. Ma and Pat turned away demurely, but I swear I saw them both grin. The chief watched me. He seemed to be trying not to laugh.

"Sorry," I said to Ma's and Pat's backs as I slipped through the door. "Just give me a minute to get back under the sheet."

"Don't hurry on our account," Ma said, still turned away, and I thought I heard a barely suppressed ripple of laughter from Pat.

Once in bed, I beckoned them in. Pat pulled up my desk chair, sat down beside my bed, and wordlessly took my hand. The sheriff and Ma remained standing, and it was the former who broke the silence.

"Feel like talking?" he asked gruffly.

Easing myself up on the headboard again, I said, "More than I have in the past 24 hours, Sheriff."

He glanced at Ma and back at me. "You get a good look at the men who attacked you?"

"Nossir. It all happened too fast."

"Patricia says she didn't either."

She nodded slowly, not taking her eyes off me.

"Well," continued the sheriff, "Hoss Heavener, a fella who helped break up your little ambush, says he'll swear one of 'em was Jim Moran, the postman that's got the rural route to the north of Mackaville."

"A postman?" I blurted.

"Yeah. Now, Hoss is known around town for

bein' devoted to the giggle water, if you know what I mean, and he and his friend may've been sneaking a few nips out in his pick-up when they heard Patricia's scream. What I'm saying is that he ain't the most reliable witness in the world."

He squatted down next to Pat, bringing his face closer to mine. "Doc says you ain't hurt bad. So what I want to know is, where do you want to go with this?"

"I'm not sure I understand," I returned. "Do you mea—"

He cut me off. "I mean I can drag him in, and he can come up with people who'll swear he was somewhere else, and 'round and 'round we'll go. I know you're s'posed to be leaving soon, and you might have to stay for a while instead, so you could testify. That what you want?"

"Hell, no," I said emphatically. Patricia's eyes widened. "Sorry," I added. "But no. It's like you say. I'm all right, or I will be soon enough. Maybe you could put a scare in the guy, let him know you're investigating or something, so he doesn't try it again."

The sheriff stood up then. "Maybe I could," he said. Then, nodding at Ma and Pat, he added, "Good afternoon, ladies," and walked out.

They watched him leave, and then Pat turned back to me. "Any better?" she asked.

"Sure. Now that you're here."

She made an "oh, please," face, and I said, "It's the truth. I haven't seen you for a long time, you know, and you make everything better."

The click of the door told us that Ma had left as well, leaving the door only slightly open for what I assumed was propriety's sake. Patricia leaned in and kissed me anyway, causing an electrical charge of a much more pleasant nature to careen through my body.

"I'm sure I have awful breath," I said.

"You do," she said, and kissed me again.

Well, maybe it was the buoyant presence of Patricia, who sat with me even after Ma had returned with the potion. Whatever it was – potion, Patricia, or both – I found myself slipping back into dreamland.

By the time I woke up again, it was dark and I felt still better – even though Pat was gone. I felt so good, in fact, that I got to my desk and started typing this letter to you. I even put on a pair of khakis. Ma must've heard the click of this typer, because after about 30 minutes she showed up with milk and a ham sandwich and that tin of aspirin, remarking on how good I looked and telling me Doc had called and said to change the bandage tomorrow.

Looking back now as I wind this missive up, I'm kind of amazed at how long it is. To be honest, I've taken a few breaks and laid down on the bed for a while between bouts with the typer, but I'm just not sleepy, probably because I've been knocked out so much of the past day and a half. Anyway, I'd rather write you than stare at the ceiling, so enjoy this magnum opus.

And please – keep it in a damned safe place.

Your pal and faithful correspondent,
Robert

September 12, 1939
Tuesday night

Dear John,

I'm starting to see every day as another step toward my job in D.C., and while I'll miss Pete and Ma and the guys in the boarding house – and good old MacWhirtle, of course – the day I get out of here cannot come soon enough. I think back on everything that's come at me since I've been in this town, and I wonder how I could've possibly dodged so many bullets. That sometimes leads me to wondering if I will last long enough to shake the dust of Mackaville off my feet for good – that maybe there's still some bullet or something with my name on it that's going to get me. But that way lies madness, as Shakespeare said, and when those thoughts come calling I try to dispel them with the much happier notion of Patricia leaving here with me as my wife.

Her grandmother, unfortunately, isn't coming out of the after-effects of scarlet fever as well as Dr. Chavez thinks she should. She's very weak, Pat tells me, and she's developed a cough that worries the doc. I found that out this morning, when she drove by to see how I was doing. I told her about how Ma had damned (except I said "darned") near killed me when she insisted on painting that long u-shaped cut of mine with mercurochrome. It felt like she'd turned red ants loose on my midsection, but she swore it would keep me from having a scar – like I'm concerned about having a scar in that location. Still, I've learned that when Ma Stean gets an idea in her head, it's best just to grit your teeth and go along.

I did notice that there were patches of it that didn't burn, which seems to me to signal that I'm already healing up. It's a good thing, too. This little episode has put me behind on my interviews and reports, and the quicker I get better, the quicker I can catch up and get out of this place.

Anyway, because of Mrs. Davis's condition, Pat and I aren't spending as much time together as we'd like, and I haven't found the right time to pop the question. She's worried about her grandmother, and I keep thinking that this isn't quite the right time. I know I'd better do it soon, though.

And, yeah, just the thought of it does make me nervous.

Patricia and I talked (and kissed a little, but don't spread that around) up in my room, leaving the door cracked – we figured it was Ma's house rules – and then she went downstairs to help Ma with breakfast. I'm moving around pretty well today, so I was at the table when the others came in – Mister Clark and Dave, that is. Paul's on a swing shift, I'm told.

Although it's only been a few days, Mary

Lou Castle's reign at what is now the Castle Foods plant has already impressed the hard-to-please Mister Clark. He explained over fatback and biscuits that the railroad has had to start K-balling.

"That's when they have to build, or rebuild, new box cars to meet the demand," he told me. "They take cars that are worn out, junked, and rebuild them. We've got men on three shifts doing that now. That tells you about how the productivity has increased under Miss Castle." For Mister Clark, that last sentence amounted to a slavish endorsement.

I felt so good after breakfast that I decided to climb on the old Indian and head out to get an interview or two. Plus, I've amassed several letters to you that needed to get to Harrison, and I don't like letting those pile up. Ma seemed concerned that I was going, and told me to be careful, but the residual tightness in my head and the crawly little pains that poked around my midsection didn't seem to be big enough to stop me. So I rolled the bike out of the shed and, sure enough, here came Rennsdale at a lope, from around the side of the house. Mac, curled up in a patch of sunlight beside the back steps, barely looked up as she passed him and jumped in my sidecar.

We'd made it through town and into the foothills when I was suddenly hit with a flash of the seventh sense – and hit hard. An image of a snake, a big one, flared up in my mind like a photograph of a nightmare. And the thing was that I didn't just see it, John. I felt it. It slithered obscenely across the floor of a big office – and even though I'd only glimpsed the inside of that office once, I knew exactly where it was.

Sliding into a 180-degree turn, I opened the bike up and blasted back toward Mackaville, running every stop sign I encountered. When I reached the gate of the packing plant I just yelled at the guard and whizzed on by. He shouted back for me to stop, but I didn't even look back, skidding to a stop at the front entrance of the plant, where Diffie had taken me on tour only a few days ago. The same young-lady secretary was on duty, and she looked up in shocked surprise as I ran down the hallway to the L-shaped area, past the glass bricks, to the door that now read "Miss Castle." I threw it open.

She was alone, standing in the middle of her office, a file folder in her hand. Her eyes widened at my intrusion.

"Mrs. Gabber – Miss Castle," I said, trying to keep my voice down. "Please come out here right now. Quickly. Now!"

She smiled and was walking toward me when a mitt grabbed me from behind and whirled me around. It was the uniformed gate guard, a middle-aged man with thin hair and bad breath, which was coming now in strangled gasps from his exertion. Grabbing up a handful of my shirt, he stuck his face so close to mine that our noses touched.

"Just what the hell and who the hell do you think—?" he began, and then he turned to Miss Castle. "I'm sorry, ma'am. This man refused to stop at the gate." He twisted the front of my shirt more tightly until it threatened to choke me. "I'll take care of him now."

"It's all right, Lonnie," she said. "Mr. Brown is a friend of mine. He's to be let in without question anytime he shows up."

He couldn't have jerked his hand away from my shirt any faster. "Yes, ma'am," he said.

And then, to me, "Sorry, sir." He actually tried to smooth the cloth he'd wrinkled.

"You may return to your post," she said.

He did so with haste and one final, "Yes, ma'am."

With that diversion past, she turned back to me. "What is this, Robert?" she asked.

I put my finger to my lips and nodded back down the hallway, where several young women had gathered. Then I silently mouthed the word "snake."

"If you still need to check the warehouse," I said loudly, "I'll stay here and take care of that unpacking you asked me to do."

You can say this for Miss Castle: She catches on fast.

"Go right ahead, Robert," she said at the same approximate volume. "But you didn't have to be in such a big hurry to get here. You could've hurt yourself."

Turning toward the women at the end of the hall, she shook her head and smiled, as though I were the world's biggest eager beaver. This seemed to be enough for the secretaries and receptionists, as they quickly melted away, dispersing back to their posts.

"Give me a half-hour," I whispered, and she nodded and left.

I don't suppose I have to tell you that my seventh sense was going off like a fire-alarm bell when I stepped into that office. The only weapon I had was the skinning knife stuck down inside of my boot, and I wasn't at all sure that was anywhere close to adequate protection.

Softly closing the door behind me and taking out the knife, I began a methodical search through the room, at first getting down on my knees and checking under Miss Castle's big teak wood desk. The damaged nerves around my midsection stung me in their disapproval, but the way my seventh sense was going off it wasn't hard to cover the pain with adrenaline and keep my mind on my task.

Apparently, Miss Castle wasn't yet completely moved in, because behind her desk against the back wall were stacks of card-board boxes and files. They were packed so closely together that it didn't look like a snake of any size could be hiding there. I looked back toward the shut office door, reading her name in reverse on the pebbled glass. To the left of it was a coat rack, and to the right two tall file cabinets. The one closest to the door was flush with the wall, but whoever had brought them in hadn't bothered to square them up. The second one stood a good foot away from the wall.

I knew that's where the snake had to be, coiled and waiting.

Looking around, I spotted air vents at the top and bottom of the walls on both sides of her office. It hit me that the snake would've had to come through one of those; the boxes in the back blocked her window, which was shut, and it couldn't very well have slithered through her doorway without someone seeing it – unless, of course, it had been put in the room before she arrived. But then, someone would've had to have had the key to her door.

All this flashed through my mind as I stayed on my hands and knees and moved toward the floor vent on my right. Sure enough, the wire had been cut to make an opening of about three square inches. I made a mental note to find out who was headquartered in the adjoining room.

But that was a task for later. Getting to my feet and trying not to feel the protesting pain around my stomach and in my head, I stuck my knife back in my boot, walked to the back of the room, and pulled a couple of those big boxes away from the stack, sliding them across the carpeted floor. I did that until I had about a half-dozen in a double line across the floor. They were heavier than I would've liked, but I still got them arranged pretty quickly.

Pulling my knife back out and gripping it between my teeth, just in case, I slid one of the boxes as quickly as I could against the wall behind the file cabinet, blocking the space, Then I went into overdrive. The boxes were only about three feet tall, and if the snake sensed what I was doing, it'd make a break. Before that could happen, I had to get my barrier up, and in a hurry.

If that blade had gone deep enough in my belly for stitches, I would've popped them in the next minute or so. It felt like I was doing just that as I horsed the boxes up, one on top of the other, working like a stevedore, wary and jumpy every second. I piled up those boxes like a madman, and luck was with me because the stack came up almost level with the top of the file cabinet. I hoisted a final box up on top of the cabinet, sliding it over onto the top of the pile until it completely blocked off the opening bordered by the boxes, the cabinet, and the wall. I hoped it was heavy enough to withstand any reptilian assault from underneath it.

Did I think about what might happen if I was wrong, if the snake was somewhere else in the office, just waiting for the opportunity to sink its fangs in my ankle? A little, I guess. But my senses were ringing so loudly when I approached that file cabinet, I would've bet money it had to be there.

When I finished, I was sweating like an ice-water pitcher. But my task was hardly over. First, I went to the vent at the right-hand corner of the room, the one whose screen had been cut and opened, and using the top of my knife blade pushed the wiring back until it was all reversed, the strands pointing inward. Then I went back to the stack of boxes and slid several more over to the area of the file cabinet, where I arranged them into a kind of corral that led from the cabinet to the wall. It took three boxes, packed tightly together, to get there. Then I stacked another row of boxes on top of those three. When I was finished, I had a barrier about six feet high – the height of two boxes – with the wall on the other side, giving the snake only one place to go when I gave it an opening. That's what I hoped, anyway.

Taking a deep breath, I left the knife in the office and stepped out, looking down the hallway. The secretary was trying not to peer back at me and not doing a very good job of it. She was a cutie, with a turned-up nose and a splash of freckles across both coffee-and-cream colored cheeks.

"Pardon me," I said, making my voice as even as I could. With all the jumpiness inside me, it was no easy task.

"Yes?" she said brightly.

"May I borrow your bottle of typewriter cleaner?"

"Certainly." Pulling open her drawer, she took out a brown bottle and handed it over. I thanked her and returned to Miss Castle's office, half expecting to have a snake drop down my neck. But nothing had changed – including the insistent clanging of my seventh sense.

I knew, of course, that the Gabbers had had a way of "seeing" through the eyes of the animals they controlled. Well, if Old Man Black could "see" through the eyes of a snake, he was about to get his retinas cooked.

Very carefully, I pulled the top box off and slid it to the floor. Then I stepped up on it and looked down into the opening between the file cabinet, wall, and my cardboard partition, half-expecting a fanged head to shoot up at me. Nothing. I thought I saw something stir at the bottom but I couldn't tell.

So I reached in and wrestled out another box, as quickly as I could, setting it on top of the file cabinet. Now, there was only one box left in the pathway to the wall vent. I quickly considered reaching down and moving it but rejected the idea as too risky. It was going to be risky enough anyway.

John, you know how powerful that type-writer cleaner is, strong enough to burn the caked-up ink right off the keys. It's the last thing you'd want in your eyes.

Even if you were a snake.

So, still standing atop one of the boxes and looking down into the cardboard-lined abyss, I poured every bit of that fluid into the opening and pulled my head back, just as a big rattler came streaking over the box in its way and down the chute I'd constructed toward the open vent in the wall, hissing and smoking where the cleaner had hit it. When I heard the frenzied thudding against the boxes on the way, I almost felt sorry for it; the agony was driving it nuts. I had a scary moment when it hit the wall and then tried to climb up over the boxes at the end. Its head appeared, tongue flailing, and then it dropped down again. A wisp of smoke hung for a moment in the air above it.

Then, just as I'd hoped, there was the new scratchy sound of its body writhing across wire, followed by silence, and I knew it had found the hole in the wall and gone through it in its frenzy to get away from the pain. Quickly, I slid a box in front of the air vent and then moved the rest of them back to the wall behind Mary Lou Castle's desk. But I spread them out so they wouldn't block the window, which I opened. The smell of the cleaner and the burnt snake was too pungent. Then I turned on her overhead fan and left the office.

The young lady was still sitting at her

desk at the end of the hall, and still trying not to appear too interested in exactly what I was doing in her boss's office. Smiling, I set the empty typewriter-cleaner bottle on her desk.

"I'm afraid I had to use it all," I said. "It was a big job."

She beamed at me. I want to think it was because she liked my looks, but it probably had more to do with my obvious closeness to the big boss. "It's okay, sir. I can get another."

"Good. Thank you."

Heading toward the plant via the sidewalk, I couldn't help but remember the first time I'd been there, when I'd damn near been caught eavesdropping on the meeting of the town's leaders. I'm sure some of the faces I saw belonged to people who had chased me that night. How things had changed.

When I caught up with Miss Castle, she was standing by several pallets of tinned meat, talking to a couple of young men, whom she introduced as her sister's sons, Hal and Bart. They'd just started work that day and seemed glad to be there. We exchanged pleasantries before I told Miss Castle, "I believe I've fixed the problem we talked about."

Excusing ourselves, we headed back toward the main building. When we were out of earshot of her nephews, I told her, "There was a rattler loose in your office. I'm pretty sure whoever has the room next to yours is responsible."

She didn't even seem surprised. "Rupe Atkins. The assistant manager. I'd hoped he might switch his loyalties to me, but I guess I was foolish to think that." She stopped and turned back, calling the boys by name. Then she turned back to me. "Lonnie may need help escorting Mr. Atkins off the premises," she explained.

"You might have them bring a couple of shovels," I told her. Her eyebrows arched.

"The snake is in <u>his</u> office now," I said casually.

By the time we arrived at the suite of offices, the receptionists and secretaries were up again, forming a wide-eyed, loose knot around the office door next to Miss Castle's. Somebody inside was cussing loudly and screaming in between outbursts.

"Be careful, boys," I said to the brothers, both of whom held shovels at the ready. "And you and the girls might want to step back, Miss Castle." I pulled the knife out of my boot – a little theatrically, I admit – and pushed open the door.

It was quite a scene. A skinny gee in his thirties, clad in a blue seersucker suit, stood in abject terror on top of his desk. Well, <u>stood</u> isn't the right word. He was dancing with fear. He'd already kicked most of the papers off his desk, down to the carpeted floor where the four-foot-long viper flipped and writhed and rattled.

"Get that son-of-a-bitch outta here!" he shouted, pointing a quivering finger at the reptile. One look told me the snake in its pain and sightlessness had lost all reason and was now just looking for something to tear into. As it twisted around toward us, one of Miss Castle's nephews neatly severed its head, driving the point of the shovel deep into the thick carpet. Blood pulsed and spurted as the young man's brother made a couple of thrusts of his own. Then it was over, and the sweating, shaky man climbed down off his desk, uneasily eyeing the knife I slipped back into my boot.

Miss Castle was waiting for him.

"You brought that snake in, didn't you, Rupe?" she said quietly.

His eyes, already wide, got even bigger, and he swallowed. "No, Mrs. Gabber – Miss Castle. No. Why would I do something like that?"

The boys had started looking around the room, and one of them pulled a flat wooden box from under the desk. It was something he could've carried in without attracting any attention.

"'Bout snake-sized, I'd say," the nephew commented, holding it up. "Little door here on the end."

Rupe Atkins looked wildly back and forth

from Miss Castle to her nephews. You could smell the fear oozing out of him.

"I – I don't know...what–"

"Better get out of here, Rupe," she said, and there was ice in her voice. "These two young men will escort you to the gate. We'll box up your belongings and send them to you with your final check. Do not try to set foot on these grounds again."

"B-but, Mrs. – Miss–"

At her nod, her two nephews came up to him, one on either side, and nudged him toward the open doorway, where the young ladies who'd gathered there parted like the Red Sea. Then Miss Castle turned to me.

"Robert," she began. "How did you know?"

Nodding toward the door, where a few stragglers still stood, I said, loudly enough, "Gosh, Miss Castle, I knew you had a lot of snakes around these parts, but I didn't know they could get inside buildings."

She nodded and a smile played briefly across her face.

"I hope we won't see any more of them, Mr. Brown," she said.

"I hope not," I returned, as I went to one of the abandoned shovels and scooped up the pieces of the snake, depositing it in the wastebasket. The carpet was splattered with crimson gore, already turning darker.

Miss Castle turned toward the door, addressing the young ladies hovering around outside, some of whom were glancing surreptitiously in and then looking away. "All right, girls," she said. "I believe the excitement's over now. Please return to your desks."

They melted away immediately. When they were gone, I said softly, "Old Man Black. And likely Barney Gibson, too. How many more accomplices could they have here?"

"Rupe Atkins was very loyal to my husbands," she said. "I know there are others here like him. Some may just not want a woman for a boss. They'd listen to anyone who wanted me gone." Then, "I'll keep my eyes open. And thank you."

"You're welcome, Miss Castle. I'll help any way I can." I started to pick up the shovels, but she laid a hand on my shoulder.

"I'll have Hal and Bart take care of all that. You've already helped enough."

Nodding, I left, smiling as I felt the stares of the secretaries and receptionists on me.

Kicking the Indian to life, I rolled out to the gate and stopped beside the guard. Neither the former assistant manager nor Miss Castle's nephews were anywhere to be seen.

The man — Lonnie, I remembered — stood a little straighter when he saw me. He even whipped off a salute.

"They get that assistant manager out of here?"

"Yessir, Mr. Brown," he said. "Them two boys escorted him to his auto. They oughta be gettin' back about now."

"They told you never to let him back in, didn't they? Miss Castle's orders."

"Yessir," he repeated. "If you don't mind my sayin' so, I never liked his sorry ass anyway. Always lordin' it over us like he was the king of Persia or somebody."

I couldn't help grinning at his metaphor. "All right, then, Lonnie," I said, "carry on," and I gave him my own salute as I revved the bike. I was just about to take off when a streak to my right caught my eye. Without so much as a pause, Rennsdale flat-footed it right into my sidecar, gave me one look, and then settled herself in. By the time I got into the mountains, that little cat was sleeping the sleep of the just.

And now, I plan to do the same.

Your pal and faithful comrade,

Robert

September 13, 1939
Wednesday evening

Dear John,

Today was the day of the big Gabber double funeral (the 13th seems damned appropriate) and everybody within a 15-mile radius of Mackaville must've shown up. The Baptist church is the biggest one in town, and it still didn't have room for all the, well, <u>mourners</u> isn't exactly the right word. There didn't seem to be many tears shed over the brothers' demise; in fact, the whole event took on a kind of carnival atmosphere. Honestly, John, there were people in town for the services that looked as though they hadn't been out of the mountains since McKinley was shot.

When I dropped by the Castapolous Cafe around noon, after completing two of my few remaining interviews, Mr. Castapolous was doing such a land-office business that he put me to work out front, taking the orders and giving them to him in the kitchen. When things got <u>really</u> backed up, I even cooked a few hamburgers on the grill. We undoubtedly violated a few of the sanitary codes of the state of Arkansas, but we got the job done, and I got a great free meal out of it after the crowd was all served.

I'd intended to ride over to Ma's and go to the funeral with her — both she and Patricia had mentioned my doing so at breakfast this morning – but staying and helping Mr. Castapolous put me behind, and by the time I finished eating my lunch it was only thirty minutes before the service was supposed to start.

"I'm gonna shut down this place," Mr. Castapolous said, pulling the shades. "Not because I loved the Gabber brothers, but because I'm gonna take a little rest in the back. After they get those two buried, I'm sure I'm gonna have some very thirsty people come through the doors. Gonna be a good day for beer."

I told him I understood and made my way over to the Baptist church. Even with just a motorcycle, the closest spot I found to park on the street was two blocks away. The front yard of the church was teeming with people, and the organ was already going. I could hear it through the building's open windows, which already had people gathered around them. To me, that meant the church was full.

As I drew close to the building, I saw I was right. In spite of the heat and the humidity, people were packed like pilchards inside the open double doors at the top of the steps, talking and fanning themselves and craning their necks to try and see inside the sanctuary. This funeral was the biggest thing to happen to Mackaville in a month of Sundays.

I stood under the window long enough to

hear that Ma's prediction was on the money: The preacher, who had one of those voices that can go from a roar to a whisper and back again in the space of a few seconds, eulogized the Gabbers as town leaders, openhearted and generous souls who were responsible for making Mackaville what it was. I agreed with the last part. They carried a lot of the responsibility for making Mackaville what it was, all right – the good and the bad. I wondered about Miss Castle, who was surely sitting in there on the front row. What was she thinking about it all, about the canonization of the men who had virtually held her captive for decades?

Ma had predicted that the reverend wouldn't finish the service without an altar call, and she was once again correct. When he started talking about being saved, and how if you weren't and you died you'd be spending eternity in a burning Hell, begging endlessly for only one drop of water to cure your fevered tongue, I drifted away, got on the bike, and drove over to Pete's.

I wasn't sure if he'd be open, but he was, although there wasn't a car to be seen on the streets. I found him in one of the bays, changing the oil on an old robin's-egg-blue Hupmobile.

"Looks like we're the only ones in town who aren't at the funeral," I said to his feet. "Guess you didn't want to go?"

He peered up from under the auto. "The

only reason I'd've gone was to make sure they was dead," he said. "How 'bout you?"

"I heard enough. Had to listen at a window. Church was full to the brim."

He slid back underneath the car. "Getcha a Cleo Cola," he said. "On the house. You're gonna need that sugar energy for the rush after the funeral."

He wasn't wrong. I took my time finishing the bottle of pop, and I was just swallowing the last of it when vehicles began pulling up at the pumps. For the next half-hour or so, I was as busy as I'd been at Mr. Castapolous's. The Gabbers' last rites had sure turned out to be a boon for Mackaville business.

Things had slowed considerably when Ma pulled up in her big yellow Hudson. As I said, it was a hot day – they've been mostly hot ever since I got here, seems like – and the car windows were down. Patricia stuck her lovely head out of the back and waved as Ma stopped at the pump closest to Pete's office. I saw that Miss Castle was a front-seat passenger.

I said hi to Ma and Miss Castle and then took Pat's hand and squeezed it, grinning in at her.

"We waited for you," she said, only a slight admonishing note in her voice.

"I'm sorry, Patricia," I returned. "As W.C. Fields would say, 'Things happened.'"

She smiled then. "Did you go?"

"I did, but I had to listen through a window."

"You were probably better off. There were so many people inside it was hard to take a breath. How are your wounds?"

"I'm fine," I said. "How's your grandmother?"

"She's doing a lot better. Mrs.— Miss Castle has a job for her, and I think that's helping Grandma get well, knowing she's needed."

From the open window on the front seat passenger's side, Miss Castle said, "She's already helped out. She suggested we put cats in and around the plant to keep the…vermin away, and I think that's an excellent idea. I've asked her to help screen our current employees in the hopes that we don't have any more incidents like we had yesterday. Thank you again for your help with that."

"You're welcome."

While Pete bustled around under the hood, she added, "I called both the sheriff and the police chief and told them about what happened yesterday. They assured me that Mr. Atkins will be out of Mackaville within 48 hours. I just wanted you to know what's going on."

"Thanks. I appreciate that. And I'm glad Mrs. Davis is in this with you." Then, to Patricia, "Will you be around later on?"

"Why don't you come by?" she said. "We're

not contagious anymore, so Doctor Chavez says, and Grandma would be glad to see you."

"It's a date." I let her hand go and waved as they left.

Pete came up and stood beside me. "She's a good one," he said.

"Yeah. I'm a lucky guy. Or did you mean Miss Castle?"

"Both of 'em. And Ma, too, for that matter."

They had no more than left when another auto pulled up at the pump island closest to the street. It was a late-model Plymouth sedan, white on top and dark blue on the bottom, with some suitcases and other stuff tied down on top.

"Okie or Arkie coming through?" I asked Pete.

"Car's too new for that," he replied. "I've seen that vehicle before, too."

"I'll get it," I said.

As I got closer, I saw that the turtle hull was tied down, with more baggage sticking out. It seemed to have been tossed in randomly. There were two people in the front seat, a man at the wheel and a woman beside him. I walked up to the driver's side and started to ask him if he wanted me to fill 'er up – but the words caught in my throat when he turned his head and I saw it was the assistant manager who'd turned the snake loose on Miss Castle yesterday. His phiz was bruised and cut; someone had roughed him up.

"Have a good look, you bastard," he said. "I took it from the cops, thanks to you, and don't think I'm leaving before I pay you back." And up came a .22 six-shooter.

Funny what you see in situations like that, John. It was like the scene was a painting, with the woman beside him showing a complete lack of expression, looking straight ahead, not at the little pea-shooter in his hand.

That lasted a millisecond. Then I shot my fist out and grabbed the barrel of that little piss-ant six-shooter and bent it up and back as hard and fast as I could. The guy screamed and I heard a snap that I knew was his trigger finger. I jerked the gat away, and then I knew I'd had the bulge on him all the time: it was a single-action. You had to cock it before you could shoot it.

This genius didn't know that, thank God.

As I stood looking at the pistol, he popped the clutch on the Plymouth and roared out, the load on top of his car shifting and bouncing. I stood watching as the car shot down the street, nearly hitting a lamp post, and roared away.

Pete was in the office smoking a Spud when I walked in and dropped the .22 on the counter beside the cash register.

"For your toy box," I said.

"What the hell, Robert?" he said, just as we heard the squeal of another auto outside. Pete ducked behind the counter – going for his .38, I knew – but when I looked out I saw it was a cop car, old "Trout" Lawson himself at the wheel. He climbed out at what was, for him, a high rate of speed. I stood in the doorway.

"Was that Atkins that just left here, endangering innocent civilians?"

"Yep. He endangered me, too." Holding the door open for him, I pointed to the pistol on the counter. "Threatened me with that weapon, such as it is. I broke his finger jerking it away from him."

Apparently, Chief Lawson wasn't too concerned with fingerprints. He picked up the pistol, looked it over, and set it back down.

"Attempted murder would put that guy away for years, Brown," he said. "I guess you saw it all, Pete."

"Enough," Pete said, taking a drag on his Spud.

I shook my head. "Aw, hell, let him go. Looks like he's been punished enough, and his wife seemed scared to death. He won't give Mackaville or Miss Castle any more trouble."

Trout picked up the gun again, dumped out the shell into a big palm, and stuck it in the front pocket of his khaki uniform. "All right," he said, shrugging. "It's your call." As he got into his car, he turned to me again.

"I don't know what you mean by 'punished,'

though. After he got thrown out of the plant, Mrs. Ga – Miss Castle called us, just in case he had any ideas about making any more trouble. We took him in for questioning, but it's funny. He had trouble getting up the stairs to the second floor. He fell down three, maybe four times."

Then he grinned.

I'm glad I'm on the right side of the Mackaville law – for now, anyway.

Your pal and faithful correspondent,

Robert

September 14, 1939
Thursday night

Dear John,

Spent some time in the Davis parlor with Patricia after I wrote you yesterday evening, and I came this close to popping the question. But I just couldn't find the right time or the right words. I'll see her again tomorrow, so maybe then. I know I'd better do it soon.

If I sound a little wobbly, it's because I'm not altogether sober. I'll explain later. Right now, I hope the discipline of typing helps me to focus and concentrate on what I have to tell you.

Mrs. Davis, who still looks awfully gaunt to me, says she's well enough for Patricia to spend a few hours away from her, so we're going to the Palace Friday night, where the single-feature offering is The Return of the Cisco Kid. With Pat by my side again, that small-town movie theater really will feel like a palace.

This morning as I was getting ready to leave the boarding house I got a call from Dill Jolley, the Falstaffian character who runs Jolley's Mercantile. You may remember him from a few of my previous letters, including the one about my first snake attack. The phone service was terrible and I guess it was long distance to his store, because he was uncharacteristically brusque. That must've meant it was costing him money.

The gist was that an old man named Brady had told Mr. Jolley he'd gotten a letter from the "gummit" some time back, telling him he was going to be interviewed by someone from the WPA. He'd been waiting for that person to show up at his doorstep ever since. Mr. Jolley knew the old geezer was talking about me, so he said I ought to come out and get the interview while I had the chance.

As fate would have it, Mr. Brady was one of the last people I had on my list, because he lived in a remote place in the mountains that had no other homes around it; I've put off going to those areas because it takes hours of traveling just to get one story, with no guarantees it's going to be any good or even that my interview subject is going to be home. So I told Mr. Jolley I was on my way and took off atop the Indian, my faithful feline companion by my side.

When I got to Jolley's Mercantile, it was like old home week. I hadn't been in for a while – maybe since back in late July, when I'd bought that wind-up flashlight from him – but it was like I'd been in there yesterday. The hill-billy Greek chorus lounging around the cracker barrel looked as though it hadn't left for the past two months – same faces, same overalls, same old slouch hats and toothless grins. One of 'em even asked me if I'd run into any snakes lately, which got a big laugh. I had to admit I half-expected Black to be there, as had been the case the first time I'd visited Jolley's Mercantile.

The old gentleman, Mr. Brady, was a character right out of the Lum and Abner radio show. He even talked like Abner. He was 93 years old, he said, and sharp as a pin. He also told me he was Mary Lou Castle's great, great uncle on her father's side. As I've told you before, everybody in these hills seems to be a cousin, uncle, or aunt to someone else.

He was sure proud of his great-great-grandniece, telling me how she'd "gone away to school up in Fayetteville" for a year before marrying into the Gabber clan.

"We'd all expected big things of her," he said, "but ol' Jeb put th' rush on her and hooked her good. She liked the lettuce, y' know. Allus did. But pay fer whatcha get, and she sure did."

The others nodded in sage agreement, and I kept still. If any one of them knew she'd been passed between both the Gabbers for decades he wasn't saying, and I saw no need to bring it up either.

After that pronouncement, Mr. Brady launched into a great story about how his father and older brother had run into a "swamp devil" back in '78 and had killed the demon by stuffing their muzzle-loader shotguns with silver coins and blasting it at point-blank range.

That made me recall loading my own sawed-off Remington with cut-up dimes, back a lifetime ago, when I had thought the cats in this town were somehow the villains. I'd learned a lot since then, and I was still a hell of a long way from knowing it all.

Old Mr. Brady hopped around the store like a wizened crow, acting out the whole story, egged on by the crowd and Dill Jolley himself. It was a grand performance, and when it was over the onlookers actually clapped. The atmosphere was so pleasant that I didn't want to leave, so I dragged my heels, smoking a couple of cigarettes, drinking a Nehi Orange (Mr. Jolley doesn't carry Cleo Cola), and then buying a chunk of rat cheese as big as your hand and two inches thick and some crackers out of the barrel, three for a penny. It was enough to share, and I did, which made me the hero of the day. I actually got another usable story out of one of the group.

It was toward the end of my visit that one of the loafers, a weathered old farmer in a floppy straw hat, asked, "How you been gettin' on with Old Man Black?"

Of course, they all knew. When I demonstrated a willingness to talk, they began peppering me with questions about things that had happened between him and me. As is usual with gossip and second-hand tales, they got a lot of things wrong, but I corrected them where I could and even told them about the snake in the box sent to me at Ma's boarding house. Even though I didn't go into any of the supernatural stuff, I could tell by their captivated faces that this was the most exciting narrative they'd heard for a good long time.

"I figured you fellas would've heard all that by now," I said. "Doesn't Black hang around here?"

One of them spit in the tarnished cuspidor beside the counter. "Ain't seen him in a while," he said, and the others nodded.

"Never liked him anyway," said another.

Dill Jolley shook his head. "Anyone's welcome here – even these here useless ole boys," he said, gesturing vaguely with his thumb toward the layabouts. "But when ole Black came in my door, it was like a storm cloud floatin' across the sun. And he never hardly bought nothin' nohow."

Several of the others shared negative observations about Black's character, and a couple pumped me up for daring to take him on. It was kind of nice having people "flock to my standard," so to say. Then old Mr. Brady reached in the side pocket of his overalls and pulled out an amulet he insisted on giving me. It was a silver three-cent piece on a dirty piece of twine, and he assured me that it would help me in any future battles with Black. Thanking him, I slipped it over my head and around my neck, as he and the others nodded their approval. I left the place on a high note, but got a little sad when I realized it would probably be the last time I'd be there in my life.

I'd spent longer at Jolley's than I'd planned; when Rennsdale and I hit the Mackaville city limits, it was almost 1:30. Even after the cheese and crackers, I had one of Mr. Castapolous's chicken-fried steaks on my mind, but first I thought I'd run by the depot and pick up a schedule so I could actually start planning my trip to D.C.

The buzz of my seventh sense came too late.

As I stepped onto the platform, two big bruisers stepped around the corner of the station.

I immediately turned and headed the other way, only to confront another pair of thugs in my path. We were the only people on the platform; even the ticket window was vacant. And since it was the heat of the day, there weren't very many people on the streets, either. I could be pounded into hamburger before anyone took sufficient notice.

The two I'd turned to face were closest, so I thought I might as well try breaking through them. Reaching up, I pulled my cap down tight over the leather aviator's helmet I wore, tugged on Mr. Brady's amulet for luck, ducked my head, and slammed into the one on the left, knocking us both off the platform and jarring the cut around half my stomach into a lit fuse of pain. I was on top when we hit the sidewalk, and I pounded at his chin with my right fist until I took a hard, numbing blow to the shoulder that I knew came from a leather-covered sap. I recalled Doc Chavez's notion about my having a concussion – and a good head blow from that weapon, I thought, might just do me in. Plus, the blackjack had rendered my right arm momentarily unusable.

Hearing the roar and whistle of a train, I knew that any cries for help would be lost in that cacophony, so instead of shouting I rolled over hard and pulled my assailant over on top of me, just in time for me to hear another slap and a simultaneous scream of pain that told me I'd rolled just in time for the other gazabo to be hit by the sap meant for my noggin.

Even with my weakened right arm, I was holding my own with the guy I'd knocked off the platform. I knew that couldn't last forever. As soon as his partner drew a bead on me and unloaded, I'd be on the canvas. Still, I fought, giving my attacker a good left jab to the throat – dirty, but this was no time for the Marquis of Queensbury. Grabbing his collar, I jerked his oily face down and at the same time brought my head up and forward, smashing it into his nose. If I was going to get another concussion, I wanted it to do some damage.

His cry of pain mingled with the noise of

running footsteps, and I figured it was all up.

Instead, it was the cavalry arriving.

I could hear confused shouting, some slamming noises, and I shoved my suddenly immobilized attacker off me and looked around, just in time to see one of my would-be assailants get knocked spinning by a blow from a suitcase. Two big galoots, who'd apparently just got off the train I'd heard coming in, were cleaning up on these guys, using their luggage as clubs. Then someone – I later found out it was the station master – hustled out of the depot door with a stout brake club. I glimpsed two of the thugs running away. The one I'd tussled with was down, and the other, still gripping the leather sap in his hand, had slid down the side of the platform and was looking dazedly out, his hand pressed to the side of his head.

I was wobbly myself, but I managed to get to my feet just in time for one of the guys to step up to me, holding me by the shoulder.

"You ok, pal?" he asked. "We saw those guys jump you and figured the odds needed some evening." Damned if there wasn't something familiar about his face. It was a little lighter than the coffee-and-cream complexions of most of Mackaville's citizens, but I knew I'd seen it before.

"You got here just in time," I said, hearing a siren in the distance. The railroad people, or someone, hadn't wasted any time in calling the coppers. "I don't think those plug-uglies meant to leave me breathing."

A police car rolled up then, and a couple of Trout Lawson's finest rolled out. While the guy next to me had been talking, he'd kept an eye on the thug down on the pavement. I saw now that his pal had been doing the same with the stunned hoodlum against the platform. Gesturing and talking importantly, the boys in blue had the two cuffed and in the car almost before I knew it. One came back, asked me what had happened, and then left. The whole session took about two minutes. Then he turned to my new friend and asked his name.

"Bill Knowles," he said.

The cop, a squat middle-aged guy with a build like a rutabaga and a button missing on his uniform, asked what Mr. Knowles was doing in town.

"I'm going to work at Castle Foods," he said. "My great aunt, Miss Mary Lou Castle, runs the plant now." He gestured toward his companion. "This is my cousin Donnie. He's here for the same reason."

The mention of Miss Castle's name had an effect on the copper, who almost genuflected, snapping his notebook shut and telling them, "Fine, boys. Glad to have you in town." Then he left.

When Bill Knowles had told the cop whom he was, my memory snapped immediately into focus. As we watched the cops and their prisoners pull away, I said, "You're 'Basher' Knowles, aren't you?"

He grinned. "It's just plain 'Bill' now. But – wait a minute. You're a boxer. I've fought you. CCC? Shoulda known from the uniform."

I'll spare you the usual quip about how it's a small world, but it turns out that Bill "Basher" Knowles and I had boxed one another on three separate occasions while we were both doing time in the Civilian Conservation Corps. In case you're wondering, he won two of 'em. He was a tough cookie and one hell of a boxer, a Golden Gloves guy.

I ended up taking the two over to Mr. Castapolous's cafe and treating them to a couple of hamburgers and beers. The couple of beers turned into several more, and by the time we parted with solemn vows to get together again, I didn't feel like I'd better go work at Pete's, so Rennsdale and I came back to my room. I looked at my notes from the interviews at Jolley's Mercantile for a while, then gave up the idea of working on them tonight and instead decided to write you. Now I'm out of gas and I'm hitting the sack. There were exactly two Bayer aspirins left in the tin Doc Chavez sent, so I'm taking them and going to bed, hoping they'll dull the pain that's started back up again around my midsection after the alcohol started wearing off.

I hope I can sleep, because I've got a

couple of things bedeviling me. First of all, I wonder who was responsible for those thugs attacking me. And second, why have I not been able to pop the question to Patricia? I've got to do it, and soon. Maybe tomorrow. But I'm running out of tomorrows.

Your pal and faithful correspondent,

Robert

September 15, 1939
late Friday night

Dear John,

It has been a long, long day – out in the morning and home well after dark. I miscalculated how long I would be gone and, as a result, I couldn't make it back in time to take Patricia to the movie, so obviously I didn't propose either. She didn't seem awfully upset when I stood her up – at least, she appeared to understand when I finally got to her door to explain, two hours after the movie started. I apologized profusely and asked if I could make it up to her tomorrow night, and she said yes, that'd be fine. I'm determined now to ask her and quit pussyfooting around (a term that takes on extra meaning in this town).

The trip took more than three hours one-way, with the place I was visiting on the very edge of the territory the WPA had mapped out for me. It was way west, nearly to the Oklahoma state line, and the guy was supposed to be over 100 years old. It was one of the very last interviews on my list, and to tell you the truth, I hadn't done it for the same reason I put off visiting Old Man Brady's domicile. They were both a long way from Mackaville, there were no other potential interviewees around either of their places for miles, and even though I knew the longer

I delayed my trip the better the chance he wouldn't be in the land of the living once I did get there, I just couldn't bring myself to commit to such a long jaunt. This morning, I even stayed and ate breakfast with Ma and the others (including Patricia) before starting out, and then I piddled around in my room for a while, so I didn't get on the road until after 10 a.m. I guess I was still putting it off.

But I knew I had no choice but to go see if the old geezer was still kicking and amenable to being interviewed, so finally I strapped on my aviator's helmet and headed for the shed and the big Indian. Rennsdale's taken to barreling out from underneath the front porch when she sees me, so she was right by my feet when I unlocked the door and rolled out the bike.

For all of my heel-dragging, it turned out to be a fascinating day. Even the long trip felt good. I saw some new country, and even though it was all uphill and then downhill, just like all the other excursions I've made for this job, I passed a lot of sweet-smelling forested areas and noticed that a few leaves were already beginning to change color, signaling the beginning of autumn. I did have to stop at two different hill-billy stores like Jolley's, general-notions places with a gasoline pump or two out front, to get directions.

John, you cannot begin to believe how

astonished I was when I finally reached the farm. I should have known from the strange looks both store proprietors gave me that this wasn't going to be a "normal" call, but I wasn't prepared for what happened when I pulled up to the short road to the big two-story farm house and at least a dozen big dogs came billowing out to meet me, barking and howling. Rennsdale was unprepared as well; she shot off the bike and up a big catalpa tree before the first hound made it to me.

That's right, John. Dogs! Except for my faithful pal MacWhirtle, I hadn't seen any in a long time, and you know how I am about 'em. I was so happy to see them that I didn't even consider they might attack me, and they must've picked up on my emotions – like dogs do – because they crowded around the bike, wagging their tails and whining and licking me wherever they could find a spot. All of them seemed to be mongrels with different colors and fur thicknesses, German Shepherd and husky and mastiff and some kinds of retrievers and others, all mixed up. I shut the bike down and got off, and that's when they really got friendly. In fact, they inadvertently knocked me to the ground in their joy and started crowding in to lick my face. It felt so great I wanted to laugh. You know how I love the canines, and in mostly dogless Mackaville I'd forgotten about what I'd been missing.

Through their happy growls and grunts and slurping I heard the voice of a woman. I couldn't make out what she was shouting, but it seemed to be directed at the dogs.

"It's okay!" I yelled from my sprawled-out position, trying to make myself heard through the din. "They're not hurting me!"

Struggling to my feet in the midst of the benign onslaught, I saw an attractive woman on the young side of middle age, dark complected with tightly curled dark hair, standing on the porch in a slacks-and-shirt ensemble that could've come right off the pages of a Sears & Roebuck catalogue. She was smiling even as she snapped out another one-word command. The word didn't sound English, and I didn't understand it.

But my new canine pals did. They stopped roughhousing with me immediately, and then – I'm not lying, John – lined up in two rows on either side of the dirt road, forming a lane to the porch, their bodies still vibrating with ecstasy at having a new friend, tails going like propellers. She didn't say another word; in fact, she seemed to be controlling them with some sort of silent command.

For a second I was a little apprehensive. This reminded me of what had happened at the Gabber farm the day of the snake and pig wars. But my seventh sense stayed quiet, so I pressed on toward the porch, between the two columns of panting pooches.

"It's been many weeks since I've been

around a lot of dogs," I told the woman as I stopped before the short series of steps. "I love dogs. They're my kind of people."

She nodded, still smiling, and then turned to the door of the well-kept two-story. "Gran'pa, it's that young man from the government. The one you got the letter about."

Turning back to me, she asked, "That's right, isn't it? You're Mister Brown?"

"I am. How'd you know?"

"Why, that's the name the government sent us – and we try to keep up," she said with a twinkle in her eye, just as the door creaked open and an ancient old fellow with a cane hobbled out. You know how the drawings in the Spider magazine sometimes show him as a wild-haired guy dressed all in black? Add about sixty years to the picture and you've got Larva Destruidora, which is the man's name.

As soon as he appeared, he swept a glance across the dogs, and they all lay down where they had stood, their tails still thumping the ground.

"Come up here, young 'un," he said. "My eyes ain't as good as they use to was." He had a rich deep voice, especially for a man of his age, and his grip was strong when he offered me his hand. "I can tell them dogs like you, and they ain't never wrong. Our home is your home. This here's Loba, my daughter. I am Larva Destruidora. Come inside."

I nodded my thanks and held the door open for Loba, which earned me another nice smile.

Although it had been plenty warm on the trip, the house was cool, undoubtedly because it sat in the middle of a pine forest, with giant dark-green trees blotting out the sun on all sides. Mr. Destruidora motioned me to a rocking chair, and as I took out my notebook a couple of black Labrador-looking puppies skidded around from another room, greeted me, and then went back to doing whatever puppies do. Glancing out the front window, I saw that the dogs outside had gotten up and were going about their own business as well.

We started talking, and I checked with him about the spelling of his name. When I'd first seen it on my list, I'd figured someone at the WPA had made a typographical error. I mean, what kind of a first name is "Larva"? But it turned out the government had gotten it exactly right. I figured it was Spanish, but he corrected me.

"Portuguese," he said proudly.

After the pleasantries, Mr. Destruidora's first story out of the box was a fairly mundane one. He told me how his grandparents had hewn this place out of the wilderness, although the way he said they met was kind of interesting. His grandpa, it seems, was a sailor, and his future wife was a passenger on a ship that docked at Charleston, South Carolina. Although Mr. Destruidora didn't say it, I got the feeling his grandmother may have been a Negro who came in on a slave ship. He was sure dark enough. Then again, I guess a lot of Portuguese are of a duskier hue, although I haven't seen enough of 'em to know.

I almost asked if he'd had a colored grandmother, but I didn't want to offend him. Besides, something else about this man and his daughter was on my mind. So when he was finished with his story, I said, "Mr. Destruidora, I couldn't help but notice that you and Loba seem to have a real rapport with your dogs. I know that dogs and their masters are like that, but yours seems to be something more."

The look that passed between the two told me I'd hit pay dirt, so I pressed on. I can't tell you why I volunteered the next bit of information, but I did, and it opened the floodgates.

"I've been living in Mackaville. You probably know the place. There are people there who have the same kind of communication with pigs and snakes and cats. There aren't many dogs in Mackaville."

He smiled then, showing a perfect set of teeth. That was something I hadn't seen a lot in my Folklore Project travels. As he reached over for a corn cob pipe, I glanced at Loba. She was smiling, too, showing the same flawless set of choppers, and suddenly I realized a dental resemblance. Both father and daughter had canine teeth, eye teeth, that were a lot bigger and longer than the norm. And, in the dimness of the shaded house, the Destruidora's eyes, which I first thought were light brown, had taken on a brilliant amber color that was almost orange.

I waited while he fired up his pipe. Then, he spoke. "You'd be talkin' about them dead Gabber brothers, wouldn't you? And Old Man Black? And maybe Mrs. Davis – the grandma of that pretty girl you're seein'?"

I tried to hide my surprise, but I didn't do a very good job.

"Gran'pa knows all about Mackaville," she said. "That's where our people lived."

"I'd like to hear that story," I told her.

They exchanged another glance as I quickly added, "Not for publication, if you want it that way."

He seemed to relax at that. "All righty. Don't see why not. And you might as well make yourself comfortable. That rum-cured crook ain't doin' you no good there in your pocket. Go ahead and smoke it, youngster. Little of the weed relaxes a man." As if for emphasis, he drew deeply on his corn cob pipe.

John, that cigar was in an inside breast pocket. There wasn't any way he could've seen it. Suddenly, he chuckled. "Right, ain't I?"

"Yessir."

Turning to his daughter, he said, "Still got it, daughter. I smelt it right off, soon's I got near him."

"I think Mr. Brown would like to know why there aren't many dogs in Mackaville," Loba said, flashing her orangish eyes at me and smiling.

"That right?" the old man asked me.

"Yes, sir. I would."

"Well," he said, leaning back and taking another puff. "There wasn't many of us'ns in the first place. Plenty in the hyena clan, once't. But once they got over here, it all got changed around."

The hyena clan? I thought. What's he mean? Then all at once I thought I understood: The former slaves brought to Mackaville to start the packing plant, I reasoned, had come from four African clans, not three.

"Do you mean there were four clans?" I asked. "I only know of three: the cat, the snake,and the pig. There was a hyena clan originally, too?"

He smiled, giving me another glimpse of those big bone-white eye teeth. "Only three," he said, counting them on his fingers. "Pig, snake, hyena."

"But…"

"The hyena, see, is 'bout half dog and half cat. When them folks got over here where there ain't no hyenas, well, sir, they had to make 'em a choice. Do you go with cats, or you go with dogs? They was lots of catamounts and bobcats around then, so most went the first way. But grandpa, he was always partial to mutts, I guess. He and a few of them others cast in with th' dogs, and that's how it went 'til th' Cleansin'. You know 'bout that."

It wasn't a question. "Yes sir," I said again.

"Between th' snakes and th' hogs and th' jus' plain vicious people, we was damn near wiped out." He nodded toward Loba. "Her daddy and momma both got kilt, same night, and I snatched her up and got her out. She was just a little thing, less'n two years old."

I did a quick mental calculation. Loba was older than I'd originally thought.

"A few more of us, well, we went to live with th' Indians, who had the same kind of feelin' for dogs that we did. What they was left of us just kinda lay low for a while. But we knowed what was going on in town. I reckon dogs and cats ain't s'posed to get along, but we do. We both hyena people in our hearts."

The old man knocked the dottle out of his pipe and repacked it. "We knows all about what's gone on in Mackaville, and your part in it. For what it's worth, you on the right side." A big kitchen match flared into life above the bowl of his pipe as he added, "They's still a few of us around. Some went off in th' world, like Loba here, and come back with some dough-re-mi. They been buyin' up land around these parts, kinda on th' sly, waitin' to see how it all plays out."

"Well, you already know this, I'm sure," I

said, "but with the death of the Gabbers it seems to me that the cat people have taken control of Mackaville. Since you both have the same origins, I'd think that'd be a good environment for the return of your own clan."

"Mebbe so," he said, puffing on the pipe. "What you think, granddaughter?"

She leaned in, holding me with those amber eyes. "I think you're right," she told me. "But you know there's something left for you to do."

I wasn't following her. "What's that?" I asked.

"Kill Black."

I couldn't contain my surprise at that. "Kill Black? Me? Why me?"

"You really don't know, young'un?" he asked with a chuckle. I turned to him.

"No, I don't. He's been trying to do me in ever since I arrived in Mackaville, and I'm not sure why. How come you think I drew the straw to kill that sorry old bas…" I stopped in confusion, not wanting to use that word in front of a woman.

"He isn't a bastard," Loba said, smiling. "You have to have parents to be a bastard."

That was an odd thing to say, I thought, and as I pondered her statement the old man leaned over and put a hand on my knee. A palpable shock hit me, like a big dose of static electricity.

"You the only one can kill him," he said. "We can't. We got powers, but they limited.

He can get inside our brains, know when we comin' for him. But they's one brain he can't get inside of, and that's yours." He took his hand away, grinning again. "I can't neither. Jus' tried."

John, this was all getting very strange. But my seventh sense didn't seem to think anything was untoward and remained dormant, although there seemed to be a little buzzing going through my head.

I looked back and forth at the two of them. "Look," I said finally. "I don't understand what you're getting at."

"Sure you do," said Loba. "You just don't know how to put it into words. Maybe this will help: You know how you get a kind of warning from inside when things aren't right, or something bad is about to happen?"

My seventh sense, I thought. *How in the hell—*

"You got a gift," Mr. Destruidora said, "somethin' the rest of us ain't got. Gives you a smart bit o' power." He set his pipe down in a big ceramic ashtray. "You ain't just throwed a scare into Black; you got ever'body a mite uneasy. Witch power that's scared don't work right."

"This Black, he's by himself now," added Loba. "The sons aren't coming back. He's weakened, weaker than he's been in a long, long time. It's all because of you."

It seemed like I ought to have had a

response to that, John, but I didn't. I wasn't sure what I was supposed to say.

While I was still mulling, the old man creaked up off his wooden chair. "You best be on th' road," he said. "It's a long way to Mackaville, and even with your gift, ain't no sense you bein' on the road after dark. I've got to visit th' little house out back." He held his hand out. "Nice to make your acquaintance," he said, and when we shook hands I got that same static-like shock.

Then, as Loba put a hand on my shoulder to usher me to the door, I felt the tingle again in the skin under her fingertips.

Although it was hard to tell there in the shadows of the pines, my strap watch told me it was getting on toward dusk. As we stepped through the door and onto the porch, the dogs once again snapped to attention and assembled in those same two columns, like some sort of tail-wagging, four-footed military escorts. Loba held out her hand, giving me the same little jolt that her grandfather had transmitted with his grip. It was like they both were concealing joy buzzers in their palms. I knew better, though.

The dogs followed us with their eyes, tails thumping the ground, as she walked me to my bike. Somewhere close, coyotes had begun howling.

"Listen," she said, inclining her ear toward the sounds. Then, "Let me show you something, something about yourself that you don't seem to know. Just a moment."

Throwing her head back, she yipped and yowled, echoing the sounds that pack of animals was making.

Damn, John. Just when I think I've seen and heard everything around this place, something else comes along. Cats "talking" to me, David squealing like a pig, and now this intelligent, apparently worldly woman giving out with animalistic cries. It shocked me plenty – especially when the coyotes seemed to answer her.

Then, coming down the short path in front of me, I made out the figures of a couple of animals walking toward us. As they got closer, I could see they were smaller and shaggier than the dogs on the Destruidora place. And then I knew they were coyotes. About fifty feet away from us, they sat down, their eyes catching a bit of light from somewhere, glinting yellow.

"Try to reach them," she whispered.

"What?" John, you can imagine I had no idea what the hell she was getting at.

"Try to reach them. Open your mind and see through their eyes. I think you can do it." Then I remembered how she and her grandfather had talked to me about the seventh sense, as though they knew all about it. What was it he'd said? A gift that gave me "a smart bit of power?" Did they know something I didn't?

Well, hell, I'd seen enough in the past

few months not to dismiss anything out of hand, so I stared at those two wild animals, and they stared back, and suddenly – John, this is crazy, I know, but I really was seeing through *their eyes*. I don't know how to explain it; to say I was looking at *me* doesn't come anywhere near covering it. I saw Loba and myself in black and white, like we were in a movie, but there was some sort of aura around us both that pulsed and changed colors from purple to yellow to green. All the sounds around me, even the breathing of the dogs behind us, seemed louder, and my nostrils suddenly filled with an overwhelmingly powerful mixture of earth and animal smells.

It was all too much. Spooked, I "pulled back" and was in my own skin again, watching the pair of coyotes turn and disappear into the deepening shadows. When I looked at Loba, she was grinning.

"You could get used to it, if you let yourself," she said. "It just takes practice. Good night."

Then, of all things, she kissed my cheek, giving me one final little electric jolt. I watched her walk back through the twin dog columns to the porch, still jumpy about what had just happened with the coyotes and me.

A skittering noise distracted me, and I turned in time to see Rennsdale leap into the sidecar and give me a look that said, "Get going!" Indeed, the dogs were now stirring, and the sound of the door shutting behind Loba seemed to set them free. They turned toward me just as I kicked the Indian to life. I would've loved to have stayed around and skylark a little more with the pooches, but I had a petrified cat with me, and I wasn't at all sure they'd be as friendly to her.

It was a chance I didn't want to take.

So, I waved at the dogs as I wheeled around and motored down the drive, yelling, "So long, fellas!" – and damned if I didn't hear a chorus of voices as I rode away, shouting their goodbyes back. I heard them!

There's so much I don't know.

I can't think of anything else to write after that, so I'll sign off.

Your pal and faithful correspondent,

Robert

September 16, 1939

very late Saturday night, or early Sunday morning

Dear John,

All I want to do is go to bed and let sleep carry me away. But every time I try, the events I'm about to relate to you jar me awake, so now I'm up and maybe if I get them all out on paper I can finally exorcise them from my mind and find some peace.

It all started routinely enough. I spent the morning typing up interviews. By lunch time I was all caught up, and with joy I saw that I had winnowed down the list to only two more names. Like the others I'd put off until the very end, the Messrs. Brady and Destruidora, these folks lived far away, and in opposite directions to boot, so it would take two full days to get them both. At first, I thought about just letting them go. I'd already given the government several bonus interviews they hadn't planned on, so surely I was at or over the numbers that the contract called for.

But I quickly rejected that notion. Something inside me wouldn't let me do it. It was like quitting the job just when it was ending. So I resigned myself to another few days in Mackaville and then turned my attention to the more important task at hand. I was finally going to pop the question to Pat.

I was apprehensive, but excited, too. If I'd only known.

After lunch, I shaved and took a nice long bath, thinking about how I couldn't turn back now because I'd made too many plans and Pat was going to know something was up. Pete's Hudson was outside in the driveway; he'd lent it to me for the occasion. I'd bought a new Arrow shirt and a matching tie from the little dry-goods store downtown. As I'd left there, I'd also picked up a little nosegay on impulse from the flower shop two doors down.

Patricia's a smart young lady. She'd know immediately this was not just a make-up date to see The Return of the Cisco Kid. Maybe I was going about it wrong, but it was the path I'd chosen, and, by damn, I was going to stick to it.

By the time I pulled up in front of the Davis home I was all nerves. Giving myself a good mental talking to, I walked up the side-walk to the porch and knocked on the door. Pat answered, called back to her grandmother that it was me and we were going to the movies. For a moment, I felt like I ought to go in and ask her for Patricia's hand in marriage, but then I realized that was putting the cart before the horse. There'd be plenty of time for that, I thought, after Pat gave me her answer.

Pat knew something was up immediately.

"Where's the Indian?" she asked as she shut the door behind her. "Why do you have

Pete's car? And why are you bringing me flowers?"

"Can't I bring you flowers?" I asked as she took them from me and held them up to her bosom.

"You never have before. There's a little pin in the back. Pin them on me, Robert."

That morning, the wind had shifted to the north, bringing with it some cooler mountain air. It felt like the Indian summers we get in Minnesota, and it was winsome and welcome after the stifling dog day heat that had carried through August into mid-September. In deference to the lowered temperatures, Patricia was wearing a blue wool sweater with her white skirt, and when I went to pin those flowers above her right breast I got the shakes again. She was damned sexy.

"Give me those," she said, smiling. "You're liable to stab me." And she pinned the flowers on herself with a little laugh.

At Pete's car, I held the door open for her, and halfway in, she stopped. "Robert," she said. "When are you going to tell me what all this is about?"

Well, I'd planned for dinner at Mr. Castapolous's joint and then the movie before I got around to popping the question, but with her query all of that went out the window. I managed to say, "You want to eat first?" But when she shook her head "no" I added, "Ok. Let's drive out into the hills a little ways and I'll tell you."

We both remained silent as I headed out of town, and while it was a short trip, it seemed as though it took hours. I turned the radio on, hoping to find a sweet ballad on the radio, but instead all I could pull in were pieces of dramas and a slice of war news about the French retreating from Germany. So I switched it off and a few minutes later, I pulled off a gravel road I knew wasn't used much, killed the engine, and, turning to her, took a deep breath.

"Ok, Pat," I said. "Here it is. I have to leave Mackaville soon and go to a new job in D.C."

"Yes," she said softly. "I know."

"I don't want to go without you. I don't want us to part, ever. I love you and want you to marry me."

For the first time, I realized there was a full moon out. I saw it reflected in her eyes as she gazed steadily at me. Finally, she spoke.

"Robert, I don't know what to say. I love you, too." She touched my arm, tentatively. "But I hadn't thought about it being forever."

"Please think about it now," I told her. "You're smart, and Washington is a progressive city. I know you've thought a lot about going to college. We can find one there, I know, that caters to people of your…race."

Since I said that, only a few hours ago, I've wished a hundred times that I could take it back. I've of course known for months that most of Mackaville's people, including her, are at least part Negro, and while Patricia and I had never talked about it, I just figured she knew I knew. All I wanted to do was tell her that it didn't matter to me and that I was willing to help her adjust to the outside world.

Her piercing look told me it had been the wrong thing to say. And for once, what came out of my mouth next, as I struggled to explain myself, just made it worse.

"Look, Pat, it doesn't make any difference to me. Honest, it doesn't. I don't care that you're colored. And my folks and the people that'll be around us – well, the way you look, they'll never have to know."

"The way I look?" She almost spit out the words. "What the hell do you mean by that?"

In all our time together, that was the first time I'd ever heard her cuss. I reached for her, but her body had gone rigid, her eyes hard.

"You damn fool," she said. "Take me home."

"Pat, I–"

"Take me home." Rage simmered in her voice.

I ground the starter on the Hudson and turned around, heading back to Mackaville. I couldn't understand, and I didn't know where to start.

"I'm sorry," I said finally, as we sped back to town. She didn't respond.

"I said 'I'm sorry,'" I repeated.

"I heard you," she said, the anger still coloring her voice. "And I'm sorry, too. I'm sorry that the man who wants to marry me is so worried about what other people think. I'm proud to be what I am. I won't pretend to be anything else."

"I didn't mean—"

She cut me off again. "What you meant, Mr. Brown, was that my forebears bother you. I'm not white as an Easter lily, like you and your family and friends, and you think that's a problem. It may be for you, but it's not for me."

We were in front of her house now, and it looked different to me. Everything had changed.

Except for Patricia. She opened the door, turning on the dome light, and it shone on her as she carefully undid the nosegay from her sweater and then, like a coiled spring, threw it on the front seat.

"Goodbye, Robert," she said. Her eyes glistened. She had never looked more beautiful.

I opened my mouth to speak again, but she shut the door before I could say anything. I heard her footsteps on the sidewalk, realizing it was a sound I would never hear again. The scent of her lingered.

Suddenly, I just wanted to get out of there. So through the shock and the pain I made it to Pete's station, just as he was closing up. I know he could tell from my face that something had gone terribly wrong, and since he knew why I'd borrowed his auto he also had a damn good idea what had happened. I knew he'd ask me nothing, so, gutting up, I forced a smile and threw him his keys.

"Didn't work," I told him.

He nodded. "Wanna stick around and have a pop?"

"I appreciate it, but no thanks. Think I'll take the Indian for a whirl and see if it'll clear my head."

"Ok. It's in the back. Key's in the ignition."

Thanking him for the loan of the Hudson, I got to the bike and took off. Even in my dazed condition, I knew I didn't want to wander too far out into the mountains, since I was never sure what was waiting for me when I was alone. And on this night, I felt more alone than I'd felt in a long time.

So I buzzed around the outskirts of town for a while, taking the highway and a couple of gravel roads I knew pretty well, but, as I think Hemingway wrote at the end of A Farewell to Arms, it wasn't any good. I kept thinking about what I'd said to Pat, and how she'd reacted, and I tried to blame her, and then I tried to blame this damn town, and finally I shouldered the blame myself and said the hell with it. I suddenly needed a drink, and the only place I knew to go for that at this time of the evening was to Mr. Castapolous's.

He was doing a fine business when I walked through the door, shaking off the feeling that everyone in the place knew I had been brushed off by Patricia and were laughing at me. In fact, though, hardly anyone looked up when I came in. They were too busy working over platters of Mr. Castapolous's Saturday night special, fried frog legs.

"Robert," he said with a grin as I shouldered up to the counter. "You come for some frog legs?"

"Sure," I told him.

"Just about out of 'em. These customers, they love their batrachos." He peered at me. "Something wrong, Robert?"

"Been unlucky in love tonight, Mr. Castapolous," I said.

He shook his head. "That's too bad. You eat some frog legs, have some wine. Things'll get better."

In a moment, there appeared in front of me a dinner plate full of what looked like small pieces of fried chicken, a saucer holding a couple of dinner rolls and butter and some slices of tomato and pickle, a little bowl with some kind of dressing or dip, and a water glass nearly full of red wine. Mr. Castapolous beamed at me from behind the counter. "Nothing helps a broken heart more than a full stomach – and a light head," he said, gesturing toward the wine. "This is the good vino, too. My own personal."

I thanked him and dug in. I'd never eaten frog legs before, and they were saltier than I thought they'd be. The dressing he had out for dipping turned out to be mostly horse-radish, enough to make my eyes water, but the wine went down very smoothly, and before I knew it there was a pile of shiny bones on my plate. Busy as a one-armed paper hanger, Mr. Castapolous bustled back and forth between counter and tables, making sure everyone in the place was happy, or at least content. Twice, he poured me more wine.

I knew sometimes he wouldn't let me pay, and I had no idea how much the wine was worth, so I left three singles under my plate and headed out, warmed by the alcohol and food into a kind of glowing numbness.

There were so many autos outside the cafe that I'd had to park near the end of the block, under a street light, and when I opened the door I saw immediately something different about the Indian. There was a woman, sitting in the sidecar.

No, not sitting. When she saw me she kind of rose and swayed, reminding me of a cobra coming up out of a Hindu's basket.

As I looked, Mr. Castapolous appeared beside me, trying to stuff a couple of singles in my front pocket.

"You pay too much, Robert. Take this."

I held up a hand. "No. You take it. Look down there."

"Hmmm," he said, following my gaze. "Maybe you're not so unlucky after all."

"Know her?"

"Seen her around. Sort of a skag, I'm thinking."

"Watch me, will you? I want to see what this is about."

"Sure."

As I got closer, I saw that his description fit. Her sweater, too tight by a couple of sizes, made it clear that she wore no brassiere. Her makeup was strictly Barnum and Bailey, her hair right out of a peroxide bottle, and the pungent scent of her musky perfume was tawdry and cloying.

"What are you doing here?" I asked. "I don't know you."

"Oh, but I know _you_," she returned, showing a black dead front tooth as she grinned at me. I didn't like her looks at all. The slitted cold eyes, especially.

"And you know _me_," she continued, her voice hissing as it rose. "You knew me _good_." Then, all in one motion, she ripped her sweater almost down to her belly button and threw back her head, letting go with a blood-chilling scream. I swear she was grinning the whole time.

It all caught me by surprise, and I back-pedaled away from the bike just in time to see a quartet of men come running, just as though the scream had been their cue. In the light of the street lamp, I saw that the lead bozo was one of the guys who'd tried to do me in at the train station last Thursday. He already had his sap in hand. A thought flitted across my mind: Who the hell bailed him out of jail?

Meanwhile, the cheap frail was screaming her lungs out.

"He had his way with me! He raped me!" The shrill yelling was like some kind of crazy movie soundtrack to a fight scene, as the guy from the station reached me and let go with the sap. Stepping inside his swing, I let him have a full roundhouse right to the gut, and he went down. Then the other three were on me, and I figured it was all over. But I'd figured without Mr. Castapolous, as an explosion suddenly froze them into statues. Even the tomato stopped her screaming.

I looked down the sidewalk to see my Middle Eastern friend standing with the Mannlicher, working the bolt and ejecting one of those cigar-sized shells.

"Let him go!" Mr. Castapolous shouted, as people began boiling out the door behind him, scrambling to see what the fuss was about. "Next shot goes through your heads!"

Looking at one another, they stepped away from me. The tramp even stepped out of the sidecar.

I had just started walking toward Mr. Castapolous when I saw a dark auto rounding the corner. It screeched to a halt in front of me and a harness cop in full uniform rolled his bony ass out, hollered that he was taking over, and then told me to turn around and put my hands behind my back.

Suddenly, it hit me. I'd seen that guy before. I knew, then, he was the cop who'd done nothing but watch way back when, the time my fight with the Black twins spilled out of Foreman's Drug Store and onto Mackaville's streets.

Then, the clack of handcuffs on my wrists brought me back into the moment. The adrenaline shot through me like electricity. Something was very wrong.

My assailants, instead of running away, stood almost cockily under the street light. Even the slutty wren who'd cried rape stood, looking strangely unperturbed, swaying on her feet as though there was music playing only she could hear.

Just as the cop began horsing me toward the auto, it hit me. There was no way he could've known I was anything more than an innocent bystander. My accuser hadn't said a word since he'd arrived. Then I saw that the car he was hustling me toward wasn't a police vehicle at all, but a plain black Ford touring car.

"Mr. Castapolous!" I shouted. "Look at that auto! It's not a cop car!"

My captor slapped me on the side of the head for that, but I spun around and ducked as I saw Mr. Castapolous raise the Mannlicher again, aiming it squarely at the man's chest and hollering, "Hold it! You may be a cop, but that ain't an official vehicle!"

"You said it, Mr. Castapolous. Hold these people while I call the sheriff."

"Already called him," returned Mr. Castapolous, sighting down the barrel toward the policeman. "Better put your hands up, mister," he said to the man.

"You're gonna be in trouble, greaser," the guy returned sullenly, trying to sound authoritative and not doing a very good job of it.

"You gonna be a grease spot, you don't get up your hands." Mr. Castapolous's response actually drew a couple of chuckles from the folks behind him, who were clearly enjoying this Saturday night diversion.

Muttering curses, the copper slowly raised his hands.

"You behind him," Mr. Castapolous motioned with the rifle barrel toward the four men and girl. "Get 'em up too."

They complied.

"Thanks," I told Mr. Castapolous. "The cavalry came just in the nick of time."

"I don't know about no calvary," he said softly, eyeing the group. "But this bastard's sure enough a town law."

I was still mulling that bit of knowledge when Sheriff Meagan roared around the corner in his own vehicle, siren blaring. When he climbed out, he looked as though the call might've awakened him from a hard sleep. His demeanor suggested the same thing.

"All right, what the hell?" he growled.

The cop spoke first. "This low-life" – he indicated me with a nod, still keeping his hands in the air – "raped this girl. And his wop buddy here threatened to shoot me."

"All right, Brown," Sheriff Meagan turned to me with a vinegary expression on his face, like he'd just gotten a whiff of something rotten.

"Sheriff, this is a set-up," I said. "I was leaving Mr. Castapolous's place when I saw this girl sitting in my sidecar. I asked her to leave and she cried rape. Not only have I never seen her before, but when this policeman came along, he didn't say a word to her. He just handcuffed me and tried to take me away in his auto, which isn't even an official police car."

Mr. Castapolous and several of the diners who'd gathered behind him all voiced their agreement with my version of the events.

"All right, E.V.," the sheriff said. "Put the goddamn gun down."

Suddenly, the girl materialized beside him. Sniffling and pulling the torn sweater together in front of her ample tiddlywinks, she did her best to sound hysterical. "Not an hour ago, we were parked outside of town and this man threw me down and forced himself onto me." Again, as her voice rose, it sounded more and more like a hiss. "I didn't want to do it. He made me. He made me. And then – and then he told me he'd get me something to eat but made me wait while he went in to get it." She sniffled again and tried to make pleading eyes at the sheriff. With her eyes, it didn't work. She was no Bette Davis in the drama department, either.

"This one, she's lying," said Mr. Castapolous, holding the Mannlicher with its barrel pointed downward. "I saw Robert drive down the street and park. She wasn't with him then. She got in later."

I knew that he likely hadn't seen me until I'd actually come through his door. I also figured he knew I hadn't done anything to this girl, and so his sense of values would permit a little fudging.

She started to sputter out a response, but I cut in. "Sheriff, you can check with Pete Barlow. I was there at his station right before I came here. This woman wasn't with me then, either."

"When'd you get here, Brown?"

Mr. Castapolous spoke up. "It was about 7:15. I had frog legs in the fryer and had to keep an eye on the clock."

"Bullshit!" said the cop. "Sheriff, when I came by here, this guy was trying to get rough with the girl. She was crying and screaming and I knew I had to stop it."

The murmur from the Castapolous Cafe crowd told a different story.

"What the hell are you doing here anyway, Battersley?" The sheriff spat the question at him. "You're in uniform, but you ain't in an authorized police vehicle."

That seemed to catch the man off guard. "Well…" he said, "I was just headin' home and – listen, who you gonna believe? A brother law enforcer or these here civilians?"

Sheriff Meagan turned to Mr. Castapolous. "See if you can raise Trout. He may still be at the station."

Nodding, Mr. Castapolous headed back into the cafe, still clutching the rifle.

Just about that time, here came the Hudson I'd been driving only a couple of hours earlier, motoring down the street. It stopped right in front of us, and Pete stuck his head out the window.

"Heard the siren," he said to Sheriff Meagan. "Anything I can do?"

"Yeah," returned the sheriff. "You can tell me if any of these people visited your station this evening." His gesture took in not only me but the four thugs, the cop, and the people crowded around the cafe door.

"No one but Robert, there. Robert Brown. He came by just as I was closing up."

"What time?"

"Well, I shut down at seven. We visited a few minutes."

"Anyone with him?"

Pete shook his head. "Not a soul," he said.

The tomato started to protest, but Sheriff Meagan silenced her with a gesture. "All right, Pete. Thanks."

Pete saluted and drove away, and the sheriff turned to the cop, who by this time was looking very uncomfortable. "Get those damn bracelets off this man," he said. "And then get your sorry ass out of here."

Moving quickly for a guy his size, this Battersley had the cuffs off me in a jiffy and seemed to be in a real hurry to get into his auto. He'd just stuck his head in when the sheriff slammed his open palm against the top of the door frame, knocking the door against the side of Battersley's head. The cop let out a scream of pain and tumbled into the front seat. Reaching into the open window, Sheriff Meagan pulled his head up and went nose-to-nose with him.

"I ain't your boss, Battersley," he snarled. "But I got a strong suspicion you've been terminated from the Mackaville force. You might want to get the hell outta town before you find yourself on the wrong side of the bars."

With a snort of disgust, he pushed the man back in the car. Battersley fumbled for the keys and cut out of there like his hair was on fire. Then, the sheriff turned to the four thugs and the woman. Their sullen attitude had melted considerably.

"Simmonds, what the hell are you doing out on the streets?" He barked this to the man

I'd recognized from the attack at the train station. The blackjack, naturally, had disappeared, and I thought about telling the sheriff about it and having the guy frisked. But I decided to leave well enough alone. Sheriff Meagan was doing just fine without me.

"I'm out on bail, sir," he said.

"Wanna go back in?"

"No, sir."

"Then you and your buddies better be movin' on, and in a sweet hurry, before Chief Lawson gets here."

I didn't want them to be able to leave just like that, but, again, I held my tongue as they practically ran away, back to wherever it was they'd come from. But the girl stayed. She had to. Sheriff Meagan's big hand was on her shoulder, restraining her, and all her wiggling did nothing to get her free.

Then the police chief pulled up in his official black-and-white Chevrolet coupe.

Sheriff Meagan turned back toward the crowd. "Watch her, E.V.," he said, and I realized Mr. Castapolous had returned. He still carried the Mannlicher, too.

Chief Lawson got out of the copper car, and he and the sheriff conferred for a couple of minutes. Then they both walked over to the girl, whose expression indicated she now knew that things had turned bad for her.

"What'd you have to do to get them boys behind you, Cora?" Lawson asked.

She tried to work up another sniffle but dropped it. "I ain't done nothing," she said, lowering her head. Her hand still clutched the torn sweater. She looked pitiful as hell.

"No, nothin' besides a little whorin' to get the job done," said Lawson. She had no reply.

Reaching down, he turned her face up to meet his gaze. "I ought to throw you in the slammer right now. But I know sooner or later you got to tell your Uncle Black you failed. That'll be punishment enough, I reckon."

The funny way he said "uncle" made it clear that her relationship with Old Man Black might not be familial, but I was shocked enough just to hear my nemesis's name. So this had been another of his plots. I couldn't be very surprised. The attack at the train station – that had been, too. I wondered if this tramp had had anything to do with that.

"I don't want to see you back here in town for a while," Lawson continued. "And if you so much as look at this man again" – he indicated me – "I'll lock you up, and don't think I'm bullshitting."

She nodded. "I'm sorry, Chief Lawson," she said, still looking at the sidewalk. "Is it ok if I apologize to him?"

"Go ahead," he said.

She was only a few yards away, and once she turned toward me, her face a mask of hatred and anger, the seventh sense shot through me like lightning and I almost expected the silvery flash that streaked toward my throat, followed immediately by a meaty thud. Then the girl was on the sidewalk, clutching her stomach, and Mr. Castapolous was standing beside her, ready to hit her with the butt of the Mannlicher again. Beside her, gleaming in the yellow radiance of the street lights, was a straight razor. She tried to grab it and get back up, but Chief Lawson stomped her hand and kept his boot on it, ignoring her screams, as he reached down and picked up the weapon. Then he pulled her to her feet, the sweater coming apart and exposing her breasts.

All modesty was gone now. She was an animal, writhing in his grip.

"Look here, Cora," he said. "If I ever find you in town again, you'll go up for attempted first-degree murder. And you'll be convicted." He swept his arm toward the crowd that had hardly moved since everything had begun. "Look at all these witnesses, Cora. Now get out."

She pulled away and took off, turning a safe distance away to spit in my direction. Then she lurched down the street and around the corner, and I heard the labored grind of an ancient vehicle starting up to take her away – to God knows what.

I looked down at my shirt front. It gaped open from a long slit across the chest. The bottom half of my tie lay on the sidewalk.

"You're damned lucky, Brown," Sheriff Meagan said.

"I'll tell the world," I returned. Then, to Mr. Castapolous. "Thank you. I imagine you saved my life."

"Hate to hit a woman," he said, and his eyes showed he meant it. "But she'd have gutted you like a mullet."

The show was over for the evening, and the patrons, talking among themselves, went back through the doors to their unfinished dinners. I couldn't imagine that cold frog legs would be very good.

When only the four of us were left outside, I said, "So this was another of Old Man Black's surprises?"

Trout Lawson nodded. "We've been wonderin' what he'd try next. Now we know."

"I'm thankful you were here," I said. "Can I buy you gentlemen a beer?"

"I'll toss in some frog's legs," Mr. Castapolous said. "On the house." The sheriff and the chief nodded at one another and then at me.

Hell, John, I'd have bought them beers all night if they'd wanted. The wine had worn off for me, and I just didn't feel like drinking anymore, so I got them a round and then begged off for the evening. But as I was leaving, the sheriff took hold of my arm.

"Brown, you <u>are</u> getting the hell out of town in the next couple of days, aren't you?"

"Yessir. I have a job in D.C."

"Good," he said, letting go of me and turning toward the chief, who was busy stripping a frog leg with his front teeth. "Me and Trout are gettin' tired of all this excitement."

I couldn't tell if he was kidding, and at that particular time I didn't care. I just wanted to get back to Ma's and sleep. Which, as you know, I haven't yet been able to do.

Two women tried to eviscerate me in one day. One succeeded. And life goes on, sort of.

Your pal and faithful comrade,

Robert

September 17, 1939
Sunday evening

Dear John,

Well, hell, I couldn't sleep last night. I tried, but crazy thoughts kept racing through my head and then I'd try to count sheep and take deep breaths, but none of it got me anywhere. I rolled around so much that Mac finally got sick of being on the bed with me and jumped down with a snort of disgust.

When dawn broke, I got up, washed, shaved, and was on my way to partake of what would have been my last pre-church breakfast from Ma.

Halfway down the stairs, though, I stopped short. I couldn't go to church. Patricia might be there, and it would just be too awkward and unpleasant for both of us. So I took a hard left at the bottom of the staircase and headed quickly out the front door, trying to ignore the enticing smell of frying meat rolling out from the kitchen.

I got the bike out and running in jig time, not wanting to face anyone, even Ma. It was only after I'd gotten two blocks down the road that I realized I hadn't seen Rennsdale. It didn't matter what time of the day it was or how much of a hurry I was in – that little cat always seemed to be watching and waiting for me, ready to barrel across the yard from her place under the porch and hop into the sidecar.

Not this time, though. I hadn't seen her at all, and for some reason the thought made me kind of glum. It was like maybe she knew I was leaving and had turned her back to me, knowing she'd never see me again.

As I've written you before, Mackaville still observes most of the blue laws, so there wasn't much open when I reached town. Mr. Castapolous's place, being an establishment that sells alcohol, was shut up tight for the day, and when I drove by I didn't see any sign of activity. Maybe he was sleeping in, or he might have already gone out somewhere on his day off. We'd talked plenty last night anyway.

The only thing open on the town square was Mr. Foreman's drug store, so I stopped in front and went in, thinking I wouldn't mind talking to him again, giving abstract stuff like "truth" and "faith" a going-over. It might take my mind off my little piss-ant personal problems.

As it turned out, he wasn't there. No one was in but that same teenaged soda jerker who'd been there when I'd last visited. He nodded like he knew me and drew me a cup of coffee from the urn behind him. Down the counter in a glass case sat a peach pie. As good a breakfast as any, I guess. As he cut me a slice of the pie, an organ droned from the table-model cathedral radio on the counter. It was playing some vaguely familiar hymn as he sidled up and set the plate in front of me.

"Hey, mister," he said. "I seen you talking to the boss the other day."

I nodded.

"I recognize folks and what they do," he said proudly, creasing his pock-marked face with a grin. "I keep my eyes open. I wanna be a detective someday."

"No doubt you'll be a fine one," I said around a forkful of pie.

That made him draw up even straighter. Then, conspiratorially, "Hey, you mind if I try to pull in somethin' besides this churchy stuff?" He nodded toward the radio. "Once in a while, you can get a swing program all the way from Fayetteville."

"Knock yourself out."

I took another bite while he fiddled with the knob, stopping not at a music program but for a news broadcast. The announcer's voice seemed especially tense, and as the kid and I stared expectantly at the radio, we heard how the Japs were attacking China over in the Far East while at the same time the Soviet Russians had begun invading Poland. The jerker shot a worried glance toward me, and in that moment I felt like the world I knew was on an irrevocable course toward destruction, and, like millions all around the world listening in drug stores and kitchens and living rooms and greasy spoons, we'd be swept up in it, whether we liked it or not. I felt suddenly trapped, like a bug in a jar.

He switched the radio back to the organ, still playing that same hymn. "Hell," he said softly.

"Yeah." I finished the last bite of my pie and slapped a quarter on the counter. "War is hell, so they say. Keep the change."

The escalating war was still on my mind when I kicked the Indian into life and pulled away from the curb, starting up the other side of the town square. I'd just passed an alley when I heard the grinding of gears and a bob-tailed truck with a heavy winch mounted on its short bed pull out behind me. In this place, I've learned to assume that everything is a threat until I learn differently – especially when I feel my seventh sense kicking in, as it was now – so I immediately opened the bike up and took off through the mostly deserted Main Street.

Then I saw a black sedan waiting at the corner. My seventh sense told me to avoid it as well.

In a few seconds I was approaching the courthouse. If it had been a weekday, Sheriff Meagan would've been in there at this time of the morning, and that would've solved any problem I might have had. But even a guy like him needed a day away from work.

The courthouse was quiet and probably locked tight, which I guess was ok since I didn't want anyone to see me run that Indian right through the neatly kept lawn and bounce onto the drive that led to the street outside the square. It was a shortcut I didn't think the truck could take; I'd lost sight of the car.

As I heard that bob tail clattering behind him, I realized I knew that particular sound.

Although I hadn't actually seen the getaway vehicle that had picked up the slatternly Cora Saturday night, whatever it was had made the exact grinding noise.

So it was Black again. Or maybe Black and the postmaster, Barney Gibson, in cahoots.

How would they have known I'd be coming downtown? I figured they had someone watching Ma's boarding house, knowing sooner or later I'd be going somewhere by myself on the big Indian. What mattered now was getting away, so I opened up the bike as much as I dared to in this situation. In a few moments, I'd left the truck in my dust and I was zipping down the road to the big Baptist church, where I once again left the road, cutting up the little hill toward the back of the place, which was dotted with big evergreens. The few people outside the church gaped as I passed, and I waved at them like everything was jake.

Once behind the church building in the woodsy area, I killed the engine and rolled the bike behind the biggest evergreen I could find, effectively hiding it from anyone on the street. Then I pulled the old Colt pistol out of the sidecar and stuck it in my belt under my jacket.

Peering around the side of the church, I saw the bob tail truck sitting catty cornered, rumbling like a cement mixer.

I stepped back behind the church, sure that the driver hadn't spotted me, and watched as more people began arriving, while I tried to figure my next move. It came in the form of a boy, maybe seven years old, who approached the building from the sidewalk on my side. The kid was messing with something shiny affixed to the front pocket of his white shirt as the woman beside him talked. As they got closer, I heard her say, "…you don't want to wear that to Sunday school, Jacob. It ain't right to be thinkin' 'bout no Dick Tracy when you s'posed to be thinkin' 'bout Jesus."

He was starting to protest when I stepped out. I'd just gotten an idea.

"Say," I told him, "that's some badge."

He turned his head and dug his toe in the dirt. "I'm in th' radio club," he mumbled, squeezing the object with one hand as his mother (I guess) squinted at me.

John, I'm never sure who knows me and who doesn't in the burg, but I'm confident most of the locals have either seen me around or know who I am from the town grapevine. So I'm betting the woman had an idea as to my identity. At least, she didn't grab her child and run away when I started talking to him.

"How about that?" I said. "You know, I've got a nephew in that club." I shook my head. "Sad thing, though. He lost his badge the other day, and it broke his heart." Reaching in my back pocket, I continued. "He's in a wheelchair. Very sick. And I guess that Dick Tracy captain's badge – and you fellows in the radio club – give him the courage to keep going every day."

I felt a little bad about laying it on so thick and lying like the serpent in Eden, but when I fished the ten-spot out of my wallet, the look in their eyes went a long way toward alleviating my guilt.

"I wonder," I said, holding it up, "if you might consider selling it to me. It would make him awful happy."

I've never seen bigger eyes in my life. Both the woman and the boy reached for the sawbuck I held up like it was a diamond bracelet. She snagged it, and he couldn't get that badge off fast enough.

"Thank you, mister," the woman said, voice brimming with emotion, as the kid quickly handed it over. "It's a gift from God in his mercy."

I told her she was welcome, palmed the badge, pinned it to my shirt front under my jacket, and peered around the corner again, thinking, Well, I may have lied, but at least I put some food on their table. Then I carefully made my way into the pines and came out from behind a tree down the street, where several other people were walking toward the church. I fell in behind them, always keeping an eye on the truck. As I got closer, my ears told me the vehicle wasn't running anymore and I saw that the driver was standing on the running board, peering dully at the church. These guys all seemed to be dressed the same way: overalls, boots, black hat. It was like they'd been stamped out at a factory. Hell, they even smelled the same.

As he kept a fish eye on the church grounds, I crossed the street, got behind a family group that was all dressed up, and let them shield me until I reached the side of his truck.

Fortunately, it was one of those ancient models with no doors, so I was able to step noiselessly up onto the running board and slide into the passenger's seat, grabbing up an automatic pistol that lay there and sticking it in the side pocket of my breeches. He turned just in time to get a good look into the muzzle of my Colt.

"Get in fast and be quiet about it – if you want to keep breathing," I hissed, trying to ape the speech of one of those Warner Brothers gangsters.

Looking around, he reluctantly clambered

in under the steering wheel, and as soon as he settled I jammed the pistol in his crotch.

"You move a muscle, I'll blow your balls off. You get me?"

He nodded. I knew he was in agony, but he did his best not to squirm – until I cocked the gun.

"Please, mister," he said, almost blubbering. "I ain't done nothin'. You makin' a mis—"

"You're damn right it's a mistake," I interrupted. "Yours!"

I pulled back my lapel and flashed that badge. He didn't dare turn to look, but I knew he'd caught sight of it in the rear-view mirror. I only hoped I'd been too quick for him to read the "Dick Tracy" part.

"You've been screwing with the federals, buddy," I snapped, keeping my voice low enough not to attract the attention of the people passing on the other side of the street. "J. Edgar Hoover. Melvin Purvis. Know those names?"

"Yes – yessir," he stammered.

"You think we don't know what you're up to?"

Like I said earlier, John, I don't know how many people in this town know me, but even if they only kind of know me, they have the idea I'm hooked up with the government in some way or other. And if this gee had heard of me, I'd figured that the badge would just help drive that notion home.

Meanwhile, he was stuttering like Porky Pig, trying to tell me he didn't know what I was talking about. I would've felt sorry for him if I hadn't known he was one of Black's hired thugs who would've joyfully gutted me and dismembered my corpse if the old man had told him to.

I interrupted his sputtering monologue.

"How many gunsels in that boiler you got waiting on the square?"

"H-honest, I—"

That was as far as I let him get. Giving the Colt a hard twist, I said, "Honest, hell! You've been grifting since you were weaned. We know your whole story. Now I ask one more time and you sing like Kate Smith or your blood'll be all over this seat. How many?"

"Two…two," he stammered. "For God's sake—"

And John, believe it or not, at that exact time the bells in the Baptist church tower started ringing.

"Don't use that gat on me!" he almost shouted.

"Put your head down on the steering wheel! Now!"

He did, and I busted him good with the barrel of that heavy old six-gun, clipping him over the right ear. Even though the bells seemed to have the attention of everyone on the street, I worried that someone could've seen me, so quickly I drug his unconscious form over to my side, climbed over him, and cranked up that old truck. A couple of blocks up the street I turned into an alley that led back to the town square, close to where I'd first spotted the sedan.

Halfway down, I stopped and ground into reverse. Those old chain-driven trucks are slow, but they can be pretty powerful; I'd horsed lots of 'em around in my CCC days. Like all the rest I've driven, the throttle was on the dash. I pulled it out just a little, backing the bob-tail up until it was at a slight angle across the alley. Letting it idle, I set the hand brake even though it was still in gear – something you can do only on those old chain drives. Then I watched the mouth of the alley.

It wasn't long before the sedan came rolling through the alley's mouth, its occupants undoubtedly wondering what the hell was going on. I jerked the throttle out, released the brake lever, and cut the wheel so the truck straightened out and began backing down the alley at a very slow rate of speed. It was so slow, in fact, that they didn't realize it was headed for them until too late. That high truck bed rolled into their radiator, smashing it, and began slowly but relentlessly caving in the whole front of the auto. The driver tried to throw it into reverse, but he'd missed his opportunity. Their engine was dead.

I gave the truck a little more gas and slewed them into a telephone pole, keeping up the pressure until the vehicle stalled. Then

I jumped out and ran, doubling back to get my bike from behind the church, and took a different route back to Ma's. Funny, but I felt damned exhilarated.

I didn't think my assailants would be in any shape to chase me, but just in case I zigged and zagged through several neighborhoods, and then – well, I don't know if I want to call what I got an idea, but I suddenly became aware that I was near Barney Gibson's place. In a moment, I was cruising by it. It was one of those shotgun-style houses with the rooms all in a row, no hallways, and doors at either end. A good-sized portion of the east end was gutted and charred, with lumber stacked beside it, indicating it was being rebuilt. I figured the affected area was probably the den, or, as they say here, the sitting room. The rest of the house didn't seem to have been fire damaged at all.

I drove by pretty fast, not wanting to attract attention to myself, and I saw all I needed to see in those few seconds. Then, a few blocks away, I parked the Indian in a wooded area. The lumber was stacked so high around the blackened part of Gibson's home that it was easy to hide behind. I wasn't there 10 minutes before I'd found what I was looking for.

Afterward, I drove on back to the boarding house, put up the bike, and went to my room. Ma was gone to church, of course, and I didn't hear any other evidence of life in the place, so I had plenty of time to myself to do a little bit of research.

Once again, those books you sent me were a godsend (if that's the right word). I studied them, and did some typing, knowing everything had to be worded just right in order for what I had in mind to work. It took a few hours, but at last I had a script that I thought would do the job.

I felt some urgency because I didn't want Ma to be around when I made the phone calls I needed to make. Sunday afternoons were generally quiet around the boarding house: Ma usually went to some friend's place to eat and visit (maybe she was at the Davis house, I thought, with a pang of sadness), and the boarders often worked, or went out, or just stayed in their own rooms. So I got everything together as quickly as I could, prowled around a little to detect any other signs of life in the boarding house and, finding none, went to the living room, picked up the phone, and gave the operator Gibson's number. It was possible she'd listen in, but I had to take that chance. I decided I'd be a little cryptic just in case, using the word "message" for "spell" or "demon," for instance.

After seven rings I was ready to quit. But then he answered.

"Mr. Gibson?" I asked.

"Yeah. Who's this?"

"Someone calling to save your life."

"What?" he snorted, but he didn't hang up, so I continued.

"This is the man who sent you that fiery messenger the other night." I was being a little obtuse, but I figured he'd get it.

"Fiery messenger?" he sputtered. Then, "Listen here, you little—"

"I have another one ready to go. It's about the size of a small horse." The sputtering died away.

"There's a way out for you," I continued. "This new…messenger has a five-day delay. If I'm still alive in five days, I'll cancel the message and you'll never have to receive it."

He said one word in a gravelly whisper. It was, "Brown."

"Yeah. I plan on taking a train out of this stinking town in a couple of days. If you and Black let me do that, I promise you'll never see me again — and no message, no…delivery boy. Otherwise, well, if you didn't like the last one, you damn sure won't like this one."

"Two days?" he asked in that same whisper. "That's all?"

"Wednesday, I'll be leaving. So it's more like three. Then you won't have me around anymore, ever."

"By the way," I added, "the thugs you and Black sent had an accident this morning. I don't know what kind of salary you get from Uncle Sam, but you're going to need some ready cash for auto repairs. Not to mention doctor bills."

Silence. I figured he was mulling things over, and I gave him a few seconds to do it. He knew I'd sent that demon; he knew I could as easily send another. Maybe he was wondering if he (or Black) could cancel the spell himself. I was counting on him not knowing enough about my particular brand of magic to be sure.

Finally, he spoke, in that same low whisper. "How do we know you'll keep your end of the bargain, Mr. Brown?"

Well, at least he was calling me "mister" now.

"You don't," I said. "But turning loose something that big requires a part of my soul and some of my blood, two things I'd rather keep intact. You leave me alone, and we'll both be much better off. Otherwise, you might just get the message tonight. I've secured a few items of yours that were in that burned room. I can give them to the messenger, just to make sure the message gets to the right place."

If the operator was listening in, she'd just gotten an earful. So had Barney Gibson.

"That's it, Mr. Gibson," I said. "Yes or no?"

"Yes, yes, dammit!" His voice had risen from a whisper to a near-scream. "Yes, I'll lay off! Just get out of town! That's all we want!"

"How about Black?"

"I can't talk for him."

"For your sake, you'd better be," I said, and hung up.

For all my leaning on Gibson, I knew that he – or anyone else in Mackaville, for that matter – couldn't control Old Man Black. He was the ancient snaky patriarch, and even though he knew I still had the wax effigy and certainly had figured I'd sent the demon to Gibson's place, I had the feeling he wasn't going to scare as easily. He knew I could've killed him with the doll, and I hadn't. He figured I didn't have the guts to murder anyone, even him.

Maybe I didn't. Still, I figured I'd better try to call him as well.

I'd just picked up the receiver when Ma came bustling through the front door. Hanging up, I greeted her.

"Missed you at church, Robert," she said. "Lots of folks wanted to know if you was all right."

"I'm fine, Ma. Just had some business to take care of. Hope you don't mind if I used the phone."

"Not unless you called Nome, Alaska." She grinned, but her eyes told me she knew about my break-up with Patricia. "I hate it you're goin' away, Robert."

I stood up. "I know, Ma. You've been awfully kind to me, and there's no way I can pay you back."

We looked at one another for a moment, and I felt a sudden tremendous affection for this good woman. Then she grinned again. "You can start by puttin' the ice truck card in the window. Twenty pounds up, please."

She was talking about this square yellow card with large black numbers printed around the borders. You set it up in a window so the ice man can see it; whatever number that's standing straight up is the amount of ice you need. It's pretty efficient.

So I got the card out of the kitchen and set it in the back window. While I was doing that, she asked me if I wanted some cold salt pork for a sandwich, and I said sure, so that's what I'm munching on right now as I type this letter to you. Ma bustling around downstairs kind of queered the notion of my calling Old Man Black, and I'm not sure it's necessary anyway.

Gibson's probably already told him all he needs to know.

Even with the threat of that old bastard lurking in the background, all I can think about right now is Ma, and Mr. Castapolous, and Pete, and even Sheriff Meagan and Chief Lawson – all people I hate to say goodbye to. If I let my mind drift too much, it gets filled with images of Patricia, and that's when I realize that leaving her forever will be the toughest thing of all. But then I tell myself she's already gone, and there's nothing left to keep me here.

Not that I'd stay. If I get out of here with my skin intact, I'll consider it a victory. Good night. I hope like hell I'll be writing you from D.C. in a few days.

Your pal and faithful comrade,
Robert

September 18, 1939
Monday evening

Dear John,

One more day. That's what I keep telling myself. <u>One more day</u>, and then I'm on a rattler out of this God-forsaken town forever and on my way to a brand-new life. (A rattler. Ironic as hell, isn't it?)

I had a deuce of a time going to sleep last night, and I expect tonight won't be any different. Even though nothing has triggered my seventh sense – not yet, anyway – I'm on edge and jumpy as a kangaroo.

Today, I was up a little before dawn and on my way. As I've written you, I put off doing the interviews that are the farthest away until the very end of my time here – and they're in opposite directions to boot. This one was down south, more than a hundred miles through the mountains. It doesn't seem like that's a very good use of the gasoline the government pays for, but I guess there aren't any Folklore Project scribes closer than me, and that's why I got the assignment.

Rennsdale didn't show up again this morning. I haven't seen her for a few days. Being the farthest thing from a cat lover, I can't explain why not having her riding along in the sidecar hit me so hard this morning, but it did. A lonesome feeling, I guess it was. I'd really gotten used to her being around, looking up at me from her little nest in the sidecar as we rode along.

The Noble farm, my destination, turned out to be about the most prosperous of any I'd visited for the WPA. They ran cattle as well as hogs, chickens, and even a few goats. As I pulled up I noticed there were fairly new farm machines in the lot beside the barn. (Yet for all of that they didn't have a telephone, so I hadn't been able to call them to arrange the visit.)

As I pulled up, idled the Indian, and hallooed the house, a big dog came running out, tail wagging like a windshield wiper in a thunderstorm. I'd been cautioned by the WPA that a lot of these farm dogs would have no compunctions about snapping a couple of pounds of hamburger out of your carcass, but the ones I'd met in my travels had been nothing but lovable pooches.

Not that I'd met any until just recently; before, any animal attacks had come from pigs, not hounds.

This dog seemed to be a sweetheart, too. It looked about half wolf – a white body a little thicker than a greyhound's and a long nose; pointed, mostly tan ears; and intelligent brown eyes. He didn't jump up on me like the ones had at the Destruidora place, but stood right at my feet, tail going and big eyes looking up at me and then glancing away, like some dogs do. A man who appeared to be on the far side of sixty – although I've learned, Lord knows, not to judge ages around here by appearances – came out of a large two-story whitewashed house and ambled toward me.

"Hello," I said. "I'm Robert Brown, from the WPA Folklore Project. You folks should've gotten a letter about my coming to see you." I patted the animal on the head and scratched his ears.

"Yessir," he said. "I 'member. Name's Noble. William Noble." We shook hands.

"Fine dog you got here," I said.

"Thankee. Been hard to keep 'em 'round here. Snakes always bitin' 'em, and they gotta be tough to live through a rattler or copperhead bite. Big 'uns like ol' Duke here got the best chance. Still, we been lucky to have one last a year. Usually, it's been about two-three months."

He was a big man, dressed in overalls like most of the rest of the farmers and country people I'd interviewed, with little rivulets of chewing-tobacco stains down from the corners of his lips. He spit, then reached down and tousled the head of the dog, who responded with unbridled joy.

"It's kinda funny about ol' Duke," Mr. Noble said, nodding at the happy animal. "We got him in May this year and he ain't never been bit yet. Truth to tell, I ain't been seeing as many snakes 'round the place since he came aboard, neither. Kinda strange, but I hope it keeps up."

"Me, too," I said, my mind racing. May was when I'd come to Mackaville. Did Old Man Black and his reptiles bedevil people this far away from the town? And if he did, had things gotten better because of how I'd incapacitated Black?

"He's a damn good dog, this 'un. Caught a chicken thief and tore his drawers off a couple months ago. If'n I hadn't got there in time, no tellin' what Duke woulda done to him." He spit on the ground. "He was a sorry sight when the sheriff showed up to take him in."

"Sheriff Meagan?" I asked.

"That's right. You know 'im?"

"I do know him. A fine man." So I wasn't the only government employee who had to cover hundreds of miles to do his job.

"He sure is. After he talked to me, he gave that young fella a choice: chain gang, or work off his time here with me. I took him on, and damned if he ain't makin' a good hand, even if'n he's just a kid."

Spitting again, he added, "Done so good, fixin' machinery and my old Ford and all, I started payin' him a salary with his room and board." Then he turned, cupped his hands, and shouted toward the barn.

"Hey, Benjamin! Come on out here a minute!"

A tall lanky kid of about sixteen, who'd likely been watching since I'd driven up, exploded out of the barn door and double-timed it to where Mr. Noble stood.

"This here's a man from the gov'ment," Mr. Noble said, indicating me. Benjamin shook my hand solemnly. "He's here to take you to Cummins Farm."

The kid stiffened into a statue, his eyes flashing back and forth from me to his benefactor. "Naw," said Mr. Noble. "I'm just shittin' you." He spit again, grinning. "He's here to get some stories 'bout the old days."

Benjamin relaxed then, grinning. I couldn't blame him for clutching up. I imagined there were lots of miscreants who'd done time at the Cummins Prison Farm for crimes no worse than chicken-snatching. I'd heard the place made Leavenworth look like a suite at the Ritz.

"That's right," I said, pulling the by now tattered list from my front pocket and nodding at Mr. Noble. "I'm here to see a Mrs. Dennis Porter. That would be your mother?"

The look that passed between him and Benjamin told me all I needed to know. "I'm sorry," I said.

"Hell, don't be," said Mr. Noble. "Momma was eighty-nine when she passed. It was only a few months ago. She had a good life right up to the end." He nodded toward a well-kept little house between the barn and the home he'd come out of. "Even had her own little place over there. Didn't want for nothing."

"You can talk to my grand momma, mister,"

said Benjamin. "She's eighty and she knows some of them old stories, I bet. She and Aunt Cissy told me some of the same ones, about ghosts and stuff."

"Whyn't you go see if she's up to it?" Mr. Noble told him, and he took off. He seemed to have two gears, neutral and fourth.

I watched him run, thinking how he'd referred to "Aunt Cissy." Did that mean that he was somehow related to his employer?

"Yeah, he's kin," said Mr. Noble, as though he'd read my mind. "That's one of the big reasons I didn't want him on no chain gang. His daddy wasn't no damn good, and his ma died from worry. His grand momma's my ma's sister, and she was tryin' to take care of him, but she didn't have no money neither. I'd've given 'em chickens and eggs – hell, I'd let 'em have ham, too – if only they'd asked. But they was too damn proud, so he tried to steal from me and got caught."

He spit again and continued. "It wasn't too long after Duke caught 'im in the henhouse that Momma died. And after I dropped the charges and got 'im released to me, well, they wasn't so proud that they wouldn't live in Momma's house. My own boy, he got kilt in a auto wreck ten years ago. Buried my wife just about eight years ago. Benjamin keeps goin' like he's been goin', this place'll be his someday."

In my weeks and months at this job, I've noticed a couple of things. People in the country tend to talk a lot to you, maybe because they don't see very many folks outside their own group. And more often than not, most of them are related to one another in some fashion. This visit was a perfect example of both.

I watched Benjamin come running back up to us. He told me to give his grand momma five minutes to "do" her hair and then go on up to the little cottage and she'd talk to me. Then the two of them, Duke prancing along, showed me around the farm a little bit, the hog pens and the big chicken house and the rows of grain sorghum which Mr. Noble said made dandy feed for the pigs. It all looked and felt idyllic, and I couldn't help but wonder if the lack of snakes had something to do with the peace I felt there – and if it did, had I actually played a role in making it what it now was by my dustups with Old Man Black?

I was pondering that, watching the multi-colored chickens peck and scurry around us, when Benjamin said, "Looks like Grand Momma's ready, mister," and I looked toward the little house to see an old lady standing in the doorway. She beckoned me to come in, and when I reached the cottage I saw that she was dressed in a dark gray outfit that was just barely out of style.

"You are Mr. Robert Brown?" she asked as I entered. Her little home was a model of clean, tidy housekeeping, and she seemed awfully spry for an octogenarian.

"Yes, ma'am."

"Mary Lou has told me all about you."

Well, John, to say I was surprised is an understatement. I managed to get out, "Mrs. – Miss Castle is a friend of yours?"

"Oh, yes. 'Course, she's much younger, but she was the littlest sister of my best friend. I was never so shocked in all my life as when she married Gabber." She sniffed. "He had plenty money, but trash with money is still trash in my book. She was way too good for the likes of him. Too smart, too – or so I thought – with her goin' off to college and everything."

Sitting down at a heavy wooden table, she motioned toward a cozy that held tea cups and a kettle.

"You take sugar in your sassafras?" she asked.

I nodded yes. Sassafras tea, which I hadn't ever tasted before hitting Arkansas, isn't bad at all – kind of like drinking hot root beer. I took a sip, she took one, and then she set her cup down and said, "All right, young man. Get out your notebook. Mary Lou and I have talked about this, and I'll give you a story that's true. I 'spect it'll match whatever she and others have told you. She thinks you can be trusted. Hope she's right."

And for the next three hours, that old lady told me about ghosts, spirits, and bog monsters, all as a prelude for her own stories about the Cleansing, the battle that raged back "afore her time" involving the cat people and their related dog people, the snake people, and the pig people. Most of it buttressed what I'd heard from Miss Castle, David Jefferson, and, recently, from the Destruidoras, who'd been the source of information about those who favored dogs.

Benjamin's grandmother explained that the dog faction of the hyena people had let their animals get too thinned out and had been driven from the valley by the pig and snake factions after the carnage was over. Not too different from the version I'd gotten from Mr. Destruidora.

She finished as quickly as she had begun, standing up and saying, "Now, Mr. Robert Brown, you got your stories, and I hope Mary Lou's right – that I can trust you to know which ones to tell and which ones to keep to yourself. I got work over at the main house, so please 'scuse me." And with that, she ushered me to the door and politely kicked me out. I believe it was the nicest bum's rush I've ever had.

No one was in sight, even Duke, when she shut the door behind me. So I just got on the Indian and drove off. It was a long trip back to Ma's, but I had a lot to think about.

I started this letter right after I got in, and now I see it's nearly midnight. I know I'm going to be here only one more full day, and I'm sure that's why my surroundings have taken on the quality of things you see in a dream. Even MacWhirtle seems unreal to me now, as he sits watching – unreal, and more than real. He looks at me like he knows I'm leaving.

Or maybe I'm just too damn tired to be rational anymore. I doubt I'll get much sleep until I'm on that passenger car headed toward D.C., just about 36 hours from now.

Of course, a hell of a lot can happen in 36 hours. Thank you, God, for the seventh sense, and please let it keep working until I'm out of this place for good.

Your pal and faithful comrade,

Robert

September 19, 1939
Tuesday morning, 4 a.m.

Dear John,

Well, I was right. I can't go to sleep at all. I tried for a couple of hours but no soap, so I got up and stirred around and looked at a couple of pulps – a Dime Detective and a Double Detective – that I haven't finished reading. But while I'm sure the stories were good, I just couldn't get involved in them; my mind kept running down all kinds of different trails. I thought about leaving, and I wondered if Black was going to fling any last-ditch assault at me, and while I kept trying to keep her out of my thoughts Patricia circled always through my mind, and sometimes the sense of loss was so bad that I felt my eyes watering, and it was all I could do not to break down and bawl. I sure didn't feel like transcribing the notes I got yesterday, either. In fact, I'm not going to do any of that until I get out of here. I just don't have the discipline right now. I've got one final interview, way up north, and I won't write that one up either. Not until the city limits of Mackaville are forever behind me.

Something that doesn't take any brain power, like packing, would be perfect for me right now, but I got that done a long time ago. So all that's left is to write you, even though I did that, too, four hours ago.

So, let's see. What should I say? I don't know much about where I'm going to do the interview tomorrow, or what the people will be like, so that's a dead end for a conversational topic. I don't think I want to talk about the war in Europe, either. They're fighting and killing each other in Poland and China, and maybe those countries won't last much longer. Then what?

I really want to get out of here, John. I think about all I've escaped and all I've heard and seen, and I wonder how I've managed to keep my carcass intact, and then I get a little chill when I consider that maybe at the end, when I feel like I've jumped slick, some final unexpected thing'll get me, like in the ending of a gangster picture. I don't mean I'm having a seventh-sense chill; it's just a shiver of fear coupled with messages from my adrenal glands urging me to get the hell out. But then I calm down and tell myself: One more day. One more day. That's all.

You've been a great friend through all this. When I get away and we see one another again, I'm going to buy you enough beer to float the Titanic. That is, if I don't sink like it did first.

Enough of all this. I'm going to try the Dime Detective again. Maybe this time, it'll work.

Your frazzled but faithful comrade,
Robert

September 20, 1939
Wednesday evening

Dear John,

Praise the Lord and pass the ammunition! I am now out of Mackaville for, God willing, the rest of my life!

Please excuse the penmanship, which I know is even worse than you remember it. This train takes turns like a roller coaster and besides that, just now as I began this letter I noticed that my hand is shaking a little. It's nothing serious, just some sort of residual nervousness I guess, but it's unwelcome.

I expect you know why I'm writing you in long hand instead of on the typer. Besides the jolting, twisting trip through the mountains that would make typing difficult if not impossible, there are people sitting all around me in this car and a few are trying to sleep. I wouldn't want to click and clack them out of their reveries.

There is so much to tell you, and since Little Rock to Washington, D.C. is a very long ride, I hope I can tell it all by the time I reach my new home. (Once again, God bless FDR. I have an apartment waiting for me, courtesy of Uncle Sugar.) I know I'm going to have to stop writing every few minutes and take a deep breath before going on, and I'm so exhausted I can hardly hold my head up, but by damn I'm going to get it done.

First, the relatively mundane stuff. I don't think I got a total half-hour of sleep yesterday morning; by the time six a.m. rolled around I was on the Indian headed north. (Once again, no Rennsdale.) This house was about as far as the Noble place, only in the opposite direction, so after around three hours I found it. Although it wasn't quite as grand a spread as the one I'd been to the day before, it seemed neat and well-kept, certainly better than many I'd seen.

This family was full Negro, and while I've gone on my expeditions expecting to find people of darker hues for some time now, these folks were very black, almost ebony, like Africans. The family name was Thurman, and the ones I was assigned to talk to were a nice old man and woman with lots of extended family around them. They'd lived together for so long that they often knew what the other was going to say, and sometimes in their enthusiasm they both told the story at the same time. That makes it harder to take notes, but I managed. It helped that their main story was a dandy, all about some ancient gods who came back every thousand years or so to re-establish their religion. According to them, their Dark Continent ancestors had been intimately connected with these supernatural entities, which made Mr. and Mrs. Thurman high priests of a sort.

Although their tales of these gods were a little more ancient than what I was supposed to be getting, I let that go and simply took down what they had to tell me.

The way they ended that part of the interview still gives me the creeps. In unison, they said, "It's jest about time for another visit, too."

If they were trying to spook me, it worked. Since they didn't go on nearly as long as Benjamin's grand momma, I got back in town around dusk, and even the lights of that damned town looked somehow reassuring to me.

Like I wrote you earlier, I was already packed and I craved human company anyway, so I decided to drive straight through to Pete's Skelly, return the Indian, and give my friend a final couple hours of work if he needed me. Turns out he did. Since Diffie's old man became a high mukluk at the plant, Diffie himself has taken on a heightened sense of his own worth and hasn't been spending much time as a pump jockey for Pete.

I didn't mind, though. The reassuring presence of Pete and the familiar work helped calm the swell case of nerves I'd acquired on my last day. As closing time rolled around, I was planning to ask Pete to join me for a goodbye beer at Mr. Castapolous's.

I was inside the office, getting what would be my last Cleo Cola out of the station's pop box, when Pete opened the door and stuck his head in. "Black's here," he said.

In the last half-hour or so, I'd begun feeling a kind of low-grade apprehension or nervousness, which I attributed to my changing circumstances and having to say goodbye to Pete and this station, which had been a kind of oasis for me. Now I realized it was maybe about something else.

"He's just standing outside that ol' truck," Pete said, watching out the doorway. "Reckon he wants to see you?"

Taking a deep breath, I sat the pop bottle on the counter. "I wouldn't be a bit surprised," I said.

Old Man Black and I spotted one another at the same time. As I stood in the doorway next to Pete, he came walking up, kind of stiff-legged. Warning bells began to ring inside me as he approached.

"Need to see you," he said to me, his eyes flicking toward Pete and back to me. "Alone. Won't take but a minute."

"All right," I told him, as coolly as I could. My heart had begun to accelerate. Here he was, my No. 1 enemy in Mackaville, capable of anything, standing face-to-face with me on the eve of my departure – and wanting to "see" me. Alone.

Pete nodded toward the first bay. "You can go in there, shut the door." He shot a meaningful glance my way. "I'll be around if you need me."

"He ain't gonna need you," Black said sullenly. "I just wanna talk to 'im a minute."

I led the way into the grease bay, the place with the elevated auto rack where I'd put on scores of new tires and changed plenty of oil as well, working from that little rectangular pit underneath.

When Black shut the door behind us, I suddenly felt as though some sort of bug had flown down the front of my shirt, jumping and fluttering.

"Damn!" I said, grabbing a handful of my shirt front. It was that little silver three-cent coin old Mr. Brady had given me at Jolley's Mercantile a week or so ago, jerking around as though it were alive. It stopped when I grabbed it, although I could still feel it vibrating against the inside of my clasped hand. Pulling it out from under my shirt, I flipped it out, where it continued to quiver on its lanyard of twine. Its action matched the electric charges going off inside of me.

Black's eyes widened when he saw it.

"Where the hell you get that witch charm? You better throw that damn thing away." His eyes seemed to dance as he watched it.

"I think I'll keep it," I said, my voice a lot calmer than I felt. "This is the first time it's acted like this. I don't think it likes being around you."

I didn't, either. For the first time, I

realized how bad he smelled. It was a pungent, peculiar odor, part outhouse, part musty animal that brought the snakes I'd killed to mind.

I knew he was angry. But was he angry enough to try to kill me right here, to take one more shot? I knew Pete stood just outside the door, ready in case anything happened. God bless Pete Barlow.

"I don't give a good goddamn if you wear a dozen of them damn things," he spat. "I come here to have final words with you, and that's all the hell I care about." Still, he eyed the quietly vibrating three-cent piece as he spoke. "I hear you're finished with this town, and I came to make sure we was parting company for good 'n' all."

"That's right. I'm leaving tomorrow. I won't be back."

He nodded, his eyes flickering between me and the coin that hung around my neck. "We had our differences, Brown. You sent my boys away and damn near killed me. Put me in the damned hospital."

"You did the same to me. And your boys took off on their own. I had nothing to do with that."

He started to say something, but I continued. "Don't forget that I let you get well, too." A travesty of a grin broke across his face, and he flicked his tongue over his lips. And John, I'll swear his tongue was split in two parts, like a snake's!

"Yeah," he said. "Yeah."

He shrugged. "Well," he said, "me and Gibson don't want no delayed spell worked on us, so I come to tell you we wanna part friendly-like."

At this point my seventh sense started really going nuts, and the vibrating inside me was picked up by the little coin, which began bouncing around as though it were in an earthquake. My ears began to ring – to sing, actually – with a high-pitched whine that slowly transformed into a near-deafening scream. I suddenly remembered blasting rock in the CCC and how a big explosion sometimes left me with this kind of noise echoing through my ears for hours.

Black had become transfixed by the three-cent piece again. "Cain't you make that damned thing stop?" he said, agitated.

"No. Like I say, it doesn't like being around you."

That seemed to anger him.

"I got no more time to waste," he said. "I come to shake hands and make friendly and that's it." With that, he stuck out his gnarly right hand.

I'll tell you, John, I had such an aversion to shaking that old bastard's hand that I couldn't bring myself to respond. Now that I think about it, maybe it was the seventh sense. Or the dancing coin. Or both, telling me not to touch him. Whatever it was, the feeling was so powerful that I actually jerked my hand back.

"Th' hell's wrong with you?" he hissed.

"We don't need to shake," I said. "It's fine. Tell your partner I'll drop the spell. Thank you for coming by."

All I wanted to do at that moment was just get rid of him, and as quickly as I could. The air in the bay was thick with his rank smell. I wanted to hold my breath until he left.

Then things began to pop.

I was watching his eyes when it happened. They were a watery blue, but as I looked they grew darker and deeper, taking on a brown hue even as the pupils squeezed together, elongating into vertical slits of pure black. Then his nose — it melted into his face, John! All the time his whole head began shifting under the black hat, changing into a blunt, rounded, scaly visage that was purely reptilian.

He stood between the door and me, between me and freedom, his clothes falling to the floor of the bay like shed skin. The coin was practically jerking the twine away from my neck.

I had no choice but to go the other way, toward the second bay, even though I knew that the garage door, my only exit, was shut. Maybe I could get it opened in time. Slowly, I started inching backward, around the pit, almost transfixed as he continued to metamorphose.

Suddenly, from behind his head, parchment-like skin billowed out into a stiff, vibrating hood and all at once I was looking at a huge cobra, rearing up as tall as a man, its body thick as the calf of your leg. It stood there swaying, rippling with power. And then, like the hiss of steam, or compressed air escaping from a valve, it began to speak.

"You ignorant goddamn fool," it said. "Don't you think I know if you die, there's no spell? No more pain from you and your little doll. No more demons. Ever! It all dies with you!"

I leapt just before it struck, taking off for the other bay and running to the work bench at the far end. The overhead door was down, as I'd figured, and I had no time to try and pull it up.

The snake that had been Black was on its belly now, crawling rapidly toward me, its eyes gleaming. Vaulting atop the bench, I began throwing anything I could get my hands on, trying to slow it down. It kept twisting and I kept missing until I managed to bean it with a generator, right at the top of its head between its beady damned eyes. That stopped its forward progress, and I hoped it would be stunned long enough for me to get away, but in a second or two it shook its head and resumed its relentless crawling toward me. I hadn't even drawn blood.

As it advanced, I retreated to the end of the bench, my back against the wall in the corner of the room. There was no place else left for me to go. Reaching down behind me, I felt what I'd just spotted there: a four-foot section of steel pipe. It was a "cheater" we slipped over four-way lug wrenches to loosen stubborn nuts. I picked it up, keeping it behind my back.

Seeing I was trapped, the abomination rose up in front of me, swaying, again speaking in that hissing spray of words.

"I'm going to pump you so full of poison you'll turn black," it said. "Then I'll do the same to Barlow." As it spoke its head rose above the top of the bench where I stood, its slitted eyes meeting mine. "Too bad you'll never get out of—"

Bringing the pipe around hard, I swung it like a baseball bat, every ounce of terrified energy in my body funneled into that one last-chance blow. It smacked the neck of that thing, just below that inflated hood, with a loud and sodden crack. I actually heard the bones snap as the head actually whipped around the pipe. It dropped to the floor of the bay, hissing and writhing in agony, and I slammed the pipe into its head, again and again, until a greenish fluid sprayed from the broken skull. Then I leapt over the still-flailing body and ran for the grease bay and the door to the office. I was halfway through the bay before I realized I was hollering at the top of my lungs for Pete.

A noise like a giant balloon deflating came from behind me, and I turned to look. All I could see from that vantage point was a section of the snake, still writhing but slowing now. I had no idea Pete was beside me until he grabbed my arm and I jerked away like I'd been scalded.

"Easy, Robert. Easy," he said. Then: "Holy Mother of God! What the hell is that thing?"

"Black," I said. That's all I could say.

We both stepped slowly to the door between the two bays and stood, watching the creature go through its death throes. And then, another nightmare piled on. The thing began changing again, and in only a few moments it was the naked body of Black, still twisting and slithering and turning – and dying before our stunned eyes. It seemed an hour before he finally lay still, his blood – now red – oozing out onto the concrete floor. In death, he was as repulsive as he'd been in life.

As we advanced on him, another shiver went through his body. I instinctively clutched the coin around my neck. It, too, still vibrated, although much more quietly.

Black's head lay bent at a ninety-degree angle, the broken neck bone raising his skin like a tent pole. It was not something you'd want to see. And I thought for all my moral back and forth about killing him, when it came down to cases I'd finally done it. It didn't matter if he was… something else when I let him have it. Maybe it didn't even matter that he'd been attacking me. I'd taken his life, and nothing could change that.

Suddenly, all I wanted to do was get out. In fact, I turned to flee. But Pete brought me back to reality.

"Damn, you can't leave him here," he said. "Even Sheriff Meagan'd have to hang you for this one."

"Yeah. What'll we do?"

"Let's get his clothes back on him. Then I'll hose all this down." For the first time, I noticed the liquid green splotches on the floor, spattered across my shirt and pants and tie as well.

When Pete retrieved his clothes and we bent down to dress him, I almost threw up. The stench was overpowering. We got him into his overalls, but I wouldn't even try to put his filthy shirt back on his body. Pete didn't insist. I was putting his second shoe on him when he suddenly kicked.

"What the hell!" I shouted.

"Easy," Pete said again, holding down the leg.

"Can't he stay dead, Pete? Can't he at least do that?"

"Ain't you ever heard that old story?" Pete asked. "Some snakes, they won't die until sunrise."

Somewhere, I <u>had</u> heard that. Of course, I hadn't believed it.

I do now.

After we got that stinking, repulsive body clothed, Pete hosed the bay down and then he brought in a big tarpaulin. Using our feet, we rolled Black up in it, throwing the vile shirt in with his body. Then Pete turned the ends up at the top and bottom and wrapped a rope around it, tying it off in a trucker's knot. There was movement, and crinkling noises, underneath the tarp.

"Now what?" I asked in a weak voice. I was dog-tired and sick to my stomach, but I knew I couldn't weaken now.

"I'll bring his truck around," he said.

Pete left and I turned out the lights in the bay and pushed up the garage door. Standing there in the darkness, smelling the outside air, I started to feel a little better, but the rustling sounds coming from underneath the tarp still unnerved me. The seventh sense had abated, along with the thrumming of the coin, but there was an edge to the calmness inside me, a sense that things were only momentarily quiet.

Then I heard Black's ancient truck cough into life, and in a moment Pete pulled up in it.

Another moment, and we'd pitched the still-quivering body of Black into the truck's bed, shoving aside some ancient-looking tools and a big gas can, handling the corpse as though it were on fire.

"Get the Indian and follow me," he said.

"Hurry. You get lost, meet me up on Witch Mountain by the Gabber place, where we met that whatever-the-hell it was."

I nodded ok, the truck belched a cloud of smelly exhaust, and he was off, taking the side roads out of town. I'd already put the bike in the shed behind the station, not figuring I'd ever ride it again, so it took me a minute or two to get it out and get it going. I knew Pete wouldn't slow up just to wait for me, not when he was driving a truck carrying its owner's body in the back, so I wasn't too concerned when I didn't catch up with him in town. Thankfully, I knew how to get to our rendezvous spot.

Still, I felt some reassurance when I reached the foothills outside Mackaville and glimpsed the single red taillight a hundred yards or so in front of me. I followed it for what seemed like forever before it stopped at the exact place we'd encountered the panther. I pulled up beside him, and he stuck his head through the open driver's-side window.

"Stay with me," he said. "It's a few more miles to the cliff I got in mind."

Falling in behind him again, I tailed him onto one of those high ridges, and we continued on for a short while, climbing higher, until we reached a point where the right side of the now-dirt road skirted the edge of a tall cliff. The state highway crews and their conscripted convicts hadn't gotten to this stretch yet; there was no curbing, and only wooden posts set at intervals marked the edge.

Pete was out of the truck and beside me before I could even horse the Indian up on its kick stand. He'd killed the lights on the pick-up truck and told me to do the same, adding, "Ain't gonna be no one on this road, prob'ly, but the sooner we get this done the better I'm gonna like it. C'm'on."

I hustled along behind him, the two of us bathed in the cold light of a waning moon.

When I got to the rear of the truck I swallowed, reached in, and grabbed one end of the tarp. Pete took hold of the top part of the bundle, and as we hoisted the body out of the truck bed, I thought I could feel it quivering. Or maybe it was me. Hoisting a corpse in the moonlight, like grave robbers — the enormity of what we were doing struck me like a sledgehammer blow. I'd killed this man, and now I was disposing of his body. I was a killer.

Then, another realization. I may have had a few tremors going through my body, but there was definite movement coming from the bulk under the tarp, and it was getting stronger and more insistent.

"The son-of-bitch is still alive!" I hissed. Pete stared at the moving mass between us and then at me, his eyes white in the pale light.

"Just a snake," Pete said steadily. "He — <u>it</u>'ll be dead at sunrise."

We sat our burden down, just at the cliff's edge. Now, whatever was inside was practically thrashing.

"Kick your end off," Pete said, holding the rope. "I'll pull the tarp away."

John, I'd like to tell you I stopped right there, told Pete no, and pulled old Black or whatever was in that tarpaulin out of danger before we got the hell out of there. But instead, I reared back and kicked as hard as I could with the flat sole of my boot. I put so much into it that the tarp and its contents shot straight out into the darkness at the edge of the cliff and Pete, holding onto the rope that tied it all together, stumbled a couple of steps toward it with an oath. Then the rope went tight.

He began jerking. "Damn thing…won't let go…" he said.

I knew he'd tied a trucker's knot, which is designed to unravel when you jerk on it. So something was wrong. I ran to the edge of the cliff to see if I could pull it loose, bent down, and there – by heavens, John, I'm not lying – the face of Black looked up at me. No, no, it wasn't Black. It was part snake, part human, luminous in the light of the moon, and so full of pure poisonous evil it seemed to be on the verge of exploding. The knot was just beside the face, one end of the rope sticking up toward me, and as I jerked at it and the tarp came free, the thing swiveled its swollen head and tried to bite me.

Then, it screamed. The sound echoed and echoed in my mind, mixed with the sodden thud of the body as it hit and slid down jagged rocks hundreds of feet below.

The next thing I knew, Pete was dragging me away from the cliff's edge, telling me to stand back. I watched as if I were in a dream, a nightmare, as he ran back to the truck and, leaving the door open, jerked it into gear and sent it after Black. Jumping out and running toward me as the pick-up scraped between two of the barrier posts, Pete stood with me, watching, as it teetered on the brink for a long moment before tipping over into a downward plunge.

Wordlessly, we stepped to the edge and looked over it. From where we stood, the flaming wreck appeared no bigger than a campfire. Then, something else. In the fire, a tiny figure, twisting in agony. The screams were tiny, too, like the tortured noises a trapped and dying insect might make.

Then the figure went up like a torch, and the screeching from below stopped. All of a sudden, I could hear real insects – tree crickets, cicadas, katydids – as well as the soft insistent call of a whippoorwill. It all hit me somewhere deep inside, giving me a feeling that the balance of nature had now somehow been restored, that maybe everything was going to be all right. I can't describe it more than to say it was a sense of tranquility, of peace. I didn't even feel so much like a murderer anymore.

"Let's get the hell out of here," Pete said.

The feeling of the mountain air flowing past my face, the smell of the outdoors, the roar of the wind as I gunned that motorcycle toward Mackaville – all of that had a calming effect, too. But as we drew nearer to the town, I felt tremors once again taking over, growing inside me.

This manifestation of the seventh sense – it was different. It's like, well, like I saw something in my mind, a loose end like the strand of rope on that trucker's knot, something I needed to take on and clear up before everything could really be all right and I could leave Mackaville with a clear conscience. As I drove, this tenuous vision began to coalesce, becoming clearer and clearer until, finally, I saw the cemetery, the images I'd first glimpsed from the train window, including the old calico cat, all mixed up with the big tombstone that held the victims of the so-called "cholera epidemic" and the cats I'd seen on that night as well. I knew then that's where I had to go to piece everything together before I left town. It's hard to explain the feeling; I was being warned about what could happen there, but I was being pulled toward it as well.

As I rolled all that over in my mind, I

realized I'd pulled behind the station and beside Pete's car. As he climbed off the Indian, I turned to him. "Pete," I said. "I couldn't have made it without you."

He grinned a little. "Sure you could've. And don't worry about nothing. He was gonna kill you. Nothin' else you could do." He nodded toward the bike. "I'll wait 'til you put 'er up and give you a ride back to Ma's. You got one more night in that big comfortable feather bed of hers, so you better enjoy all of it you can."

"Thanks, Pete," I said. "But if you don't mind, I've got one more thing to do tonight. Can I bring the Indian back tomorrow morning?"

He started to say something, thought better of it, and simply said, "Sure."

Thanking him again, I took off. The thoughts and images danced in my mind, prodding me, and I knew now exactly where I had to go. First, though, I drove to Ma's shed and loaded up a pick and shovel. Luck was with me; nobody came out to see what I was up to at that time of night.

As I rode toward the cemetery, I checked the radium dial of my wrist watch. Ten forty-five. I'd seen precious few autos on the road, which was good. I was scared but driven, if that makes any sense.

Topping out of the uphill drive, I pulled in through the arch of the gate and, after a short survey of my surroundings, parked the bike behind a mausoleum. I think it was the very same one I'd seen the cats perched on when I'd first come to town. Had I known then…

After I dismounted, I took out my tools from the sidecar and wound up the hand-cranked flashlight. Hearing rustles in the grass around the tombstones, I flashed my light around but spotted nothing. Somehow, though, I knew the rustling was cats; they were out there, watching me but not wanting me to see them. Why they weren't friendly now, why they wouldn't show themselves when they'd been my protectors for weeks, was something I'd have to try and figure out later. Right now, I had more urgent concerns.

In front of me was the path that ran through the place, laid out in the moonlight, winding around the stones and the family crypts and, here and there, another mausoleum jutting up in the darkness. I heard the skittering noises around me again, and this time I stood still for a moment, listening.

And then, John, I swear I heard a voice – voices – in my head. *Yes*, they said. *We are here*.

Then: *What do you want?*

I stood there in the darkness, listening to the voices in my head, smelling the slaughterhouse-scented air, my final night in Mackaville, Arkansas. This time tomorrow, I'd be on a train and far away.

If I lived that long.

"You'll find out soon enough," I said into the darkness.

I stood for a moment. I'd had a plan, but now something was drawing me away from what I'd intended to do, and toward a squat mausoleum of white stone. As I got close, I noticed there were no tombstones or any structures at all around it for a good ten or twenty feet. Then, as though I had passed through some sort of barrier, I was suddenly enveloped in cold.

I'm sorry I can't describe it any better, John. It was just cold. Bone-numbing cold, like stepping into an ice house. It felt as though the temperature had suddenly plunged fifty degrees.

I was only a few feet from the structure when that happened, and a sudden fear came with the chill. The cold held evil; it beat at me in waves from that white mausoleum. I pressed on, trying to shut out a sense of mounting dread, and in an instant I felt as though I were wading in icy water up to my knees. The cold and the terror beat on me with incredible force. I could hardly move. Just about a foot from the door, I stopped. I could not get any closer.

Holding the flashlight with some effort, I aimed it at the door, pumping the little lever on the bottom to keep it going. The beam should have been strong, but it seemed feeble, as though the building were absorbing all its light. Above the door, I read Roman numerals: MDCCLXXXIX.

Seventeen-hundred-eighty-nine. A hundred years, exactly, before the Cleansing. Then, the name below the numerals: BLACK.

A hard chill ran through me, colder even than my surroundings. I wanted to leap back, but my legs felt frozen and useless. Although I kept pumping the lever, it did nothing to brighten the light. Even in the weakened beam, though, I could see that the door itself was solid iron with inlays I knew – don't ask me how – were silver. There were symbols etched into the metal of the door, silver snakes running through them. I had no idea what the marks stood for, but – again, don't ask me how – I was sure they represented spells or incantations designed to keep something in, not out. If it was really filigreed in silver, and I was sure it was, then it should've been a magnet for thieves. The fact it hadn't been touched spoke of the dark forces surrounding this crypt, which now held me in their power as though I'd been entombed in an iceberg.

I managed to flash my feeble light around the door, illuminating the ancient padlock that bolted it as well as the rows of names chiseled into the rock at the top. They all ended with "Black." The last one carried a death date of 1840.

Then I became aware of voices, faint and unintelligible, as though someone was calling to me from down a long, empty hallway. Somehow, I got the strength to take a step back, away from that white stone structure, and I found that after the first agonizing backward step I became less mired, less cold. At last, I stepped clear of whatever had gripped me. The big breath I took of late-summer air brought me back to the reality of the moment.

Pocketing my light, I ran my hands up and down my arms to restore some semblance of warmth, stopping when I got to the sleeves. Holding them up in the moonlight, I saw that they were covered with a rime of frost.

And the voice, the voices, came back. You're a fool, they said.

I couldn't disagree.

Then, my original plan reasserted itself. I picked up the tools I didn't remember dropping and headed for the huge tombstone I'd discovered months earlier, the one over the mass grave that held the victims of the "cholera epidemic" of 1889, including Rupert Davis, Mrs. Davis's husband. The further away I got from the Black mausoleum the better I felt, but I still fought a deep sick feeling that rose from my stomach to the back of my throat.

When I reached the spot, I took a long pace away from the big stone and then began my work. My plan was to dig up squares of sod and stack them in front of the tombstone before I actually began digging in earnest. If I could do that skillfully enough, then I could replace the grass above where I'd dug and it'd look like it had never been disturbed. It was important to me to leave things looking as they had when I'd found them.

Why had I decided to do all this? Hell, I didn't know. It wasn't even a real decision on my part. I was driven by some force — driven to dig down into that decades-old grave and pry open that tomb, to find out for myself what was in it. It was something instinctive, something I hadn't planned on doing on this unimaginable night, but something I had to do.

John, I know it doesn't make any sense. But there I was, sticking the blade of the shovel into the cold, damp earth in front of the massive headstone. There was a "pressure" on me now. Again, I can't find the right words, and that's the best I can describe it. I felt somehow as though the darkness around me was deeper, the shadows moving in ways they shouldn't. The wind had grown stronger; it whispered and hissed around my ears. Then, as I carefully cut around a square of grass and dug in with the shovel, I began to hear a different sound.

This wasn't the wind. It was coming from the ground underneath me. Lovecraft would've called it a susurration — a kind of muttering and rolling of voices, all blended. Soft at first, they rose as I listened until I thought I could hear muffled shrieks, cries, wails of misery, even a pleading word or two. I stopped digging, shaking my head to clear it, but when I stuck that shovel back into the earth they returned. It took every bit of will power I could muster to keep digging, but I did. Working like a madman, sweating and panting in the night air, I dug and stacked until there was a dark patch of bare earth before me, squares of turf stacked neatly against the marker.

The wind rose, pressing in on me from all sides, until it seemed to be a living thing. The sounds from below squirmed like earthworms under my feet, voice and movement all mixed up.

As I threw shovelful after shovelful over to the left side of the grave, the odor of ancient mold and mildew and, yes, rot assailed my nostrils. But curiously, the smells I'd uncovered seemed to steady me and drive me onward.

Then the wind abruptly stopped. And the noises, closer now, turned to screams.

How long was I there, the wails echoing all around me, whirling inside my head, as I dug like a grave-robbing fiend fearful of discovery? Hell, John, I don't know. I just know that when I finally came to myself only my head was above the ground of the cemetery. I stood, panting like a wild animal, the screaming and wailing so loud now that I was sure they would attract attention. They were so intense, so full of agony and sorrow, that they stabbed at me like blades.

I will have nightmares for the rest of my life about what I heard. Through the cries and screams, voices pled hopelessly for mercy for their babies, their children, entreaties turning to long wails of agony. I responded by digging with an even greater frenzy, somehow hoping that the agony of labor would mute the shrieks reverberating through my mind.

As I dug, I realized something: there were no coffins here. There were no bones. Nothing but the voices, released now, finally, long buried, long dead, rising again. But why? I felt as though I had been plunged bodily into a subterranean hell and was digging to get out of it. But like in a dream, I couldn't dig fast enough to escape, no matter how I tried. Whatever it was I feared was gaining on me, and the screaming grew all around me, and still I dug — and through that cacophony, I heard a solitary voice, coming from what seemed a long distance away, making an attempt to warn me of something.

Then — with the rumble of an earthquake, the bank of earth around my shovel blade collapsed and I was awash in a flood of bones and skulls. The sheer force knocked me onto my back, and as I struggled up I saw that my hands were bloody from the shoveling, leaving crimson fingerprints on the skeletal remains around me.

When I got back on my feet, I was looking into a yawning black cavity, now empty, its former contents piled knee-high all around me. And then I realized the noises, the voices, had ended, as though some great switch had been thrown. I don't know how long I stood there, but I remember finally reaching down and picking up a tiny human skull, a baby's, and noticing the cuts and nicks in it.

This mass grave — I now knew it was what I'd come out here to find. But I'd also found that something was not right about it. There swirled around me a sense of evil that made me sick.

Not physically sick, John, but sick in my soul, sick to the depths of my very being. Something hideous, something unspeakable, had happened here. It was what no one wanted to tell me about the Cleansing.

Then, as I turned that little skull over in my bloodied hands, I realized exactly what it was.

The wind came up again, moaning and sighing around me. I took a step and felt a twisting in my heart as bones snapped under-foot, but I had to get out of there. I wanted more than anything to get out of there, to fill that grave back in and hurry away, never to return.

But I was too late.

They were there, standing above me. Three women and two men, gray and pale in the moonlight, staring into the deep trench where I stood. Mrs. Davis. Ma Stean. Miss Mary Lou Castle, née Gabber. Then, Gibson, the postmaster. And McDermott, the high school principal and history teacher.

The seventh sense ran wild inside of me, rising like the mercury in a thermometer.

I knew these must make up Mackaville's ruling body, the ones who controlled the town and its business and people. With the Gabbers and Black gone, their ranks had thinned considerably, and I knew some of those left held me responsible.

I deeply suspected that number included Barney Gibson, who stood above me with a double-barreled shotgun pointed directly at my heart, the moon painting his face dead white.

"You couldn't let it go, could you, Brown?" he said drily. "Well, that's good. You're way too dangerous to live."

"Wait a minute, now." It was Ma. "That ain't been decided yet, Barney." The look she shot me was impossible to decipher.

Gibson didn't take his eye, or the shotgun, off me when he answered her. "I got th' votes," he said. "You know I do."

In the midst of all this, the thought came: How the hell can he have the votes. Ma and Mrs. Davis and Miss Castle are on MY side.

"We ain't officially voted," Ma said.

"Don't need to," he returned, sighting

down the barrel at me. "Ever since this peckerwood hit town, we all been at one another. Animal killin's. People killin's. Tearin' each other apart, after living together for so long. What you think's gonna happen if we let him outta here with our secrets?" He looked at Ma and Mrs. Davis, and then sighted in on me again.

"Mr. Gibson's right," added McDermott, his voice dry as kindling. "I commend your pursuit of knowledge, Mr. Brown. In fact, when this whole dust-up began, and the first votes were taken about you, I abstained. As a fellow historian, I wanted to see where your thirst for learning would lead you." He sighed audibly. "But it's like I told you in the cafe, when you were kind enough to give me that ledger book. Best for some things to stay buried. It's even more than 'best.' It's necessary."

"So you two are all for killing me and leaving me here," I said, trying to keep my voice under control. "If all of this is so democratic, where's your deciding vote?"

Silence fell like a shroud. Ma looked away from me, while Mrs. Davis kept her eyes on the ground. Then, standing beside the two women, Mary Lou Castle took a step toward me.

There was pain in her eyes, but it was mixed with resolve, and I knew before she opened her mouth that she had been the deciding vote.

"This town is finally on the right track

again, Robert," she said softly. "We're going to grow, and the kids are going to start staying around instead of leaving for other places. Mackaville is alive again."

"And you're going to kill me to make sure it stays that way?"

The words seemed to hit her like buckshot. "Believe me," she said. "It was an agonizing decision. We just can't take the chance of you getting out and telling everything you know about us."

Ma stepped forward to stand beside her friend. "This ain't a good option we got. We don't want you to die. We know the gov'ment might come around looking for you—"

"I told you we got that taken care of," interrupted Gibson.

She turned, glaring at him.

I knew I had to do something. So I shouted, "Wait a minute! If you're going to kill me, don't I deserve a last word?"

"You don't deserve nothing," Gibson said. "You're a murderous bastard, a mad dog. Wouldn't surprise me if you finally got Mr. Black. He ain't here, and this ain't somethin' he'd wanna miss."

I was thinking frantically about how to respond to that accusation when Ma Stean stepped forward and pushed the barrel of that shotgun down. "Let him speak," she said. "He has a right."

John, again, it was one of those times. I knew I was in deep, and <u>they</u> knew I knew it.

I had discovered the final and most hideous piece of the Cleansing, and there was an overwhelming chance that the knowledge would be what finally got me killed.

As I looked up at Gibson, and, behind him, McDermott, they suddenly looked ancient in the cold light, as though they'd been carved out of pale, porous rock. Perhaps it was just a trick of moonlight. But more likely it was my seventh sense, telling me that, like the Gabbers and Black, they were old beyond their years, two more still-living eyewitnesses to the Cleansing.

"All right, Mr. Brown." said McDermott.

I looked toward Ma and Mrs. Davis. Miss Castle didn't return my stare, but in the moonlit tableau, the eyes of the other two had taken on a glow, and in them I saw why the cats had avoided me tonight — even as they tried to warn me. The cats had known I was here, so the cat people knew, too. And so did the others.

But maybe there were some things the cat people didn't know. The thought hit me like a thunderbolt, even as I addressed Mrs. Davis.

"You think your husband died in the riot, Mrs. Davis?" I asked. "Maybe he did. But maybe he didn't."

Out of the corner of my eye, I saw Gibson raise the shotgun again. This time, Ma grabbed the barrel and held it down. She was bigger than he was, and just as strong.

"Let him go on," she said.

I spoke quickly, knowing now that Gibson wanted me dead, and in a hurry. "Here," I said, thrusting a leg bone into her hands. "Look at this. Feel this."

She took it, running her palm over it.

"Feel those nicks and cuts," I asked. "You know what that is? That's the mark of the knives, where the meat was cut off!"

She dropped the bone, and Gibson tried to raise his shotgun again. Ma prevailed.

"Your husband – all these people – they weren't just killed! They were slaughtered!" The wind had come up again, and I had to shout to be heard. "Slaughtered like hogs, their meat canned and sold and shipped out with the hog meat!"

At that, Gibson really began to struggle with Ma. But McDermott raised his hand, signaling for him to stop, and then his lips opened in an ugly grin.

"Well, isn't that just a fine bit of deducing?" he said, looking at me like a snake looks at a mouse. His voice sounded like dust being poured over stone. Ma and Mrs. Davis stood open-mouthed, staring at him. Mary Lou Castle, too, appeared stunned, her eyes on the scored bone Mrs. Davis held in both her hands.

"You're right, Einstein," McDermott said. "We moved a lot of meat over those few days, didn't we, Barney?" His eyes had taken on a wild quality that would've scared the hell out of me if I hadn't already been as afraid as I could get. "You'll notice I said 'we.' Why, Barney and I are hardly mere civil servants. We have been silent partners in Gabber Meats for decades. The powers behind the throne, as it were." Shooting a glance at Miss Castle, he added, "And we know that will continue, what with the untimely deaths of your husbands." The "s" at the end was very clear.

If she heard, she didn't acknowledge it. She only looked up briefly and returned to studying the bone.

"Easy now, Butcher," Gibson said.

McDermott leered in at me. "Nickname. Never cared much for it, but when you've had it for 80 years, it kind of sticks." Then, to Gibson, "This man is one of my intellectual comrades, a seeker of historical truths. Might as well give him the whole story. He won't be taking it anywhere else."

Looking over at the women, who still seemed transfixed by the bone I'd handed Mrs. Davis, Gibson said, "I dunno. What about–"

McDermott cut him off. "He won't be taking it anywhere else," he repeated.

Then, he leaned in above me, smiling that evil smile again. "They went to the plant alive and dead, colored and white alike. If they were alive, we hung them on trolleys and dropped them in the vats. The screams that came when they dropped off into that boiling water were quite impressive. It had to be boiling, you know, so we could slip their skin off and cut the meat from the bones.

"It was a very…challenging time, and it got tricky for us because we and the Gabbers finally had to turn on the white Rebels they'd brought in. That's when the bodies on the racks went from mostly black to mostly white. Of course, it's finally just all meat, isn't it? Black or white or in-between – what difference does it make? Once it was spiced up, it was all uniform, and quite flavorful. Sending it out all over the country wasn't only the best way we could see to get rid of the evidence. It was also an affordable and tasty treat for consumers all over the country. The masses gobbled it right up. Of course, all that kid and baby flesh – salted with mothers' tears – made that big batch of 'potted meat' a rare dining experience for anyone." He laughed, a hollow rasping sound that raised the hairs on the back of my neck.

"I didn't know," Mrs. Davis said, looking out over my head into the darkness beyond. "I was confined to the house, about to give birth. I didn't know." She turned to Ma. "Did *you* know?" she asked, her voice as soft as a child's.

Ma stepped over and put an arm around Mrs. Davis. "No, honey," she said. "Lots of us didn't."

"Don't matter." It was Gibson, lifting the shotgun again. "What matters is, we was all getting along before this Yankee carpetbagger come in, and we'll all get along again once he's gone."

Abruptly, Mrs. Davis wheeled on Gibson, her eyes blazing. As she dropped the bone, her lips drew back from her teeth. Gibson brought the gun up toward her.

"Now look here," he said. "You get back. Just get back."

From deep within Mrs. Davis came a kind of sustained yowling, muffled at first, but then gaining in volume until it became an unsuppressed shriek of rage and pain. Although she made no move toward him, Gibson began backing away, holding the shotgun on her. Ma reached toward Mrs. Davis, as if to restrain her. Behind them, Miss Castle had picked up the bone and stood staring at it.

Then, something else grabbed my attention. Beneath me and beside me, the bones and skulls and fragments began to rustle, moving of their own volition. They danced in the moonlight, clinking against one another. My mouth went dry. I couldn't bring myself to move. All around me, the dance of the bones, hopping and falling, flowing with jerky clacking motions toward the side of the trench closest to the people standing in the cemetery.

Above it all, I heard a click and looked up – into the barrel of Gibson's shotgun.

"You're finished," he said.

Then, another click. And a voice, in the beautiful rolling tones of a sermon, said,

"Lower that shotgun, Mr. Gibson, or I'll fill you full of silver."

There, stepping out from behind a tombstone, was David Garland Jefferson, the Colt Walker .44 in his big hand.

"Please step back, Mrs. Davis," he said, as Gibson sullenly placed the shotgun on the ground in front of him. And then, to McDermott, "Remember me? I remember you. Raise your hands and get over here next to your friend."

As he did so, around me and underneath me the bones chattered and clattered and flowed. Gibson was the first to catch on to what was happening. His eyes wide with sudden fear, he backed away from the pit I'd dug — just as the first phalanx of bones flowed up and over, onto the ground in front of him, between us.

For a moment, I had the horrible feeling I was going to die there after all, myself and my soul tangled and buried in a pile of long-dead bones for all eternity. Then I was up and out of the trench, rolling onto the ground, hearing the crunch of bones powdering beneath my body. I felt a hand on mine, and Ma Stean was helping me up, along with Mrs. Davis, who seemed to have returned to normal. Then another hand: Mary Lou Castle's.

With David's attention diverted to the pit and me, Gibson and McDermott broke away and began running with all the haste they could muster.

But the bones were faster. They not only scrambled and rolled along the ground now; they actually flew, or jumped, until they whizzed around the two like volleys of arrows. I heard a hard thunk next to me and saw Gibson go down, the jagged end of a femur sticking out of his forehead.

"Hurry! This way!" David shouted, as the three women and I ducked our heads and began scurrying toward his voice. As we reached a big tombstone, David reared up from behind it and pulled us down.

Bones flew and rolled and slithered raggedly all around us. It was like in the movies, when a plague of locusts descends on a farm. You couldn't see anything beyond them, these airborne and crawling and swirling pieces of long-dead humans.

And then, they seemed to all pull together into a twisting gray-white mass, a tornado that swirled toward McDermott. He screamed, and it fell in on him, and then – John, I have to stop a minute. I'm shaking so hard now that it's drawing the attention of some of the other people here in the day coach. I hadn't realized how intense reliving all this would be…

Back now. I went for a walk through the other cars – of course, I kept this letter with me – and I feel a lot better now, well enough to tell you that what I saw next was something I didn't actually see so much as feel. Once again, I don't have the right words to describe it, but what happened was that the trench I'd dug — John, it became a mouth, an obscene maw with lips of earth and teeth of splintered bone, and, still screaming, McDermott slid beside Gibson's prone body on a conveyor belt of skulls and bones to the waiting abyss. They went in as though they'd been poured, bones piling in on top of them, earth filling in over bones. And then — the ground moved.

Chewing. Chewing.

It seemed to take eons before the frenzied cries of terror and agony muffled and died away, but finally, all was silent. In the moonlight, the graveyard looked as it had before, when I had come into this place to find for myself, for good and all, what had happened during the Cleansing.

And now that I'd found it, I wished deeply that I hadn't. I still do.

Your pal and faithful comrade,

Robert

September 24, 1939

My first Sunday in Washington, D.C.

Dear John,

Well, I start the new job tomorrow. It took me well over two days before I arrived in this booming metropolis, and since I hadn't booked a sleeper, I was pretty well done in when I reached the platform. But a friendly taxi cab driver took me to the right place, dropped me off at the gate, and after the Marine guard checked me out, I was able to report.

The big boss was out of town, but his subordinate was there, a guy about our age named Fletcher. He took one look at me, told me to get some sleep and report on Monday, and then gave me a key and instructions on how to get to my new digs. This apartment isn't bad. Pretty spartan, but clean and comfortable enough. The building's full to the brim with other guys and gals. I think I'm going to like it here.

The bed's good, anyway, and I stayed in it for the night Saturday and all of Sunday, barely getting up during that whole stretch. I'll admit to a few rough nightmares over that period, but I feel better now, and I've resolved to send you this final letter about Mackaville to wrap up the loose ends — for you <u>and</u> me. I hope, by writing you about the end of it, I'll be able to lay that episode of my life to rest in my own mind. Soon, I suspect, I'll be treating it like a movie or a dream, something I saw and felt that didn't really happen.

After the…experience I told you about in my last letter, David accepted my offer of a ride into town while Ma, Miss Castle, and Mrs. Davis left in Ma's Pontiac. I offered to have him stay with me again, but he declined and asked to be put off at the hotel. When I stopped the bike in front, he climbed off and grabbed my hand.

"Goodbye, Robert," he said, above the idling of the Indian.

"Goodbye, David. You saved my life tonight."

"I'm not so sure about that." He grinned. "But if I did, we're closer now to being even."

"How did you know? I mean, why are you even in Mackaville? I thought you were back in St. Louis."

"I am," he said. "Miz Evans and I have us a nice storefront church up there. But — well, I could say I knew you was leaving and came back to tell you goodbye, and maybe that's part of it. But maybe I could also tell you that once I got to town, I didn't lack for information on where you were and what you were doing."

"The cats?" I asked.

He only smiled.

I nodded. "However it happened, thank

you," I told him. "Maybe I'll visit that church of yours sometime, after I get settled into my new job and earn some vacation."

"We'd both like that," he said. "Goodbye, Robert Brown." And with that, he turned and walked into the hotel.

Ma's automobile wasn't yet in the driveway when I reached the boarding house. So I put the Indian up and crept in through the kitchen door. MacWhirtle was curled up asleep outside my room, and the sight of the little pooch gave me my first real pang of sadness about leaving Mackaville behind. He followed me in, and I guess he jumped up in bed with me; truth to tell, my head had hardly hit the pillow before I was out.

That morning, I ate my last breakfast at Ma's. I'd half-hoped that Patricia would be there, but I knew better. She hadn't worked at the boarding house since our split. I imagined she'd return, though – as soon as I was gone for good.

Somehow, Ma had found the time to bake a cake. I guess maybe she'd done it before the events of the night before. But there it was on the breakfast table, with "GOOD BYE ROBERT" written in frosting on the top. All three of the other boarders were there, and I knew they'd stuck around just to tell me so long. Mister Clark handed me an envelope with a card inside they'd all signed, wishing me the best in my new job. Solemnly, we all shook hands and then had big slabs of cake, even though it was just shy of 8 a.m.

I had an 8:50 train and a couple of things left to do, so I went up and got my two big suitcases, lugged them down the stairs, and met Ma at the door. With her standing there, MacWhirtle looking up from her feet, I found it suddenly tough to say goodbye. For a woman who didn't do much hugging, she was sure good at it. In fact, she almost smothered me in her ample bosom.

"Now, Robert," she said, "don't you worry about nothing that happened here. We bury our own dead in Mackaville. We're puttin' a lot of trust in you to understand."

"I do understand, Ma. I'll leave 'em buried. I solemnly promise you that."

"Thank you, Robert. You been a good boarder."

Surprisingly, I found my eyes brimming and my throat suddenly constricted. I reached down to pet MacWhirtle for the last time, but that didn't do me any good. When I stood up, Ma kissed me on the cheek.

"Goodbye, young man," she said, and I saw tears in her own eyes. Quickly, I left, dragging the suitcases to the shed and getting out the bike. Managing to balance both pieces of luggage on the Indian, I took off.

Leaving had hit me harder than I'd expected. All of a sudden, I didn't want to see anyone else. I just wanted to go, and leave all this emotion behind.

When I got to Pete's, I was surprised to see the "closed" sign still up in the office window. That was unusual, but I didn't dwell on it, parking the bike and leaving the key in it after navigating my suitcases to the pavement.

It wasn't a long trip to the train station, and along the way I started kicking myself for not running by and saying goodbye to Mr. Castapolous, even though I knew I was simply out of time and sure as hell didn't want to miss the train. Still, I was thinking about leaving my bags at the depot and running down to the cafe when I spotted Pete and Diffie, along with Mr. Castapolous, standing on the platform. Mr. Castapolous was the first to greet me, rubbing his hand on his apron before sticking it out to me.

"Gotta get back, Robert," he said. "Breakfast crowd. But I wanted to say goodbye and God speed." The handshake changed suddenly into a hug as he grabbed me. "You're a good man," he said. "Write me sometimes." With that, he took off back down the street, toward his cafe, another person I was sure going to miss.

"Don't expect that from us," Pete said as I turned around. "We ain't huggin' you."

Both he and Diffie laughed at that. Since the ascension of his father at the plant, Diffie had taken to dressing like a San Francisco dandy, and what was funny about that was he still worked at Pete's station, pumping gas and fixing flats while clad in those suits of clothes.

"I'm not hugging you bozos either," I returned, shaking hands with them both. "Might get fleas."

They laughed at that, too, and we joked around for a few minutes before my train pulled in. While Pete knew plenty about what I'd been through and was hep to Mackaville's undercurrents, I wasn't sure whether any of that knowledge was shared by Diffie. So I kept things light and made no reference to the secrets Pete and I would forever share.

A final goodbye, punches on the shoulder and slaps on the back, and I was horsing my luggage toward the train. I seemed to be the only passenger getting on at Mackaville.

Then the sheriff's car roared up, screeching to a stop just beside the platform. In an instant, Sheriff Meagan was climbing out of the front seat, hollering, "Wait a minute, Brown!"

This close to freedom, I thought, *and I'm cooked. He found Black and he's pinning me for it.*

And sure as hell, the first words out of his mouth were, "Black's dead."

I did my damnedest to look surprised. He didn't look like he was buying it.

"Went off a road in the hills," he said. "Wasn't much left of him. Thought you might want to know before you leave."

"You know I'm leaving for good?"

"Hell, yes," he said, "It's hardly a secret. Whole damn town knows."

"Well, I'm sorry about Old Man Black," I returned, hoping he wasn't about to put the hammer down on me. With Sheriff Meagan, you never really knew.

"Yeah. A shame." He looked hard at me. "But, you know, the old bastard zipped around those hills like a bat outta hell. It was really just a matter of time. And you know something else?"

"What?"

"I was thinking this morning how he'd oiled up that road that you found and cleaned up before anyone got hurt. I ain't no writer like you, but if I was, I'd call that poetic justice."

He grinned then, briefly, and stuck out his hand. I took it and said goodbye, the relief beating through me in waves. Then he turned away, and in a moment he and his car had disappeared down a side street.

The conductor for my train was calling out, and just before I boarded, I took a final look at the place. Sitting there in the early morning sunlight, it didn't look sinister at all. Just another little town in the mountains, with people being born and living and dying and the community going on its way, free from the prying eyes of the rest of the world.

Then, I saw Rennsdale.

She had planted herself at the very end of

the platform, where she regarded me with a level, unblinking stare. It seemed that she'd been watching me for a long time, as though she were making up her mind about something. And then, with a haughty flip of her head, the pretty little calico turned and bounded away, down the dusty Arkansas street I would never walk again.

God willing.

Your pal and faithful correspondent,

Robert

October 14, 1939
Washington, D.C.

Dear Richard:

I happened to run onto a copy of Story magazine the other day and was happy to see that you were in there with what I feel was an autobiographical piece, dressed up like fiction.

Congratulations! I know this is just the first of many publications you'll have in your career as a writer. And in such a prestigious magazine as well. Good work. And good work, too, in getting on with the Federal Writers' Project.

Reading your very powerful tale made me think about the last conversation you and I had together at Mrs. Evans' boarding house, right before I left for Mackaville. It seems like years ago now, but I've thought again and again on what you said that night, about how being true and telling the truth are the most important things a writer can do. If I wrote something telling the truth about what happened to me while I was in those Arkansas hills for the WPA, no one would believe it. But I'm beginning to understand that what people think isn't all that important, and that I should tell it anyway and damn the consequences. If readers want to take it as fiction, fine. It just needs to be told, and, more important, it needs to be told truthfully.

So I think I'm going to do it like you did your narrative, as a piece of fiction that's really not fiction at all, and maybe I'll get lucky and see it published. Meanwhile, I've got my hands full up here in the Nation's Capitol. I can't say too much about my job, but like everyone else in the world, we're watching the sinister clown with the toothbrush moustache and what's happening in Great Britain right now. I wish I could say I think it's all going to blow over, but we're going to get into this war, and soon. I know it.

When it's all done and the world gets straightened back out, I hope we can have a good visit. Maybe we can all meet in St. Paul, where my friend John lives, and spend some time jawing about the craft. John's a newspaperman, but he's sold a story to Weird Tales and just wrote me that another pulp has bought one of his detective yarns. These aren't highbrow markets like Story, but you two have a lot in common. I think you'd like him.

Keep that typewriter burning. We all need more of the truth.

Your friend,
Robert A. Brown

ACKNOWLEDGMENTS

We extend our deepest thanks to Lara Bernhardt, Steven Wooley, Ray Riethmeier, and Bill Bernhardt for their time, insight, observations, and expertise.

ABOUT THE AUTHORS

Robert A. Brown has spent most of his working life in public education, serving as both a reading specialist and a principal, but he has also authored several nonfiction pieces dealing with the Great Depression and its popular culture, including western movies and the so-called "Spicy" magazines of the period. His work includes a piece on the legend of cowboy-movie star Tom Mix commissioned by the National Cowboy and Western Heritage Museum. An internationally known collector of nostalgic items such as movie paper, radio premiums, and pulp magazines, Brown supplied the art and wrote the text for Kitchen Sink Press's popular trading card series *Spicy: Naughty '30s Pulp Covers* and *Spicy: More Naughty '30s Pulp Covers*, which quickly became sold-out collector's items.

Brown initiated what became *The Cleansing*, writing letters on authentic period stationery to his old friend Wooley, using his deep knowledge of the 1930s to portray himself as the WPA employee beset by rural horrors who became *The Cleansing*'s protagonist.

John Wooley made his first professional sale in the late 1960s, placing a script with the legendary *Eerie* magazine. He's now in his sixth decade as a professional writer, having written three horror novels with co-author Ron Wolfe, including *Death's Door*, which was one of the first books released under Dell's Abyss imprint and was also nominated for a Bram Stoker

Award. His solo horror and fantasy novels include *Awash in the Blood*, *Ghost Band*, and *Dark Within*, the latter a finalist for the Oklahoma Book Award.

Wooley is also the author of the critically acclaimed biographies *Wes Craven: A Man and His Nightmares* and *Right Down the Middle: The Ralph Terry Story*. He has co-written or contributed to several volumes of Michael H. Price's Forgotten Horrors series of movie books and co-hosts the podcast of the same name. His other writing credits include the 1990 TV film *Dan Turner, Hollywood Detective* and several documentaries, notably the Learning Channel's *Hauntings Across America*. Among the comics and graphic novels he's scripted are *Plan Nine from Outer Space*, the authorized version of the alternative-movie classic, as well as the recent collections *The Twilight Avenger* and *The Miracle Squad*.

www.ingramcontent.com/pod-product-compliance
Lightning Source LLC
Chambersburg PA
CBHW051946240626
47153CB00005B/1646
* 9 7 8 1 9 4 8 2 6 3 6 9 6 *